Summoned to Thirteenth Grave

Summoned to Thirteenth Grave

Darynda Jones

ST. MARTIN'S PRESS ✷ NEW YORK

SUMMONED TO THIRTEENTH GRAVE. Copyright © 2018 by Darynda Jones. All rights reserved. Printed in the United States of America. For information, address St. Martin's Press, 175 Fifth Avenue, New York, N.Y. 10010.

www.stmartins.com

Library of Congress Cataloging-in-Publication Data

Names: Jones, Darynda, author.
Title: Summoned to thirteenth grave / Darynda Jones.
Description: First edition. | New York : St. Martin's Press, 2019.
Identifiers: LCCN 2018036267| ISBN 9781250149411 (hardcover) |
    ISBN 9781250149435 (ebook)
Subjects: | GSAFD: Occult fiction.
Classification: LCC PS3610.O6236 S86 2019 | DDC 813/.6—dc23
LC record available at https://lccn.loc.gov/2018036267

Our books may be purchased in bulk for promotional, educational, or business use. Please contact your local bookseller or the Macmillan Corporate and Premium Sales Department at 1-800-221-7945, extension 5442, or by email at MacmillanSpecialMarkets@macmillan.com.

First Edition: January 2019

10 9 8 7 6 5 4 3 2 1

For my hunny bunny
Robyn Peterman
because life is too short to take seriously

Acknowledgments

Dear Grimlets,

Wow. This is it. This is the big one. The one we've all been waiting for. (Or is that just me?) I gotta be honest, writing this book—the last Charley Davidson novel ever—brought me to tears on more than one occasion. I love her. I love everything about her. I love Reyes and Cookie and Uncle Bob and Garrett and Amber and Quentin and Angel and . . . I could go on and on.

But according to rumor, all series must end. Eventually. And we felt that ending Charley on the number thirteen would be fun and fitting.

That being said, I have a few accolades I must hand out.

Thank you so very, very much to my agent, Alexandra Machinist, who has stuck with me through many ups and downs, and to the lovely Monique Patterson, who edited this book with encouragement and enthusiasm. I appreciate both so much.

Thank you to the lovely Lorelei King for giving a voice to the world inside my head.

Thank you so much to my family, who have gone on the roller coaster that is Charley Davidson with me and have disembarked the better for it. After all, what doesn't kill us makes us stronger, right?

Thank you to my very own cheer squad, known to most as Netters, Dana, and Trayce, and includes the likes of Robyn, Eve, Jowanna, Trish, Quentin, the Mercenaries, my Ruby Sisters, my LERA chapter mates, the numerous book clubs who have invited me to be a part of their lives, and my SMP and ICM siblings.

Trayce and Dana, I can't tell you how much I appreciate your thoughts on everything I write. These books would not be what they are without your incredible insight and honesty. Thank you from the bottom of my ticker, which ticks so much easier thanks to you.

A special thanks goes out to Amanda Santana for her entirely true "bra" story, immortalized within these pages, and to Aili Gomez and her wonderfully creative son for naming our incorporeal child Ghost Boy. Which totally worked!

And last but certainly not least, thank you to Grimlets everywhere. (For those who don't know, if you read anything by yours truly, you're a bona fide, card-carrying [metaphorically] Grimlet.) I would never have gotten this far without the encouragement of readers like you. You've made every hair-pulling moment of angst, every late night in which I was certain I'd never make my deadline, every sob wrenched from my body when I was equally as certain that a scene I wrote was sure to end my career, so very, very worth it.

Gracias, merci, arigato, maholo, danke sehr, grazie, takk, spasiba, terima kasih, do jeh, efharisto, toda . . . thank you.

Summoned to Thirteenth Grave

1

What, pray tell, the fuck?
—T-SHIRT

It wasn't until I felt the sun on my face that I knew, really knew, I'd made it back. The bright orb drifted over the horizon like a hot air balloon, blinding me, yet I couldn't stop looking at it. Or, well, trying to look at it. After giving it my all through squinted lids, I gave up and closed them. Let the warmth wash over me. Let it sink into my skin. Flood every molecule in my body.

God knew I needed it. I hadn't had a drop of vitamin D in over a hundred years. My bones were probably brittle and shriveled and splintery. Much like the current state of my psyche.

But that's what happens when you defy a god.

Not just any god, mind you. No siree Bob. To get booted off the big blue marble, one had to defy *the* God. The very One a particular set of children's books called *Jehovahn.*

The Man had some serious control issues. I bring one person back from the dead and *bam.* Banished for all eternity. Exiled to a hell with no light, no hair products, and no coffee.

Mostly no coffee.

And, just to throw salt onto a gaping, throbbing flesh wound, no tribe.

In this dimension, the one with the yellow sun and champagne-colored sand on which I now walked, I had a husband and a daughter and more friends than I could shake a stick at. But in the lightless realm I'd been banished to, I'd had nothing. I floated in darkness for over one hundred agonizing years, tormented by dreams of a husband I could no longer touch and a daughter I could no longer protect.

She would be gone by now. Our daughter. I will have missed her entire life. The thought alone shattered me. Cut into me like shards of glass every time I breathed.

But I'd missed more than her life. It had been prophesied that she would face Lucifer in a great battle for humanity. That she would have an army at her back and, fingers crossed, a warrior at her side. And that she would stand against evil when no one else could.

I'd wondered for dozens of years if she'd won, the pain of not knowing, of not being able to help, driving me to the brink of insanity. Then I realized something and a peculiar kind of peace came over me. Of course she'd won. She was the daughter of two gods. More to the point, she was her father's daughter, the god Rey'azikeen's only child. She would've been wily and cunning and strong. Of course she won.

That's what I'd told myself over and over for the last thirty-odd years of my exile. But now I was back. An exile that was supposed to be for all eternity stopped just short, in my humble opinion, of its goal.

Unfortunately, I had no idea why I was back. I'd felt myself being drawn forward, pulled through space and time until the darkness that surrounded me gave way to the unforgiving brightness of Earth's yellow sun. That big, beautiful ball of fire I'd so often complained about as a resident of New Mexico, where sunshine was damned near a daily occurrence.

The horror!

And here it was, bathing me in its brilliance as my feet sank into dew-covered sand with every step I took. I walked toward it. The sun. Craving more. Begging for more.

"I will never complain about you again," I said, tilting my face toward the heavens, because the thought of my daughter growing up without me wasn't the only thing that had driven me to the edge of sanity. Nor the heartbreak of missing my husband. His hands on my body. His full mouth at my ear. His sparkling eyes hooded by impossibly thick lashes.

No, it was the perpetual darkness that pushed me so far inside myself I could hardly stay conscious.

I'd tried to escape. To find my way back to my family and friends. Boy, had I tried. But it seemed like the harder I struggled, the deeper I sank. The realm in which I'd been cast was like an inky, ethereal form of quicksand. If not for the wraiths . . .

I stopped and bent my head to listen. Someone was following me, and for the first time since materializing on the earthly plane, I tried to take in my surroundings. With my vision adjusting, I could just make out the sea of peaches and golds that stretched out before me. Sand as far as the eye could see.

Then it hit me. The Sahara. I'd been here before. With him.

I started walking again, slowly, making him come to me as I used every ounce of strength I had to tamp down the elation coursing through my veins.

I'd dreamed about this moment for so long, a part of me wondered if it was real. Or if I was hallucinating. But I felt the warmth radiating from his body and I knew. Heat—his heat—pulsated over me in rich, fervent waves, stirring parts of me that hadn't been stirred in decades. Or churned. Or even whisked, for that matter.

I dared a glance over my shoulder. My knees weakened and my stomach clenched at the sight. Dressed as a desert nomad in traditional, sky-blue garb, he followed at a leisurely pace. A light breeze pressed his robe against his body, outlining his wide shoulders, long arms, and lean waist.

A turban of the same sky blue had been wrapped around his head and face until only his eyes shone through.

Dark. Shimmering. Intent.

Like that could fool me. Like I wouldn't know my husband from a thousand miles away. His essence. His aura. His scent.

Of course, the ever-present fire that licked over his skin, the lightning that arced around him, didn't hurt.

He moved like an animal. A predator. Powerful and full of confidence and grace. Every step calculated. Every move a conscious act.

And he was closing in.

I turned back to the horizon, my heart bursting with the knowledge that my husband was still here. Still on Earth. Still sexy as fuck.

And yet, there was something not quite . . .

I whirled around to face him when I realized part of what I was feeling, part of the tangle of tightly packed emotions that made Reyes Reyes, was anger.

No. Not anger precisely. *Anger* would be far too tame a word. He was livid. Furious. Enraged. And it was all directed at me.

I'd stopped, but he continued his advance. The stealth with which he moved was born of an instinct millions of years old. He was a predator through and through. A hunter. He knew how to stalk and kill his prey before that prey could detect even the slightest hint of danger. But dangerous he was. On a thousand different levels.

Still . . .

"Are you kidding me?" I asked, holding up a finger to both stop him and give attitude. Two birds, one stone, baby.

Unfortunately, he didn't stop. He only tilted his head, the scarf making it impossible to see the expression underneath, and continued his trek toward me. But I could still feel it. The anger simmering just below the surface.

I didn't know if my ability to read the emotions of others was a part of my grim reaper status or my godly one. Either way, I'd had the ability to feel emotion pouring out of people since I was a kid. But Reyes was usually much harder to read.

Usually.

He kept walking, his gait so casual one would think he was out for a morning stroll. And yet purpose filled every step he took.

I had no choice but to retreat. I'd been exiled to a hell dimension for a hundred years. I wasn't eager to visit another here on Earth. And an angry Reyes was a . . . a what? A panty-melting Reyes? A ravishing Reyes? A god?

I stumbled backwards then righted myself and stood up straight to face him. I would not cower in the face of my enemy—a.k.a. my husband.

Five feet away.

"Now, listen up, Mister Man."

Four.

"I'll have you know—"

Three.

"—that I did not come back here—"

Two.

"—to be accosted by an angry—"

Wait. A veil of sheer white flowed in my periphery, picked up by a soft breeze, and I looked down, wondering what the fuck was I wearing. "What the fuck am I—"

One.

An arm wrapped around my waist, and Reyes pulled me against him, his hard body molding to mine. There was nothing gentle about his hold as he studied me.

I studied him back. I reached up and pulled the scarf down to reveal his perfect nose, full mouth, darkened jaw. His irises, eclipsed by the shadow of his own lashes, shimmered a deep, rich brown sprinkled with green and gold flecks, and I sank into him. It had been so long. So very, very long.

When I wrapped both arms around his neck, he lowered his head and buried his face in my hair. I basked in the feel of his body against mine, reveling as well in the fact that I actually had a body. A corporeal one. A corporeal one that had urges and impulses and desires, traitorous carcass that it was.

"Can we just put the anger aside for a little while and see to my needs?"

He pulled back and stared down at me, his gaze intense enough to start a fire. Then he lifted the robe over his head and tossed it and the turban onto the sand. The solid frame on which he'd been built, the wide shoulders and slim waist, the soft highlights and deep shadows of muscle and sinew, dissolved the bones I'd only recently reacquired.

"I'll take that as a yes."

Before I knew it, the world tilted. His strong arms lowered me onto the robe, a pair of nomadic trousers in the same startling blue as the rest of his garb his only attire.

And I apparently wore a white gown of some kind, the material like gossamer as he raked it up my body, his mouth, hot and wet, following its path.

Every kiss caused tiny quakes to ricochet against my bones. When he lifted the gown up over my arms, he stopped at my wrists and used the material to bind my hands above my head, holding them there with effortless ease.

A cool morning breeze washed over every exposed inch of me, as did his gaze. Both induced a wave of goose bumps that rushed across my skin, prickling as they blazed a trail wherever his attention landed. Even the heat emanating out of him and into me couldn't squelch them.

But I couldn't get enough of him. This man I'd dreamed of every minute of every hour for one hundred years.

His dark skin still bore the tribal tattoos that doubled as a map to the underworld. And the scars that lined the surface of his body attested to the many hells he'd endured. To the many lives he'd lived.

First, he was a god, the god Rey'azikeen, also known as the Hellmaker—

long story—and little brother to none other than Jehovah Himself. Then he was Rey'aziel, a demon, the son of Satan, in fact, and a general in Lucifer's army. Lastly, he was Reyes, a human for all intents and purposes. He became human to be with me. And he'd paid the price.

But he was here with me now. Reyes Alexander Farrow. My soul mate and my lover and my husband. So when he shoved his trousers past his hips, pushed my legs apart, and buried himself inside me in one, long thrust, the explosion of pleasure that washed over me was both achingly familiar and astonishingly novel.

He swallowed my gasp, kissing me long and hard and deep, siphoning every doubt I had that this was real. That he was here. On me and around me and inside me.

He began a slow, rhythmic offensive, burying his thick cock with painstaking precision. Taking his time. Exploring every inch of me with his hands and his tongue until the pleasure pooling in my abdomen convulsed and threatened to break free.

But his need seemed greater than even my own. It had been an entire century, after all. I could hardly blame him. So what began as a slow seduction of my senses quickly escalated to an exquisitely furious assault.

He abandoned all thoughts of propriety as his thrusts grew quicker and shorter and more desperate. He buried his face in my hair, his breaths warm against my cheek as he uttered the one word I would've given my life to hear not thirty minutes ago, his nickname for me: "Dutch."

His voice was as beautifully rich and stunningly sensuous as I remembered, the tenor alone driving me even closer to the brink of orgasm.

I dug my fingers into his steely buttocks, urging him deeper, the movement luring me toward that piercing edge.

"Please," I begged, whispering in his ear.

He shoved even harder. Even faster. The pressure building and building until his entire body stiffened beneath my hands.

I felt his orgasm as strongly as I felt my own. It crashed into me, his guttural growl heightening my own pleasure, mingling with the sweetest sting known to mankind.

Holding on for dear life, I clasped my arms around his neck and rode out the undulating waves of sensation, my spasms milking him as he emptied himself inside of me. He curled his fingers into my hair and panted into my ear, his warmth spilling into me. His fire engulfing me.

After a long moment of recovery in which the world slowly came back into focus, he wrapped his arms around me and rolled until I lay atop him. A place I loved to be.

"Welcome back," he said softly, his breath stirring my hair.

Hiding the fact that I was on the verge of tears, I buried my face in the crook of his neck and let my lids drift shut.

I was back. I didn't know how or why or for how long, but I was back and that was all that mattered. For now.

I awoke an hour later in my husband's arms, reveling at the feel of his skin against mine. There was so much I needed to know, so much I'd missed, but I asked the one question that had driven me to near lunacy.

I rose onto an elbow, peered into his infinite eyes, and asked, "Did she win?"

He didn't answer at first. Instead, the barest hint of a grin softened his features, giving him a boyish charm that I knew firsthand could be both endearing and lethal, often simultaneously. I'd seen that charm in all kinds of situations, from disarming a deranged stalker to coaxing a viperous demon out of a human host, and every time, it worked in his favor.

Crazy thing was, he wasn't the slightest bit aware of it. He had no clue what he did to men and women and demons alike. Or, if he did, he only took advantage of it in dire situations because his face could've opened so many more doors. He was, after all, the son of the most beautiful angel ever to grace the heavens.

He traced my mouth with his fingertips, and my chest filled to capacity with such a deep, eternal love, it threatened to burst. Which would kill the mood entirely.

I pulled my lower lip between my teeth, then asked again, "She won, right?"

He tucked a wayward strand of my brown hair, the same hair that hadn't seen the inside of a shower in over a hundred years, behind my ear.

I stifled a cringe at the thought when he asked, "How long do you think you've been gone?" His voice was all deep and rich and smooth. Like caramel. Or butterscotch. Or Darth Vader.

I leaned back to look at him. "Think? There's no thinking about it. I know exactly how long I've been gone. Right down to the second. Give or take."

"Yeah?" He flashed a smile that blinded me almost as much as the sun had. "And how long is that?"

"One hundred seven years, two months, fourteen days, twelve hours, and thirty-three minutes." I was totally lying. I might not have known the exact time served down to the minute, but I knew it was within shouting distance of my quote. "I was floating in darkness for over one hundred years."

He nodded, gave my answer some thought, then asked, "If you were floating in darkness, how do you know you were gone for a hundred and seven years?"

I looked past him, almost embarrassed. "I felt every second. I counted them."

He pulled me closer. "Aren't you really bad at math?"

"Speaking of which, I thought I was going to be exiled for all eternity."

Anger suddenly sparked inside him. I felt it like electricity spiderwebbing from molecule to molecule inside me. "Did it not feel like an eternity?"

I lowered myself back onto his chest. "It felt like three eternities."

He turned away, his brows sliding together in thought. "You shouldn't have done it."

Ah. That would explain the anger. Rising all the way to a sitting position, I looked down at him, trying to decipher his thoughts. "You would rather have lost Amber?"

Amber, my best friend's lovely daughter, was the reason I had been kicked off the third rock from the sun in the first place. But it'd hardly been her fault. She'd been killed by an insane priest who was trying to anchor himself to Earth—using Amber as the anchor—and skip out on the trip to hell that he'd booked centuries earlier.

I could heal people. That wasn't breaking the rules. I could even bring them back from death if, and only if, their soul had yet to leave their body. But Amber had been dead for two hours when we'd found her. Her soul long gone. I couldn't do that to Cookie, my BFF. I couldn't just let her daughter die when I could do something about it.

Was Reyes really suggesting that?

"Of course not," he said, offended. "You should've let me do it."

"Yes, because being cast into a hell dimension worked out so well the last time."

The last time he'd stage dived into a hell dimension, I didn't think he was going to get out. And when he did, he came back more Rey'azikeen and less Reyes. Gods were not known for their sparkling personalities or caring natures. It took a few days to get him back, days in which I worried I'd be forced to destroy him before he destroyed the planet and everything on it.

He lifted one shoulder in a halfhearted shrug. "That was a different. That was a true hell dimension."

I gaped at him. For, like, a really long time. "I'm sorry," I said, not the least bit apologetic. "Are you suggesting that my hell dimension was less hellish than yours?"

"My Brother would never have cast you into a real hell dimension."

"It was horrible," I argued.

"Most other realms are."

"It was cold and dark and endless."

"And if it had been a paradise?"

"Even the wraiths didn't— What?"

"If it'd had white beaches and blue waters and sun every day?"

He had a point. My shoulders deflated. "Without you in it, or Beep, it still would have been horrible. Look, I know time works differently in other dimensions." I drew in a deep breath, set my jaw, and girded my loins. Metaphorically. "So, give it to me straight. I can take it. How long was I gone?"

Maybe I hadn't been gone the entire century in this dimension. Maybe, just maybe, Beep was still alive. Hope fought agony for real estate inside my heart.

Reyes ducked his head, fighting off another one of those roguish grins, then said quietly, "Ten days."

I whirled onto my feet to face him. Then stood there stunned for what seemed like an hour, the truth of what he said sinking in ever so slowly as I frowned, then blinked, then frowned some more. I'd been gone for over a hundred years. Even the wraiths helped me keep track of time. But here in this dimension I had only been gone . . . "Ten days?" I snapped my jaw shut, then asked again in a rather grating shriek, "Ten lousy days?"

The wind had picked up. Sand swirled around us, creating a dust devil in the center of which we sat, but I was too astounded to pay much attention. Even as my hair whipped about my head and the sand scraped across my skin, I could only stand in indignant astonishment that I'd spent an eternity in agony.

Then reality sank in. The sand fell to the ground around us in one powdery whoosh as I realized Beep, our beautiful daughter, was still alive. And only ten days older than when I'd left her.

I pressed both hands to my mouth, relief flooding every cell in my body and causing pools of wetness to slip past my lashes. I would get to see her again. I would get to see everyone again. My family. My friends. They were all I'd thought about for a hundred years, and I would get to see them again.

Reyes had told me a similar story when he'd been trapped in a hell dimension. He'd said he was in there for what felt like an eternity while only an hour had passed on Earth. A freaking hour. And he'd come out a completely different being. At least I was still me.

I patted my face, my shoulders, the girls, a.k.a. Danger and Will Robinson. Yep, I felt very me-ish.

"They were definitely lousy," Reyes agreed, watching me feel myself up.

The smile that spread across my face felt heavenly, and a sob wrenched from my throat. "She's still alive."

"She's still alive," he said softly, seeming to know every thought I had. Every doubt and heartache and elation.

"And I'm still me, right?" I asked between hiccups. "I mean, do I look the same? How's my hair?"

Reyes tackled me, flipped me over him, and rolled on top of me.

I laughed when he buried his face in that same mess of hair again and caught my earlobe between his teeth. But it was his hands that were doing the real damage. He slid them over my stomach, up my breasts, testing the weight of both Danger and Will before going south and crossing the border into no-man's-other-than-Reyes's-land.

"What are you doing?" I said with a weepy giggle.

"Making sure you're still you. It didn't even occur to me that you could be an imposter."

"Imposter?"

He leaned away from me. "Or possessed."

"Possessed?"

"You *were* in a hell dimension." He said that bit with a smirk, dissing my hell once again. "Do you feel possessed?"

"Not particularly."

"The possessed never do. I'm just going to have to put you through a battery of tests."

"Tests?" I squeaked. When he dipped his head and brushed his tongue over Will's peak, I grabbed handfuls of his unkempt hair. "I didn't study. Will there be a written?"

2

The tests were brutal. I wasn't sure I'd passed all subjects until my very dedicated test administrator lay on top of me, panting, his warm breath fanning across my skin. I took that as a good sign. About every third pant, he'd find something else to nibble on. Some new and unexplored territory he'd claim as his own.

And then I realized something. He was stalling. All the questions I had, all the events I'd missed, and he was stalling. I'd been gone a long time. I had things to do and people to see and—

"Where's my phone?" I patted my naked body again. "I need my phone. Do I still have a phone? Wait, do they still use phones?"

"Ten days," he reminded me.

"Right. So, yes."

He pulled on the trousers and tied them at his waist. They dipped low over his hips, and I took a moment, an exquisite moment, to appreciate the work of art in front of me.

Tearing my gaze off him at last, I looked around for my clothes and noticed something I hadn't paid attention to before. We were actually lying on a huge pool of glass. Beautiful and blue and sparkling. But I could've sworn . . .

Realization dawned, and I bit my lower lip. "Um, Reyes, did we do this?"

He looked around, and his brows shot up in surprise.

"We heated the sand so much we created a pool of glass?" I asked, my voice an octave above grating. "In the middle of the Sahara? How are we going to explain this to Parks and Recreation?"

"Who are the wraiths?" he asked, completely unconcerned.

"We gotta get out of here before someone sees this." I rose and tugged on the sheer gown I'd materialized in.

"The wraiths?"

"They were my company. The only company I had. And they knew things." I tapped my temple for emphasis.

"Like calculus?"

"Like the fact that something is going on." I stopped to point an accusing index finger at him. "Something you aren't telling me. That and the fact that I have to figure out what happened when my mother died to be able to stop . . . whatever it is that's happening."

He stopped and faced me. "Your mother? What does she have to do with it?"

"With what?" I challenged.

"What did the wraiths say?"

"They said that hell is coming, and in order to stop it, I have to find out the truth about my mother's death."

He frowned in thought. "What would your mother's death have to do with anything?"

"Reyes." I walked up to him and put a hand on his chest. Mostly because I could. "What is going on?"

He covered my hand with his and lowered his head as though ashamed. "The hell dimension. The one I accidently opened? It's taking over the world."

———

Note to self: Do not open a hell dimension within another existing dimension and expect them to get along.

Reyes wrapped me in his arms, a place I dearly loved to be, and before I could say who's your uncle, we materialized into . . . a warehouse. A dark, dust-covered concrete warehouse with fluorescent lighting, metal cabinets, and lumpy cots.

"Sweetheart," I said, stepping away from him and doing a 360, "what did you do to our apartment?"

"Nothing. Our apartment, as you well know, is ground zero." He went to a wall of metal lockers and opened one up.

I grinned and wiggled my fingers at a little boy behind the lockers, but he ducked back. I must've looked worse than I'd thought.

"Beep?" I asked Reyes.

"She's safe."

"But I can't see her," I said matter-of-factly, trying to tamp down my disappointment.

"I had to evacuate her and the Loehrs to a safe house."

"They've been at a safe house since she was born." And they had been. My light, the same light that any supernatural being on this plane or the next could see, saw to that.

"A different safe house."

I understood. I really did, but it had been so long. "So, when?"

"When this is over." Attempting to dissuade me from asking more questions, he turned and tossed a bag to me. "Clothes. Shampoo. Toothbrush. Everything a growing girl needs."

I gaped at him, then tore open the bag. It was my stuff. My actual stuff.

"My . . . my toothbrush." I took it out and cradled it. "Fitzwilliam, is it really you?"

I grinned and glanced from beneath my lashes to see if I'd won the boy over yet. He'd peeked around the corner again but didn't crack a smile. Which only made me more determined.

Reyes glanced at the boy. "Did he follow you here from . . . ?"

"Marmalade? Nope. No little boys in Marmalade that I knew of."

"Marmalade?"

"Yes. That's what I named it. My very own hell dimension."

"It wasn't actually a hell—"

"The wraiths didn't have a name for it," I said, cutting in before he dissed my hell dimension. Again. What made his hell dimension so much hellier than mine? "How can you live somewhere that doesn't have a name?"

"So, these wraiths, they spoke to you?"

"Not at first. They just kind of watched me. For a really long time. Like twenty years. But they eventually warmed up to me. Speaking of which, how did they even get there? They were ghosts, spirits of a race long past, but there were no living beings in that entire dimension, so how did they get there?"

"Even in the barrenest realms, life thrives. Entities somehow get in. Make a home for themselves."

"I take it you're speaking from experience."

He scoffed softly then tossed me a pair of jeans. Jeans! I buried my face in them. Breathed them in. A combination of denim and citrus filled my nostrils, the laundry soap stirring up a torrent of memories. Mostly of Reyes bending me over the washer.

After several reminiscent moments, I said, "Are you hinting that I need to change?"

He cast me a sideways glance. "Not at all. I love what you're wearing."

I smiled and looked down a microsecond before gasping in horror. The white gown I'd materialized in was like gauze and completely see-through. I slammed the jeans to my chest and hugged them, searching for the little boy, but he'd ducked back behind the lockers.

"That poor kid is going to be scarred for life. Or, well, afterlife."

Reyes chuckled. "Yeah, I doubt that."

"So, is there a shower in this here one-horse town?"

He showed me to a room with a wash station. The warehouse had apparently been some kind of factory that required first aid compliance. It was no George, the luxury shower Reyes had built in our apartment, but it was hot and wet and everything I'd dreamed of for decades. Well, almost everything.

I brightened when Reyes stepped into the small room, one hand behind his back. I'd dried my hair and pulled it into a ponytail for the time being, but I felt wonderful. Clean. Warm. Safe.

"It's time," he said as I slipped into a T-shirt and the jeans he'd provided.

"Time?"

He brought his hand around, and it was like the clouds parted and heaven shone down on us. Blessing us. Nurturing our deepest, most primal desires.

"One triple shot mocha latte with extra whipped cream."

I ran to him and threw my arms around his neck, but only for a second. There was a mocha latte out there calling my name.

After snatching the cup out of his hand, I lifted the plastic lid to my lips and drank the nectar of the gods. The sensation that ran through my body with that very first sip, that very first sensation of chocolate and caffeine splashing onto my tongue, bordered on pornographic.

A moan slipped past my lips, and even though the liquid was the perfect temperature—scalding—I downed half of it before taking a breath. Then I slowed down. To savor. To relish. To luxuriate in.

Panting, I asked, "So, how bad is it?"

He grabbed a remote and turned on a flat screen before removing his own clothes.

The news on the television gave a rundown of the effects of a hell dimension opening in the middle of Albuquerque, New Mexico. They didn't know a hell dimension had opened up, but the signs were all there.

"Delirium is spreading faster than hospitals can keep up," a handsome anchor in a blue suit and tie said before the show cut to a montage of people in hospital emergency rooms, waiting to be admitted, many bruised, battered, and bloody. "Dozens have been admitted with an untold number of infected roaming the streets, unable or unwilling to seek help. Earlier today, the CDC had this to say."

The screen jumped to a Dr. Nisha Dev, a tiny dark-haired woman wrapped in a white lab coat. She stood barricaded behind a podium with a bouquet of microphones sprouting from all directions and pointed at her face.

"The effects of the infection are twofold," she said, her Middle Eastern accent soft as a hush came over the crowd. "It seems to attack the amygdala, the part of the brain that processes fear, triggers anger, and motivates us to act. It first presents with mild flulike symptoms, then quickly escalates to confusion and fear. From there, the patient may or may not slip into an agitated or volatile state. If you notice a family member acting confused or afraid, seek help immediately. Do not try to subdue your loved one yourself."

A cacophony of questions hit her at once, and she pointed to a reporter who asked about the violent behaviors of many of the infected.

"If a person presents, he or she needs to be sedated as soon as possible to forestall any violent tendencies that may emerge. The timeline of this evolution varies from person to person, so it's impossible to say at this point."

I pressed Pause and turned back to Reyes. "Are you telling me that we caused this?"

He lowered his head but said nothing.

"What kind of infection? Is this viral?"

"We don't know."

"Reyes, did we just start the zombie apocalypse? Is the extinction of the human race going to be on our heads?"

"That's what we intend to find out."

"Has it spread outside of the hell dimension?"

"It's staying within the boundaries for the most part."

"For the most part?"

"There've been a handful of cases outside the city, but they were all inside the war zone prior to the infection."

"The war zone?" I turned back to the television and studied the picture I'd placed on Pause. The doctor's expression had slipped. Her concern shone through her mask of professionalism. The news crawl below her picture had frozen on the words "Panic in the heart of New Mexico."

They had that right.

"Garrett came up with that. When you see what it does to people, you'll understand. But first, you need to go see Cookie."

I whirled toward him again. "She's here?"

"She refused to evacuate with the others," he said from between clenched teeth.

I giggled. On the inside. I could just see Cookie facing off against the son of Satan incarnate. And a god to boot. David facing off against Goliath had nothing on her.

"What others?"

"Amador and his family, your friend Nicolette, and, of course, Beep and the Loehrs."

Amador was Reyes's only friend growing up. They'd stayed close over the years, and Amador's family loved Reyes as much as he did. They were so lovely.

Nicolette was one of the cooler of my friends. She actually channeled the departed before they were even departed. I'd never met anyone else with her ability.

The Loehrs were Reyes's original human family. The one he'd been born into. He should have grown up happy, but Satan sent an emissary to make sure that didn't happen. Reyes had been kidnapped when he was a few months old and given to the monster who raised him. My husband's childhood had been the stuff of nightmares.

"And all of Beep's protection?" I asked. Beep had both supernatural and human protectors.

"They go where she goes," he said with a shrug. "All except your boyfriend and his gang."

"Donovan and the guys?" Alarm shot through me. "Why wouldn't they go? They're Beep's guardians."

"They're going to. Eric went back for his *abuela*."

I relaxed. Donovan, Michael, and Eric had been a part of the Bandits motorcycle club, but they'd moved on to greener pastures (i.e., watching over my daughter). They were good guys, and if Donovan made Reyes just a little jealous from time to time, so be it. Who was I to stand in the way of insanity?

Taking another swig for the road, or the hallway, I motioned for the kid to follow me and took off in the only direction I could go: down. We were on some kind of industrial upper-level balcony that looked down into the main warehouse. Cookie had to be down there somewhere, and I had a good idea where to look.

Seeking out what would have been a break room, I found Cookie standing guard over a coffeepot. Our coffeepot from the office.

"Bunny!" I cried, running forward. I wanted to throw my arms around the Bunn coffee machine, but she looked really hot at the moment. So I threw my arms around the best friend I'd ever had instead.

Cookie stiffened, and the effect was immediate and painful.

Understanding completely, I dropped my arms and stepped back. Her child had died because of me. They were about to sedate Cookie, she'd been so distraught, when I brought Amber back to life. But she'd been gone for two hours. On the other side for two hours. I couldn't imagine what Cookie went through in that time.

She turned toward me slowly, her chopped black hair a mass of disarrayed perfection. Her attire not much better. The wrinkled mess hugged her curves in all the right places. She was chaos incarnate. But to me, she was Aphrodite, Wonder Woman, and Melissa McCarthy all rolled into one.

"Charley?" she asked, her voice barely audible. "You're . . . you're back?"

Fighting the emotion that formed a knot in my throat, I nodded and pasted on a brave smile. "I'm back."

She pressed her hands to her mouth and continued to stare.

I cleared my throat and asked inanely, "How are you doing?"

"Oh, my God, Charley!"

Before I could react, she tackled me, and we hugged for a solid ten minutes. Her shoulders shook, and I couldn't help the deluge that cascaded down my cheeks.

"I'm sorry, Cookie," I said between sobs. "I'm so sorry."

"What?" She put me at arm's length and stabbed me with an admonishing glare. "What on Earth are you sorry for?"

I tried to play it off with a soft laugh, but it came out more as a strained choking sound. "Everything. I'm so sorry."

"Charlotte Jean Davidson," she said, her tone edged with a maternal warning, "don't you dare apologize to me."

"But it was Amber."

"Who is alive and well, thanks to you."

"No," I said, my shoulders deflating, "in spite of me. Everything that's happened to her—to both of you—it's all because of me."

"Oh, Charley, when will you understand how important you are?"

"And you aren't?" I asked, shrieking at her. "Amber isn't?"

"Of course she is, but we both knew what we were getting into by sticking around. You mean so much to her. She'd have it no other way."

"She hasn't reached the age of consent yet. I'm not sure her vote counts."

Cookie snorted. "Try telling her that. She . . . she hasn't been the same since you left."

Alarm shot through me. "What do you mean? What's wrong? Is she . . . does she remember?"

"She won't say, but I think she blames herself."

"For what?"

"Charley—"

"For my being kicked off the plane?" I asked, stunned. "Are you kidding?"

"She's a kid, sweetheart. She blames herself for measles and world hunger. It's a teen thing."

I shook my head. That child. "Is she here?"

"Yes. But first, coffee."

3

Cookie and I freshened our cups, then sat at a rickety table with mis-matched chairs.

The small break room opened up to a massive commons area that held a larger table and then a living area with a sofa and a few cushioned chairs. If it weren't an actual warehouse, the industrial feel of the area would've been considered quite en vogue.

At some point in our conversation, Reyes joined us. He stood in a cor-ner drinking something much stronger than coffee. My gaze kept straying toward him. I had a hard time forcing it back, but looking at Cookie, at the most marvelous woman I'd ever known, was almost as fun. Espe-cially when I realized she'd only applied mascara to one set of lashes. It happened to the best of us.

"So," Cookie said, hedging and tugging at her bra, "you're back."

"I'm back."

"What was it like?"

The question was so loaded, the weight behind it almost knocked me out of my chair. She felt guilty, too, and that guilt radiated out of her in smothering, airless waves.

I could hardly tell her the truth. That would do no one any good. So I fudged the facts. Just a little. But not without giving her a hard time. "It was horrible, Cook."

Her puffy lids rounded, and she chewed her lower lip, anxious.

"Excruciating. Bluebirds sang to me. Fruit grew randomly on ornamental trees. Squirrels cooked gourmet meals. Mice cleaned my house and darned my socks. Which is better than damning them, I suppose, but . . ."

Her face morphed into a prime example of a deadpan. "So, you were cast off this plane into Disneyland?"

I let one corner of my mouth drift up. "Can you think of a more appropriate hell for me?"

She giggled to herself and tugged at her bra again, casting a quick glance over her shoulder at Reyes.

Any other man might have looked away, pretending not to see her discomfort, but not my man. Nope. He tilted his head for a better view. Then he looked past us and winked.

I turned. Ghost Boy had followed me into the break room and was hiding behind a small refrigerator, peeking out from behind it every so often. He had brown, unkempt hair and a dirty face. Almost as dirty as the T-shirt he wore. He stared at Reyes, his eyes huge and wary, before easing back behind the fridge.

"Can I see her?" I asked Cookie.

She nodded. "Of course. She said she was going to take a nap, but she hasn't been sleeping. I doubt she's asleep now."

Cookie showed me to Amber's room. It was one of several rooms that had served as offices and storerooms when the warehouse had been in business. She nodded and left me to it.

I knocked on the closed metal door. When I didn't receive a reply, I cracked it open. I could feel emotion coming from inside. Too much for

Amber to have been sleeping. I eased it wider and stepped into the dark room. Amber sat on a cot, staring out of a dirty window.

"Can I come in?" I asked.

Amber stilled. She didn't turn around for a solid minute, and when she did, her expression was filled with wariness, as though she couldn't allow herself to hope.

"Hey, pumpkin."

She studied me, her jaw open, her eyes saucers. So it was pretty much the same reaction her mother had, except for the—

"Aunt Charley?" She blinked as though not believing her eyes, then she tore off the cot and ran into my arms.

Nope, exact same reaction.

I caught her to me and held on for dear life, the memory of her lifeless blue eyes replaying over and over in my mind. She had been dead. She'd actually died. It was so long ago, yet I'd never forgotten her faraway expression. Amber Kowalski relished life, she sparkled with it, but that night, that horrible night, everything had changed.

All I could think of as I looked down at Amber's lifeless body was Beep. What if it had been Beep? I had been given one rule, one law to abide, and I broke it for my best friend. I'd looked up at Reyes, swore I'd find a way back, then touched Amber. Healed her. Brought her to life again.

And in the one hundred years I'd spent in darkness, alone and tormented, I'd never regretted it. Not once. And I never would.

"Hey, pumpkin," I said into her long, dark hair. "How have you been?"

She let out a choked sob and pulled me tighter. I dragged her to the cot and sat down. She crawled onto my lap and cried, and my heart ached so much for her. She was devastated, and I realized at that moment that she might not have wanted to be brought back. What if she was happy where she was? What if she'd wanted to stay and I'd ripped her away from her family?

But I also had to remember that she had been killed very violently.

Her best-friend-slash-boyfriend had been in shock. He'd seen the priest claw at Amber, tear at her, trying to stay on Earth as hell tried to drag him down. In a word, he'd beaten her to death. The trauma she must have suffered at his hands . . .

I cradled her to my chest as the pain grew inside it. "I'm sorry, pumpkin. I'm so sorry."

She lifted her head at last. "Sorry?"

"I can't imagine what you went through. When that priest, the priest that I'd let loose onto this plane—"

"But . . . but you're not sorry you brought me back?"

"What?" I leaned back. "Is that what you think?"

"You were kicked off Earth because of me."

"Oh, sweetheart," I said, pulling her to me again. "I would do it again in a heartbeat."

"Really?" she said, her voice small and unsure.

I forced her to face me again. "In a heartbeat. Amber, you are so special. You—"

"I saw some parts of it."

"Some parts?"

"Of me and Quentin and Beep."

I put my fingers under her chin and raised her gaze to mine, her huge blue eyes swimming in unspent tears. "What did you see?"

"We're supposed to help her. Beep. We're part of her army. I saw it." She lowered her head again. "Is that why you brought me back?"

"Absolutely not," I said, putting as much edge in my voice as I could. "I brought you back because I love you. I can't imagine life without you."

A small smile softened her worried expression. "One good thing came out of all of this, you know."

"Oh, yeah? What's that?"

"I can see what all the fuss is about. You're blinding."

Ah, yes. My light. The beacon that is me. The same one that any departed from anywhere in the world can see and, if they so choose, use to cross through to the other side. Those poor souls who didn't cross at the time of their deaths, anyway.

That was the gist of my day job. As the grim reaper, I helped lost souls find their way home. But mostly I tried to figure out what it was anchoring them to Earth and get them past it.

Wait. "You can see my light?"

She giggled, her nose still stuffy. "I can see everything Quentin can see. Ever since I died."

Quentin, an adorable sixteen-year-old, had always been able to see the departed. That fact led to our first meeting. But while Amber had certainly exhibited metaphysical abilities, she'd never been able to see them like Quentin could. And she certainly couldn't see my light.

She giggled again. "Now I can tell Quentin he was right. You're like that light the doctor shines in your pupils during an eye exam."

"Thanks. And I'll tell him you used to play with your belly button in your sleep." I reached over to tickle her.

She screamed and kicked and cried for help. Cookie rushed in, and the whole thing devolved into a raucous wrestling match, Cookie and me against Amber. Poor kid.

But all the horsing around did have one effect. It seemed to relax Ghost Boy. He even almost, for the barest fraction of a second, cracked a smile. Not quite, but almost.

"Hey," Amber said, noticing him at last.

We sobered and straightened up our act. Not Cookie's hair, though.

"What is it, sweetheart?" Cookie asked her, brushing strands off her face and adjusting her bra again.

"Do you have a rash?" I whispered to her.

"A little boy," Amber said, greeting him with her warmest smile.

He scooted farther behind a locker but managed to keep a weather eye on us. Smart kid. We could pounce at any moment.

Cookie was still busy fiddling with her bra. She reached into her cleavage and pulled out a pair of tweezers. "Oh, goodness. I was looking for these."

I turned away and put a fist over my mouth, refusing to ask. There was simply no need. It was Cookie, after all.

"Isn't he adorable?" Amber asked.

I recovered and rolled off the cot and onto my feet. "He is. But I need coffee. And food. And to mack on my husband some more."

Amber giggled, and Cookie threw her hands over her daughter's ears.

"Language," she said, admonishing me.

"Do you even know what that means?" I asked her.

"No, but any time there is a verb in a sentence that references your husband, it's usually naughty."

"It's not naughty, Mom," Amber said, despite the sound barrier.

I rose to hunt down my husband when Cookie jumped up and followed me a little too close for comfort.

"Charley?" she said, her voice low and hesitant, supposedly so Amber, who was right on our heels, wouldn't hear.

"Yes, Cookie?"

"I just thought you should know."

"That your cleavage doubles as storage in a pinch?"

"That I may have accidently seen your husband naked. Two days ago. In the shower. Naked."

"Wait just a minute," I said, screeching to a halt and narrowing my eyes. "Didn't you accidently see him naked a few months ago?"

She bowed her head in shame. "Yes. But it wasn't my fault. I just went in to let him know dinner was ready."

"Wait just another minute," I said, raising an index finger. "You're cooking for him now?" She was totally going to make me look bad.

"Hell, no. I went to Twisters."

"Oh. Okay, then." I took off again, only to be hit with—

"Although he really likes my cinnamon rolls."

I stopped a second time and turned toward her with deliberate slowness. "What?"

"Reyes," she said, stars in her eyes. "He likes my cinnamon rolls."

"I can't believe this. You're cheating on me with Reyes? You've been making him your famous cinnamon rolls while I've been stuck in a hell dimension, longing for the ability to chew my toenails just for something to do?"

Amber whisked by us. "And enchiladas. He loves her enchiladas."

"Cook!" The sting of a thousand traitorous daggers pierced my heart. "I'm telling Uncle Bob."

The day my uncle Bob married my best friend was one that would live in infamy. My best friend became my aunt, which was only a little awkward. Mostly because she refused to let me call her Aunt Cookie. Ah, well. Picking my battles.

It might have been dawn on the other side of the world, but it was late evening in the Duke City. We ordered takeout from the Golden Crown Panaderia, which almost defeated the purpose since customers were treated to homemade biscochitos just for walking in the joint, and took our plates into the main part of the warehouse.

The commons area did triple duty as dining room, living room, and break-room-slash-kitchen. Not to mention the fact that one corner of the room was covered in computers and books and documents. It looked like Garrett's house. So it also served as our business center and headquarters. Thank goodness it was something like a hundred thousand square feet. Give or take.

Just as I sat down to sink my teeth into a slice of the Golden Crown's green chile bread, just as my mouth flooded in euphoric anticipation—I hadn't eaten in a hundred years—a male voice drifted to us from the rooms down a hall. A male voice I knew and adored.

"Everyone's leaving," he said. "They're calling it a mass exodus. I'd just call it an evacuation, but nobody asked me. Maybe we should—"

He stopped short when he rounded the corner and saw me. Garrett Swopes. A skip tracer turned scholar and a soldier in Beep's army. His dark skin and sparkling silver irises brought my heart into a state of pitter-patter.

"Charles?" he asked, astonished.

"The one and only." I rose and rushed into his open arms for a hug.

"What? How? When?"

"Well, I'm back. I have no idea. A few hours ago."

"You just . . . you just appeared?"

"Pretty much," I said, shrugging under the weight of his arms over my shoulders.

When I craned my neck to look up at him, he was appraising Reyes with the oddest expression. But by the time I turned, Reyes's gaze had dropped to his burrito. I stepped out of Garrett's arms, but he suddenly had somewhere else to look as well.

Okay, fine. I'd get to the bottom of that look once I got my husband alone. We'd promised. No more secrets. And I intended to hold him to it.

"So, people are fleeing the crime scene?" I asked, changing the subject.

"Yeah," Garrett said, snapping to attention. "The interstates are in total gridlock while a rowdier bunch has taken up looting."

"Great," Reyes said, his anger spiking.

"What exactly is going on, guys? I mean, what is this infection doing?"

Garrett's expression turned guarded. "It starts out like the flu. But then it changes. It's like they go insane."

"From all the records I've read," Cookie said, "they all think there is something inside them trying to get out. They hurt themselves trying to get it out, then eventually, they hurt others. They become uncontrolla-ble."

I sucked in a sharp breath and turned my attention to Reyes. "Possession?"

"I don't know. I've never seen a possession like this. Most people don't know they're possessed, despite what Hollywood would have you believe."

"Has anyone—" I stopped, unable to even think it. "Has anyone died?"

Everyone suddenly had somewhere else to look.

I stilled, then insisted, "How many?"

"Charles—"

"How many? How many deaths have we caused?"

"We don't know," Reyes said. "Six. Maybe seven."

I sank onto a nearby sofa, thankful there was one there to catch me. "We did this. We caused deaths. Human deaths."

"We don't know that," Garrett said, but he needn't have bothered. A glaring truth was difficult to ignore.

"Are we sure this is from the hell dimension?"

Cookie stood and grabbed a map off the desk. "Most of the activity centers here." They'd drawn a huge circle over part of Albuquerque. And our apartment building sat smack-dab in the middle of it.

"I can see it, too," Reyes said as he came to stand beside us.

"What?"

"The edges of the hell dimension. Quentin calls it the Shade."

"He can see it, too?"

He nodded. "From the roof. It's just a little darker than the rest of the world, and it's expanding exponentially."

"I get that, but what exactly is making people sick?"

"That's what we're trying to find out," he said.

"If it's expanding," I said, a bowling ball settling in my stomach, "how long do we have?"

"Until it takes over the world?" Garrett asked. "We don't know, hon."

"Why would your mother's death have anything to do with this?" Reyes asked, repeating an earlier sentiment.

"I don't know. The wraiths didn't say it had anything to do with it specifically. Just that if I found out the truth, that truth would help us stop this."

Three voices hit me at the same time. "Wraiths?" Garrett, Cookie, and Amber asked.

"It's a long story. Let's just say they came in peace."

"Okay," Garrett said, "I thought your mother died while giving birth to you."

"She did. That's what I don't get. Reyes, did you see anything unusual?"

"Uncle Reyes saw you being born?" Amber asked, fascinated.

"That's another long story," I said to her. "But, yes, Reyes was at my birth. At my mother's death. I only remember a black robe—"

"You remember being born?" Amber asked, her eyes now like saucers.

"Long story," I reminded her. It was before I knew him, of course. Before I knew he was the supernatural being who followed me around and kept me out of harm's way as a child. Then I turned to him. "Do you remember anything unusual? Anything, I don't know, supernatural?"

"No. Your mother seized, and then the monitor flatlined. And she . . . she crossed through you. To me, at the time, the whole thing was very unusual. That was the first time I'd . . . the first time you'd summoned me. I didn't understand what was going on."

"I didn't, either. But what would that have to do with anything?"

"Who else was at the hospital?" Garrett asked.

"Just my dad. Oh! Gemma and Uncle Bob were there, too. I forgot. They were in the waiting room."

"You saw them?" Amber asked.

"No. But Gemma told me years later she'd been there. She said she'd fainted and Uncle Bob found her."

"That's interesting," Reyes said. "Why would she have fainted?"

"That's what I'd like to know. Speaking of which, where is Ubie?" I asked Cook.

"Your uncle is working late. All the chaos and vandalism. The captain called everyone in."

I nodded. "What about Gemma?"

Cookie shook her head. "I called her, tried to get her to come out here, but she said she had clients. She couldn't leave yet."

"Yep, that's Gemma for you."

"Pari, too," she added.

My breath hitched. "She's still there?"

A phenomenal tattoo artist and a queen of snarky comebacks, Pari was another of my best friends. She'd died for a few minutes when she was a kid and could now see into the supernatural realm, though she didn't have a clear picture of it like Quentin, and now Amber, did.

"Said she had clients coming in tonight, but she promised to pack a bag and be here after her last one left."

"Damn. If anyone should be wary, it's Pari. She can see them. Not like you, Amber, but . . . Guess I'm going to have to fetch the both of them."

First Reyes then Garrett slapped me with stares of incredulity.

Reyes stood so he could tower over me. Establish his dominance. He was so cute when he did shit like that.

"Like hell you are," he said.

"You said you were going in to investigate what exactly was happening to the infected. This is our chance."

"This is *my* chance," he argued. "I'll go in, check out the lay of the land, get Pari and your sister, and come back."

"Hmmm," I said, humming aloud. I put my hand under my chin in thought. "Where have I heard that before?"

"Dutch," he said in warning.

So.

Cute.

"Oh, right!" I brightened. "You said something very similar the night you convinced me to send you into that hell dimension and wait while you 'checked out the lay of the land,'" I said, adding air quotes, "and then bring you right back out none the worse for wear. Easy peasy. Only you didn't come back out."

"You are not going in there."

"You got trapped. Eons later, in otherworldly time, you broke out of said hell dimension, shattering the gate, and released it onto this plane."

"You are not going in there," he repeated, that time through clenched teeth.

"You are not stopping me. I'm getting Pari and Gemma and checking out this Shade dimension for myself."

Reyes glared. Cookie took that as her cue to clear the plates. Amber gawked, her face full of blatant fascination. Garrett went back to an ancient book he was reading, presumably for research.

"We don't have time to mess around," Reyes said.

"Now we don't have time to mess around? Where was that sentiment three hours ago when we melted sand into glass in the middle of the Sahara Desert?"

Reyes's expression remained impassive. He didn't embarrass easily.

I tilted my head in curiosity. "I'd assumed we didn't have time to mess around, considering the deaths and all. But maybe there's more? Is there something else you'd like to share with the class?"

He turned away, thought for a moment, then said softly, "We only have three days."

4

A lot of days I truly expect my horoscope to say,
"Just don't kill anyone today."
—MEME

Three days? We only had three days? And then what? No one moved as we waited for more information.

Silence stretched out so long that when a male voice spoke from the shadows, we all jumped and turned in unison.

"He didn't tell you?" Osh asked, walking forward.

I might have only been away ten days here on Earth, but for me it felt like lifetimes. Osh, or Osh'ekiel, was a former slave demon, a Daeva. And while he might have looked nineteen with shoulder-length sable hair, clear, bronze-colored eyes, and his requisite top hat, he'd been around for centuries and had probably been alive for several millennia.

True, he lived off the souls of others, but he'd made a solemn vow to only live off the dregs of society henceforth. Which was why I let him stay.

Good thing I did. He was powerful. A strong ally. And he'd saved every life in the room at least once. Also, I'd missed him.

He spared a quick glower for my baby daddy, then strolled to me, a grin full of warmth and mischief lighting his face.

I met him halfway and wrapped myself around him. "Where have you been?" I asked into his shoulder.

"Looking after your rug rat."

I lurched back. "She's okay? She's safe?"

"For now." He tossed Reyes another glower.

"Osh, this isn't his fault. I'm the one—"

"Who created that thing in the first place?"

"That's not the point." I did tend to gloss over that part. The part about how Reyes, both a hellraiser and a hellmaker in his youth, had been the one to create the dimension that was slowly eating away at my reality. "But he made it for me."

"He made it on a ruse for you. His own Brother tricked him into making it, but we both know who it was really meant for."

Anger lashed out of him and stole my breath. I hadn't seen him that mad at Reyes in a long time. But he wasn't angry for himself. I had the distinct impression he was angry for Beep. Which made sense. He was destined to be a part of her army. A big part.

If what I saw still held true, he was destined to be the Warrior. The one who would either be by her side when the war with Lucifer began, or not. Either way, his participation, or lack thereof, could tip the scales in favor of or against my daughter.

He didn't know any of that, of course, but he cared so much for her. I couldn't imagine he would abandon Beep when she needed him most. Not unless there was another obstacle I hadn't seen. An outside force keeping him from her side.

"That doesn't matter now," I said to him. "All that matters is what we do to stop this."

His jaw tightened then relaxed as he refocused on me and offered a sympathetic smile. "So, how long?"

My brows slid together. "How long?"

He ran a fingertip under my jaw, waiting for me to catch on.

"Oh. Right. The time differential phenomenon. One hundred seven years, two months, fourteen days, twelve hours, and thirty-three minutes."

"Damn."

"Yep."

"I'm sorry, sugar."

"Me, too. I missed everyone so much."

He pulled me into yet another hug. I couldn't seem to get enough of them. Delight rushed through me until I remembered what Reyes had said.

I turned to him. "What do you mean we only have three days? Three days until what? It swallows the Earth whole?"

He lifted a wide shoulder. "Something like that."

Cookie gasped. "Three days?" she asked, worry spiking within her. All the stress she'd been going through was taking its toll. I could feel it gnawing at her.

I walked over to him. He was leaning against a desk. I joined him. He reached over and hooked two fingers into the belt loop on my jeans.

"Why three days?"

"I've done the math. The more the dimension expands, the more mass it acquires. The more mass, the faster it will expand until, in less time it took to gain a mile, it will encompass the entire planet."

Damn. His answer sounded perfectly legit, but something was off. I couldn't tell if he was lying or not. His emotions were so tightly packed, so tightly controlled, it was impossible to read him at times. But I felt a niggling of deception, like he was telling the truth but not the whole truth. What was he leaving out?

I shook off my doubts and focused on the business at hand. "Well, then, I guess we'd better get started."

"What's with the kid?" Osh asked, gesturing toward the little boy hiding behind the sofa.

"I'll try to talk to him," Amber said, and I realized she'd been easing closer and closer to him during our entire conversation. "Quentin will be in soon. He can help, too."

"Thanks, Amber." I didn't have time to deal with a kid right then and there. This new ability of Amber's might come in very handy.

"I'll go with," Osh said, stealing a bite off the plate I'd abandoned.

"Count me in, too," Garrett said, closing the book he'd been reading.

"Osh, I'd rather you keep an eye on Beep," I said, only a little jealous that he'd spent more time with my daughter than I had. Though from what Reyes had told me before, Osh kept his distance. Watched from afar and let the Loehrs do the actual caretaking of Beep. That was probably best, since he'd never taken care of a kid in his very long life.

"I have Angel on it."

Angel. I'd been longing to see his sweet face since I materialized.

"As wonderful as Angel is, he's still departed. There's only so much he can do should something happen."

Osh gave me a thumbs-up, took another bite, then vanished.

"And you," I said to Garrett.

He was in the middle of shrugging into his jacket. He stopped and raised his brows in question.

"You're human."

"Not all the time," he said, joking.

"I don't want to risk you getting this infection."

"Well, I don't want to risk you disappearing again."

I crossed my arms. "And what would you do if I did?"

He looked at the ceiling in thought. "Watch you?"

"Pretty much."

"So, this is your way of telling me I'm useless?"

"No." I walked closer and put a hand on his arm. "This is my way of telling you I need you here, researching this thing."

He let his jacket slide over his wide shoulders and down his long arms before hanging it back onto a hook. I only noticed how alluring his actions were because Cookie noticed—if the little spot of drool on the corner of her mouth was any indication.

"Amber, you see what you can find out about the little one."

She brightened. "I love it when I have an assignment. A cool assignment. Not a lame one like my latest school assignment."

"And what is your latest school assignment?"

"I have to rewrite an essay about how I'm going to change the world when I graduate high school."

"You have to rewrite it?" I asked.

"Yeah, my teacher didn't appreciate my first one where I wrote about being in Beep's army and how we were going to fight Satan for the survival of the human race. He said he didn't want fiction."

I gasped. "The gall."

"Right?"

Chuckling, I turned to Cook. "And you."

She paused and turned back to me, a taco halfway to her pretty mouth.

"You see what you can dig up about my mother's death."

"On it. Wait, what?"

"I need to know who signed off on the death certificate. Who her doctor was. The nurses that were in the room when I was being born. Anything and everything you can get."

"Is there a reason?"

"I wish I knew."

"Okay, I'm on it."

Reyes and I took Misery, my cherry-red Jeep Wrangler, into battle. We had to infiltrate the war zone, and we needed a backseat to extract Pari and Gemma. I should have been a general. Or, at the very least, a lieutenant. I totally had the lingo down.

As Reyes drove closer to our old haunts, I understood what he'd meant earlier. The closer we got to the expanding hell dimension, a.k.a. the Shade, the more I could see the line between the non-occupied areas of Albuquerque and the occupied.

Looking at it from the outside in, the barrier was like the ocean at night, only perpendicular to Earth's surface. It undulated in waves of shimmering darkness, and I didn't even have to shift onto the celestial plane to see it.

Reyes sat in the driver's seat, idling at a stoplight. "As much as I hate to say this, there's another hiccup we need to consider."

I stifled a groan. "Aren't you all sunshine and rainbows."

"I'm not saying it'll become an issue, but it's worth mentioning."

"Fine," I said, taking in the sights and sounds of my hometown. Since we were headed in, and most people were headed out, we didn't come up against much traffic. Small victories. "Hit me."

"Lucifer."

"Ah, how is dear old Dad?"

"He's the best at what he does. He'll use any situation to his advantage. He'll think of ways to manipulate a situation before you or I even realize there is a situation."

"You think he'll come after her through all of this." And by "her" I meant Beep. Our daughter. The girl destined to defeat him.

"It's possible. And, again, if I think it's possible now, he thought it was possible days ago. But he won't come at her head-on. He's all about stealth. If he does try something, we'll be blindsided."

"What can we do?"

"Nothing. Just be aware. Take note of anything . . ."

"Unusual?" I supplied. "Because the ever-expanding hell dimension sparking a zombie apocalypse isn't unusual enough?"

"Point taken. Just be aware."

"What about your Brother? Where does He stand in all of this?"

"Free will opened it."

"Seriously?" I said, gaping at him.

"According to your best friend, Michael, free will opened it, free will has to close it."

I sat back in stunned disbelief. "Well, that just seems counterproductive. I mean, He booted me for breaking one little rule. And He's just going to sit back and watch His world be destroyed?"

He shrugged a noncommittal brow.

"I don't believe it." I crossed my arms in defiance.

"Doesn't matter. As of this moment, He's staying out of it. I'm not saying He'll let this continue indefinitely. This is His realm, after all. But right now we're on our own."

I nodded, still reeling at that little nugget of gold.

"What's with you and Garrett and Osh?"

"What do you mean?"

"I sensed some . . . hostility."

"I did open a hell dimension on this plane."

"And that's it?" I'd sensed more than just an accusation in their emotions.

"Unless you know something I don't."

Damn it. Once again I couldn't tell if he was lying or not. Anyone else on the planet and I'd be good to go, but noooo. Not Mr. Farrow.

Still, we did agree, once upon a time, to no secrets. Surely he'd tell me if there was something else behind their hostilities.

Reyes turned right on San Mateo, heading for Gemma's office first. Cookie pinged her cell. Hopefully she'd still be there.

He slowed when we passed through the barrier of Albuquerque and the Shade. I filled my lungs and held my breath, not sure what to expect, but nothing happened. I didn't feel any different. I didn't see anything of particular note. Everything looked the same, completely normal if not a little hazy.

Even through the mist, rays from the setting sun on our right ribboned across the horizon in reds and yellows and oranges. A classic New Mexico sunset. The perfect homecoming gift.

"Is this haze supernatural?" I asked him.

"Yes. Most humans can't see it."

He turned again, and we passed through a residential area. Kids were playing in the front yard of one house while a man was working on his car in another. "Why didn't you want me coming alone? Everything seems pretty normal."

"In case you've forgotten, you're a blazing beacon of light."

"Can the demons from this hell see it?" I asked, alarmed. I'd seen them once, the demons, while they ate the bones of the priest who killed Amber. He'd been incorporeal. The priest. And yet his bones still crunched when they ate them.

I shivered at the memory, marveling about how the colliding dimensions were wreaking havoc on my town in more ways than one.

"Yes." He said it so resolutely, I had to question his reasoning.

"What makes you think so? I mean, they don't have eyes."

"They don't need them."

"And you know this because . . . ?"

He pulled to a stop in front of Gemma's office. "Dutch, I created them for you. Their sole purpose was to sense you. To track you."

"Ah. Right. I forgot."

"There's one more thing you should be aware of."

"Is it bad? It's bad, huh?"

"We can't shift. That much I remember from my time inside. We can't dematerialize."

"So, if something goes horribly wrong, we're stuck."

"Until we can physically cross through the barrier, yes."

"And you didn't think that was worth mentioning before we dove in headfirst?"

He planted a patient stare on me. "Would that have stopped you from coming?"

"Oh, look," I said, changing the subject. "Gemma's car."

My sister's new Jaguar sat in front of an adobe office building. She was a head shrink and a darned good one if not for that tiny blemish on her record where she fell in love with one of her patients and had to stop seeing him professionally so they could date. I hated when that happened.

"Wait here," Reyes said, stepping out of Misery.

"Wait here? I'm not waiting here."

He turned and growled at me. Low and deep and guttural.

I parted my lips and took him in, all scruffy hair and wide shoulders. "Now you're just trying to seduce me."

He narrowed his lids, but his mouth softened nonetheless. "I just want to make sure there aren't any around."

"Demons?" I asked, snapping to attention. For some reason I'd never understand, I yanked my feet off the floorboard, tucked my knees under my chin, and wrapped my arms around my legs. "You think they're here?"

"I don't know," he said, fighting off an attack of the dimples.

Apparently, I was hilarious.

He walked around Misery, scanning the area as he went, and opened my door for me. "Looks clear."

I pulled my knees closer, trying not to panic. "Did you check under the car?"

He grinned, then bent to look up Misery's skirts. "No demons there."

If I didn't know better, I'd say he was enjoying my trip down terror lane. "You do remember them, right? No eyes? No noses? Just huge mouths with cracked lips pulled back to look like the smiles of those who enjoy torture and the scent of formaldehyde?"

"Creator," he said, reminding me. "I know very well what they look like."

I climbed out of Misery and glowered at him. "Let me just state for the record, Guillermo del Toro has nothing on you." I reached up and tapped my finger against his temple. "There's something really messed up in there, buddy."

"I've been trying to tell you that since we met. We should hurry."

"Right." We took off toward the door, but I stopped and looked at him again. "You created them. Why can't you just, you know, un-create them? Wave your hands and make all this disappear?"

"Because this isn't Hogwarts."

"But you're a god," I said, on the verge of whining, until I realized he'd just referenced Harry Potter and I fell a little deeper into the abyss of love. I shook it off and added, "And this is your creation."

"Two words: *Frankenstein's monster.*"

"Oh, yeah, that makes sense."

"I created the Shade with the intent that it would never be released from its boundaries. It should have remained encapsulated in the god glass for all eternity. I've never released a hell dimension. I have no idea how to close one once it's been set loose."

He'd been trapped in the Shade for God knows how long, and when he escaped, he was not the same Reyes we all knew and loved. If he could've done something about it, he would have. But I still felt there was a connection of some kind. That the answer lay within my husband and his abilities.

A line of cars drove past, honking their horns and yelling obscenities like floats at a drunken Rose Bowl parade. They held up signs about this being the end of times and how the apocalypse was nigh. Sadly, it was never nigh enough.

"If you think about it," I said as we stepped up to Gemma's entrance, "Albuquerque is the new Bermuda Triangle."

He nodded, still scrutinizing the doom-and-gloom parade.

I opened the door and walked into the wake of a tornado. The receptionist's office had been vandalized. Books and papers lay strewn across the floor. Shards of glass from a broken lamp peppered the carpet.

"Gemma!" I burst through her office door and found much of the same. Turned-over chairs. A broken coffee table. Glass from a window littering the ground.

Then I saw sneakered feet. Bare calves. A prone female body.

"Charley?"

I whirled around, and Gemma rushed into my arms. I hugged her hard, then looked back to where the woman lay on the ground. "Gemma, who is that? What happened?"

She followed my gaze. "Carolyn. She's a patient. She just . . . she attacked me." Gemma choked back a sob and buried her face in the crook of my shoulder as Reyes looked around.

I closed my eyes and filled my lungs. "Gemma, was she infected?"

After a loud swallow, she looked back at me. "I don't know. I've never seen one in person. She just went crazy. She just— Wait." Her eyes rounded. "If she was infected, am I going to get it?"

"No, hon. I don't think that's what's going on here."

I looked back at the woman. She had mutilated herself before coming after Gemma. Before becoming enraged.

After checking out the rest of the office, Reyes walked up to us, his expression dire. He put a hand on my head, blocking my vision, and brought us both into his embrace.

My chest hurt. We'd done this. We'd caused this devastation, and lord only knew how many more would die because of it.

"We have to stop this," I said to him.

He nodded, his expression impassive, but I felt the tension humming beneath his steely exterior.

I called Uncle Bob and filled him in through choking sobs so the police could cordon off the scene. I told him to check out Gemma's office personally and call it in as an anonymous tip so we wouldn't have to wait around. We needed to get to Pari's as soon as possible.

We had to practically force Gemma to come with us. Apparently, her boyfriend, Wyatt, was supposed to meet her there later. She didn't want to leave, but I assured her we would get word to him where she was.

After a lightning-quick battle of rock-paper-scissors, I won the honor of riding shotgun. Gemma climbed in back, and I took the seat next to my main squeeze. He wrapped my hand in his as he drove, and I turned to look out the window. I just needed to get through the next few days, the next few hours, before I lost it completely. Before everything we'd done, all the suffering we'd caused, sank in.

Pari was our next stop, and I could only hope she hadn't suffered through a similar situation. She was closer to ground zero than Gemma had been. Much closer. And if I knew Pari, she was right in the middle of it.

5

By the time we got to Pari's place, Central had devolved into a torrent of chaos. The infected were multiplying in droves, but with all the drinking and rowdy behavior, it was impossible to tell who was infected and who was just having fun. Lining the south side of the University of New Mexico, Central had been a designated party area for years, but this was ridiculous. I could only hope Pari had not become someone's party favor.

The minute Reyes pulled into the alley behind Pari's shop, I had my door open and was sprinting toward her back entrance.

"Stay here," I heard him tell Gemma as I tore through Pari's back door.

He was fast on my heels when I came to a screeching halt in front of Pari's office. I peeked inside. Papers strewn everywhere. A broken lamp. A keyboard sitting perilously lopsided on a stack of binders.

I breathed a sigh of relief. Nothing out of place, thank God.

"Pari!" I yelled, hurrying through her shop to the front waiting area.

"Charley?" Pari turned toward me from the reception desk. She'd been helping a gorgeous couple choose a tattoo. One man had his index finger planted on a picture of matching hearts, but his partner held up a pair of snakes wrapped around two wrists.

"Pari," I said, gaping at her, "what the fuck?"

"Charley?" she said again, speechless for once in her life. Then, snapping to her senses, she rushed into my arms. I'd been getting that a lot lately. Thank Reyes's Brother I was a hugger.

"Are you even paying attention to the news?" I scolded.

"Charley. You're here."

"Nothing gets past you," I said, kissing her cheek. "And have you noticed the ruckus outside?"

"Yes," she said, squinting at me. "But I had a client tonight. I had to see him one more time."

I gasped. "Are you hooking up with someone?"

"What? No. Well, yes, but not him. I mean, he's cute and all, like really cute, but that's not it."

One of the men spoke up then. "What if we got the snakes in the shape of a heart?" he asked his partner.

"Hey," the other one said, brightening just as a beer bottle slammed against Pari's front window.

"Sorry, guys," I said, disentangling Pari and shooing them out. "Shop's closed."

The disappointed couple started for the front door. I dove onto the tall desk, reached over, and grabbed their collars.

They both made strangling sounds and turned back to me, appalled.

"Go out the back. It's sketchy out there."

A little wasted themselves, they did as they were told, giggling and stumbling into one another. But when they passed Reyes, they stopped short and both their jaws fell open.

"I know, I know. He's a looker." I shooed again. "I hope you guys have a long and wonderful life together."

One corner of Reyes's mouth tipped up. "Jealous?"

"Please." I took hold of Pari's hand and led her toward the office before turning back to him. "Unless I should be. I've been gone a long time. Is there something you want to tell me?"

His only answer was to go to the front and close up the shop for Pari.

"Do you think I should be jealous?" I asked her.

"Charley."

"Pari."

"Chuck."

"Par." I stepped closer until we were nose to nose. "Seriously, hon, I can do this all day. Now where's your bag?"

"You're here."

"Is this it?" Reyes asked. He held up a bag he'd found hanging on a coat rack.

"That's it." I foraged through it, found her ginormous sunglasses, and pushed them onto her face.

"Wait." She grabbed my arm, suddenly ecstatic. "You're here. I was waiting for a client, but he didn't show. I wanted to tell you about him. How are you here?"

"I don't know. I just kind of materialized in the Sahara Desert."

"Wow. Chuck, you gave up your life to save Amber."

"Not really. I'm still a god. I knew I wouldn't *die* die."

She sank onto the nearest chair. "Where have you been?"

"Marmalade," I said, trying to stand her back up again. "It's a quaint little corner of the universe with wraiths and a charming view of eternal darkness. We need to get you some clothes."

She gasped and looked down, then sagged in relief. "Oh, my God, I thought I was naked again. I do that sometimes." She glanced at Reyes and winked.

He chuckled and reminded me, "We need to get to the hospital."

"Hospital?" she asked.

"Yes, we're trying to find out what's going on. What this infection is."

"Cookie said something about a hell dimension."

"Yep, and we are smack-dab in the middle of it. Clothes?"

"Oh, right."

She led us up a flight of stairs to her tiny apartment and started throwing things into a bag. Haphazardly, unless she really felt she was going to need a feather boa and a riding crop at the warehouse. Well, maybe the riding crop.

"So, Chuck," she said, going for the toiletries.

"Yes, Par." I found her underwear drawer and went to town.

She peeked around the corner and busted me holding up a pair of lace boy shorts. "I know you've been through a lot, but . . . hey, did you get brighter?"

I stuffed them in the bag. "I don't think so."

"You did." She walked out to look me over. "You're brighter. I can barely see you even with my shades on. You're burning the retinas out of my head."

"You're exaggerating."

"If you say so, but if I go blind, I expect you to heal me."

"Deal. Now, what's this about a guy?"

She headed back to the bathroom. "Sorry, right, it's just, I know you have a lot going on."

"Par, no offense, but that's never really stopped you."

Reyes picked up a pair of handcuffs.

"True. Okay, so this guy came in the other day, right?" She tossed toiletries into a makeup bag as she spoke.

"Mm-hm." I motioned for Reyes to put the cuffs down.

"He just wanted a touch-up of an old tat."

He tossed them into the overnight bag.

"I'm with you so far," I said, taking the cuffs out. "Socks?"

"Yes, please. It's just, he had a little ink here and there, but he was mostly into what I thought was branding. I mean, it's not what I'm into, but who am I to judge? I have Satan riding a unicorn on my ass."

"No way."

"Way." She came out and stuffed the makeup bag into the overnight.

"So, he takes off his shirt. The tat is across his upper back. Nice lines. Clean. But he has all these names covering his torso and arms."

I nodded, pretending to understand the dilemma.

"Dozens. Men. Women. Some even written in some kind of foreign script."

"Okay."

"So, I ask him about them. He says they're names of all the people who have broken his heart. I'm thinking, cool, he's bi and just really, really unlucky in love. And kind of a ho, if you know what I mean."

"Maybe he's a glutton for punishment."

"Maybe, but the more I look, the more I think there's something else going on. I looked at a couple of names that were fresh. Like still scabbed over. And I realized they weren't brands but cuts. Self-inflicted, if I had to guess. And one was Merry. Not M-A-R-Y, but M-E-R-R-Y. It's a very unusual way to spell it, right?"

"True."

"It's just that I remembered something in the news about a Merry Schipplet who went missing a couple of weeks before he came in. I only remembered it because of the unusual spelling. This young girl was going to graduate her high school valedictorian. She'd been accepted to Vassar. She was going to spend her summer in Tanzania helping out at a refugee camp. Her disappearance made national headlines. Chuck, her parents . . . they're devastated."

I opened a binder to look at some of her latest tattoos. "I'm sure they are. You think there's a connection?"

"I didn't until I saw another fresh one. It had scabs, too. It said Mark."

"M-A-R-K?"

Her shoulders sagged in disappointment. "Yes. That one was the normal spelling, but I looked it up. Around the same time that Merry went missing, a man named Mark was stabbed to death outside a convenience store in Gallup."

"Okay."

"So I ask this guy what he does." She grabbed my shoulders and turned me to face her, garnering my full attention. "You're not going to believe this."

Suspense hung thick in the air. I held back a grin and raised my brows in anticipation.

"Charley, he's a truck driver!"

A long, drawn-out silence filled the air, and I blinked a few times as I let her revelation sink in.

She shook my shoulders, possibly causing permanent brain damage. "Don't you get it? He's a serial killer truck driver. He must kill people while he's on the road. At truck stops and stuff."

"Oh, of course. *That* truck driver."

"And who knows what he's done with Merry. Poor girl. She's probably in a shallow grave somewhere."

"Do you have a name?"

"Merry Schipplet."

"No, his name."

"Only a first name. He paid in cash. I was so hoping he'd come in tonight. I wanted to get some pictures. Look up other names he'd carved into his flesh."

"Pari," I said, giving her my best frown of disapproval. "That's dangerous. What if he really is a killer?"

"Oh, yeah." She sat on the bed. "I didn't think of that. I just wanted proof."

"I'll get Cookie on it. You stay away from him, understand?"

She shrugged and toed a shoe on the floor. "I guess."

"Okay. In the meantime, can I please see your ass?"

One more stop and then we were so out of there. Pari sat in the backseat with Gemma, only a little cramped. Misery's backseat wasn't the most comfortable in the land, but it got people from point A to point B.

"Why are we going to the hospital again?" Gemma asked.

"Reyes and I are going to go in and check out the infected patients."

"Do you think that's wise?" Pari asked.

"We'll know soon enough. We need to see them for ourselves. This could all be connected to the hell dimension."

"Oh, yeah," Pari said, "the one you opened."

"Yes." I cleared my throat. "The one we opened."

"Twenty-twenty hindsight, yeah?"

"We didn't actually mean to open it, Pari. It just kind of—" I startled when, for the third time since we'd left Pari's shop, a swish of charcoal blurred across Misery's hood.

Reyes's hands gripped the steering wheel tighter.

"Is it my light?"

"Like moths to a flame," he confirmed. "I'm surprised it took them this long."

"The demons from hell, from Lucifer's hell, can't be touched by light without bursting into flames. What's up with these guys?"

"Remember the part about me creating the hell for you specifically?"

I pressed my lips together and nodded. "Right. You'd have to create something that wasn't affected by it."

"I guess I succeeded."

We pulled into the emergency room drive-through. "In and out," he said before looking at our passengers. "Don't move."

"Aye, aye, handsome." Pari saluted to emphasize her ability to follow orders.

He gave her a flirtatious wink.

We started to get out, but I turned back to them. "And, you know, just in case they're attracted to sound, be as quiet as you can."

"Great," Gemma said, fear evident in every line on her face.

"We'll be right back."

We left Misery running and jumped out, figuring it wouldn't take long to determine if the infection was indeed supernatural. We were right. The moment we walked in to the urgent care waiting area, we saw them. At least a dozen patients sat in various states of mania. Some pulled at their own hair or chewed on their nails. Others sat curled into themselves, afraid of their own shadows as their loved ones tried to soothe them. Two others fought while hospital staff attempted to restrain them.

Another victim was brought in by ambulance as we stood there, which was odd because the ambulance entrance was on the other side of the building. That entrance must have been jammed up. The entire hospital staff was running on fumes, and people just kept coming in.

But each and every victim had one thing in common. They were playing host to a nasty Shade demon, their powdery gray bodies shuddering inside the humans they had inhabited. I covered my mouth with both hands, wanting so much to help them.

The woman on the stretcher was in the middle of a seizure when the EMTs brought her through. She had handfuls of her own hair twisted in her fingers, and her face and arms were covered in scratches and cuts. While the demons in most of the infected were docile and barely moving, the demon in this woman was scratching and clawing at her as though it were trying to get out. It bit her, its bare teeth sinking into her flesh.

"We have to stop it," I said, rushing toward her.

Reyes held me back. "They're trying to cross," he said, astonished.

"What?"

"They're trying to cross onto the earthly plane. To escape their own dimension and enter this one through a human host."

I didn't know why I was so shocked. That was exactly how both Reyes and I entered the earthly plane. To gain access, we were born onto the plane through a human host. But we were the people we were conceived to be. We didn't take a human life to make room for ours. These demons, these monsters, were taking human lives to try to enter this realm.

I faced Reyes, glowering at him. "We have to try to stop it. We have to try."

He nodded. "You're right. We need a distraction."

Two minutes later, Pari was seizing on the floor inside the ER, God love her. Reyes and I took advantage, easing closer to the woman. They'd sedated her, but the drug didn't affect the demon in the least. He was still trying to claw his way out while the woman lay helpless, being fed upon from an invisible parasite.

I took her hand. The demon was close, and it knew it. Like a shark in the middle of a feeding frenzy, it bit and wriggled and tried to break free.

Without the ability to shift, to dematerialize, we could do nothing but watch. The woman arched her back and began to seize again. Reyes straddled her on the gurney, put his hand on her chest, and waited. If it even thought about emerging onto this plane, he could grab it.

"Hey!" a man shouted from behind us.

I brought her hand to my mouth as Reyes waited. The woman convulsed, her arms and legs thrashing, as her eyes rolled back until only the whites shown through.

"What the fuck are you doing?" the man said.

I turned. It was one of the EMTs. He grabbed Reyes and fought to pull him off the woman.

Reyes, almost trancelike himself, pushed the man away, tossing him twenty feet into another EMT who was coming to aid his friend.

In the next instant, the woman went limp and the demon broke free. It lunged at Reyes, knocking him to the ground. It was twice the size of a large man and supernaturally strong.

While it fought, its bones cracked, breaking and mending, then breaking again, as though it were growing, adjusting to its new environment. All the while, it attacked Reyes with the ferocity of a cornered animal.

It swiped at him, ripping into the flesh at his abdomen. Reyes hardly noticed the blood gushing forth from his T-shirt. He landed a right hook, but the demon was fast. It recovered from the punch and clamped its teeth down on Reyes's arm.

I didn't know what the others could and could not see, but I slowed time to keep the hospital staff at bay and jumped on the back of the entity. An icy chill swept over me as I tried to get an arm around its neck.

It shrugged me off with ease, then turned toward me and tilted its head as though curious. I stumbled but caught my balance and stared back.

A dull gray from head to toe, the Shade demon had only a mouth on its face, its cracked, chalky lips pulled back to reveal a set of thick, square teeth. The kind that could tear through flesh and grind bones to dust with little effort. A crown of gray bone sat atop its head, the protrusion the same hard material as the rest of its brittle face.

I knew my light wouldn't work on it, and I didn't think for a moment I could fight it, but maybe my guardian could. As the demon straightened to its full height in front of me, I sank to my knees, lowered my palm to the floor, and summoned her.

Artemis, a gorgeous Rottweiler who'd been my official guardian since she'd died, rose out of the ground, and relief washed over me. Unlike Reyes and me, apparently those who were already departed could materialize inside the Shade. Thank Jehovah for small favors.

Without a moment's hesitation, Artemis leaped forward and attacked the demon, her snarls vicious, her growls the stuff of nightmares.

She went for the throat, ripping and tearing at the being, and though I quickly realized she wouldn't be able to take it alone, the distraction gave Reyes enough time to position himself behind it.

When the demon's claws closed around Artemis's neck, I said in a whisper-soft voice, "Come."

She released the demon immediately and dematerialized. Just as she slipped through its grip, Reyes wrapped his arms around the being's head and twisted. He broke its neck. He twisted again, his muscles straining with effort, and pulled the head clean off the body, killing it.

Before I could wonder how we were going to dispose of the body of a Shade demon, it disintegrated into dust. Time began to take hold around us as we watched the demon crumble and turn into powder. A powder that only we could see, apparently.

Hospital staff rushed toward us in slow motion. I ignored them and walked to the woman. She was dead, her eyes lifeless, staring into nothing.

I reached out to her, and Reyes grabbed my arm so hard, he nearly ripped it out of its socket. I glared up at him.

"Don't you dare," he said, his grip like a vise, his voice razor sharp.

Then what I was about to do hit me. "I wasn't—"

He closed the distance between us and said in a low tone, "I know exactly what you were doing. Her soul has already left her body."

Which meant I would have been exiled again. Cast off the plane again. Time reset itself. The world crashed back into us.

I jerked out of his grip, ignoring the two men ordering us out. "Is that how they cross?" I asked Reyes, incredulous. "They kill the host and somehow get onto this plane?"

He offered me a barely perceptible nod. "Yes. They piggyback onto the host's soul."

We both scanned the area as three rather large security guards met us in the waiting room. They'd called the police, and they were going to hold us there. But we were much more interested in the throngs of people crowded into every available space, each with a nifty Shade demon tucked safely inside.

Artemis's hair stood on end. She growled at the plethora of demons, her very favorite thing to kill, but I kept her from attacking with a wave of my hand. I didn't know what would happen if she did her usual and dragged the demon out of the host. Would that kill the human? Or had the demon killed it when he fought to get out?

Either way, this had to end. "Reyes, we have to stop this."

"I know."

"And we have to—"

"I know."

"But first—" I gestured to our armed escort.

He nodded, and a microsecond later, they crumpled to the floor, all three of them, as though they'd fainted. He hadn't even looked back at them. We kept walking as nonchalantly as possible and found Pari sitting in a chair with a nurse close by.

"I'm feeling much better," she said when she saw us.

The woman had every intention of arguing, but she didn't get a chance. Reyes knocked her out, too, and caught her as she fell gracefully to the floor.

"You're going to have to show me how you do that one of these days," I said to him.

Pari hurried over to us. "Well?" she asked.

I shook my head.

She wrapped an arm around my shoulders. "I'm sorry, Chuck. Did you figure out what's causing all this?"

"Yes," Reyes said.

Pari gasped when her gaze landed on his abdomen.

I was right there with her.

"You're gods," she said, appalled. "I thought you couldn't be killed."

"We can't," I said with a grimace. "Doesn't mean we can't be shredded and eaten alive."

"Oh. Great. Good to know."

"We have an audience." Reyes gestured to his right.

There, hovering in the shadows, stood five Shade demons.

I tripped on my own feet and sucked in a soft breath of air. Reyes took my arm and kept us moving forward while Artemis let out another guttural growl.

Their skeletal hands were folded at their chests, their heads bowed, and yet they were looking directly at us. Even though they didn't have eyes, we could tell they were looking right at us. And they were miffed. We'd killed one of their own.

As we walked past, their heads pivoted in unison, watching our every move. Just like before, their movements were synchronized as though each motion were choreographed.

"Pari," I whispered to her, "can you see them?"

She looked to the side. "I can see a gray mist, just like any other ghost."

Thank God for small favors. If that was all Pari could see, then the regular joe would see nothing at all.

"Is that one of them?" she asked in alarm.

"No. That's five of them, and they've already crossed onto this plane."

A group of hospital staff hurried past us to check on all the unconscious employees while we made our getaway. I'd grabbed a blanket off a gurney. As Reyes shifted Misery into drive, I pressed it to his abdomen. He almost argued with me, but I scowled, so he took my hand into his instead and helped me hold it.

We drove home in silence. Stunned silence. If just one of the Shade demons could best Reyes, a.k.a. the god Rey'azikeen, what chance did we have of stopping an entire dimension of them?

6

I need something that's more than coffee but less than cocaine.
—MEME

I showed Gemma to a room when we got back so she could freshen up. She was still shaking from all the excitement.

"Can you tell me what happened?" I asked as she peeled off her jacket.

We sat on the cot together, mostly because there was nowhere else to sit in these rooms. Reyes had supplied them with the bare essentials, a temporary headquarters, so to speak. And it would definitely be temporary if Reyes's calculations of a three-day time limit came to fruition.

Which, how bad did that suck? I'd considered seeing his three days and raising him five. I mean, look what God did with six days. Surely we could destroy what Reyes had created with eight spins of the globe on our side.

Were we actually facing an apocalypse? Would it come to that? When imagining a zombie apocalypse, I'd always been one of the survivors. I supposed most people thought of themselves that way. The alternative was death. Or worse, zombie hair. Nobody wanted that.

Gemma settled onto the cot and shrugged a delicate shoulder, the tips of her blond hair brushing across it. One of her crystalline blue eyes had been blackened in the attack, and she had several scratches across one cheek. I tamped down the ache in my heart for what she'd gone through. Now was not the time.

"Carolyn came in for her weekly appointment," she began, her gaze drifting into the memory, "but she seemed upset. Agitated. Carolyn's the sweetest woman I've ever met. She had a ton of issues, but who doesn't? I told her she was a little early and went to my office to hang up my jacket when she began screaming and tackled me to the ground. It was so out of the blue." She pressed her fingernails into the palms of her hands, something she'd always done when she was upset.

I rubbed her back. "I'm sorry, hon."

"No, I was just . . . I hadn't seen any of the infected. I didn't suspect a thing." She dropped her gaze, her posture deflating. "I'm so dumb, Charley. That poor woman, and I didn't realize she was sick. She needed my help."

"You're not dumb."

"No?" She stood and began pacing. "You would have known. You're so good at this stuff. I'm supposed to be the professional, yet you were always so much better with people than I was. You could read them so fully."

I giggled. "Gem, I can read people because I can literally feel the emotions coursing through them. I cheat. I'm a cheater," I added when my words failed to assuage her doubts. "And a pumpkin eater."

She finally stopped pacing and let her mouth widen across her face. She was so beautiful. Unlike me, she could have been a model or an actress or a porn star. Well, I could've been a porn star, too, but she chose to help people when she didn't have to.

I'd had little say in my destiny. Not that I would've changed it for the world. If not for my celestial baggage, I wouldn't have Reyes or Beep or Artemis or Angel or any of the other peripherals in my crazy, wonderful life.

"I blacked out," she said, sitting beside me again. "I don't even know how she died."

Sadness squeezed my heart again. "I think I do, but that's not what matters now. She's at peace."

Gemma nodded, then cleared her throat as though bracing herself for what she was about to say. She drew in a deep breath and said, "I'm so sorry, Charley."

"For the night you cut the feet out of my footie pajamas and I almost lost my toes to frostbite?" I'd never gotten over that.

She laughed softly. "First, it was the middle of August, and second, you'd grown out of them. They were strangling you. But no. I'm sorry for running out on you last time. I was trying to become more involved in your life, in what you do every day, and I chickened out and ran."

I blinked, surprised by her need to apologize. "Gem, you have nothing to be sorry for. My world is not for the faint of heart, and you've been forced to be a part of it your whole life. I don't blame you one bit for wanting to get away from it all."

"I do." Her breath hitched with the confession. "I've known for a long time what you were, how you help people, both alive and departed. Do you know how special that is? How special you are?"

I socked her on the arm. "Stop. You're gonna make me blush."

"That," she said, pointing a manicured finger at me and shaking her head. "That's what I'm talking about. You have all these abilities, all these gifts, and you take it all in stride, like it's so everyday."

"For me it is, I guess. I've never known anything else."

"And yet you never complain."

I shifted, suddenly uncomfortable. "I wouldn't say *never*. You should have heard me in Marmalade. Oh, my God, those poor wraiths. Having to listen to me rant for decades at a time. It's a wonder any of them were still sane when I left. A hundred years of that is enough to drive anyone, supernatural entity or not, to the brink of any number of mental disorders. Know what I mean?" I snorted and elbowed her, but she sat gaping at me. She did that a lot.

"A hundred years? What do you mean?"

Oops. There were some things my sibling just didn't need to know.

"Oh, no, I just meant, you know, metaphorically. Like when I used to say I was going to stab you in the face a hundred times. I would never really have done it. Not a hundred times."

She narrowed her lids, so I took the opportunity to get to the heart of why I was sitting in the same room with my sister for so long. "I have something to ask you that might seem a bit odd at first."

She perked up. "Shoot."

"You told me that you'd been at the hospital the night I was born."

The face she made told me she hadn't expected such a random question, but she inclined her head, thinking back. "I was. Uncle Bob took me, and we sat in the waiting room forever, and I know they're called waiting rooms, but waiting for a baby to be born is brutal. We were there for hours."

I frowned. "Hours? Really?" Why would Uncle Bob take Gemma, who was only four at the time, to the hospital to wait for hours? "Maybe Mom wanted you there?"

She shrugged. "Maybe. I just remember being really bored once the excitement of the vending machines wore off. Then I fell asleep."

"I have a love-hate relationship with vending machines."

"They're so shiny," she said. "And have such pretty things inside."

I gaped at her. "Gemma Vi Davidson, I had no idea we were so much alike."

"Except I'm not a supernatural entity with crazy otherworldly skills."

"Right. Well, other than that."

"Why are you asking about that night?"

I almost skipped the truth, but she'd been so honest with me, I decided to go for it and tell her the truth about Marmalade and my quest. "Okay, so all the cards on the table. I've been in another dimension, and while it felt like a hundred years there, it was only ten days here on Earth. But that's not the important part. The point is I had company."

Her eyelids formed a perfect circle.

"There were these wraiths, and they were very friendly after the first twenty years or so. But they knew things about me. They were clairvoyant. And telepathic. And oracular. Anyway, all the stuff that's happening with the infection? It's supernatural. The wraiths warned me about it, and they said that to figure out how to stop it, I had to find out what really happened to Mom."

I pushed the Pause button to let her catch up. She stared for a long, long time, then slowly nodded. "Okay. I'm with you. I can do this. I'm not running. See?" She did a Vanna White, gesturing to herself. "This is me not running."

"Look at you." I patted her on the back, pride swelling inside me. Or a bout of the giggles. It was hard to tell. "Nobody can call you a scaredy-cat. Anymore."

"But wait." Her face grew even more serious. "What did they mean about Mom? She died in childbirth, right?"

"That's what I thought. That's what I need to find out. But if you don't remember anything unusual—"

"Well, I did faint."

"Right. Uncle Bob found you in the hall. You don't remember what led up to it?"

"No. And I've tried. I can't recall anything after the sugar rush and subsequent crash I got from the vending machine. Not until Uncle Bob lifted me into his arms in the hall in front of the nurses' station."

"Wait, Uncle Bob found you in front of the nurses' station? There were no nurses there?"

She squinted, thinking back. "No. I don't think so. Maybe they were all helping with Mom."

"Maybe." I sat back for a moment, then jumped up. "I'll let you get ready for bed."

"Ready for bed? I couldn't sleep if you tranked me."

I laughed. "Okay, we'll be in the commons if you want company."

"I'll be there in a bit."

I nodded and started to leave, but I turned back to her. "You don't have to, you know. We're going to try to come up with a plan. It's all going to be very . . . supernatural."

"Nope, I'm good. From now on, I am totally there for you."

I gave her my best, most polished smile and headed out in search of a Cookie. *The* Cookie. The one and only Cookie Kowalski Davidson. I picked up a hitchhiker named Pari on the way and found Cookie in the commons room. I didn't know what else to call it. Living room didn't quite fit. And living-room-slash-office-slash-kitchen-and-dining-area was way too long.

"Did Quentin make it back?" I asked her.

She'd been poring over a printout and started when Pari and I walked in.

"Yes. How's your sister? Oh, hey, Pari."

Pari claimed a spot on the office sofa. The sofa that was not made for comfort so much as durability. "Hey, Cook."

"She'll be okay," I said, going for the Bunn.

"Good. Quentin and Amber are playing with that precious little boy." She said that as though she could see him. When I turned back to her, coffee cup hovering at my lips, she stopped what she was doing and pinned me with her concerned mommy face. "Is he going to be okay? That sweet baby? How did he die?"

"He'll be fine, hon. I don't know, but Q&A Investigations is on the job. They'll figure it out."

A ghost of a smile brushed across her face. Q&A Investigations was Quentin and Amber's very own private detective agency. Before I'd been booted out of the Milky Way, they'd even had an employee. Named Petaluma. Not sure what they'd paid her with, though. Neither of them did what I'd repeatedly told them to: cut their hair and get jobs. That was sometimes the best advice I could offer. It seemed salient, even when faced with questions like, "How do you find a dead body if it's already dead?" or "Can we legally bug a suspect's phone?" The PI biz was so complicated.

The main entrance door opened, and we all turned to see Garrett and Uncle Bob walk into the room. My uncle Bob. The very man who liked to say he practically raised me but was more like that uncle who embarrassed the family by trying to order a chocolate sundae with extra tequila at Baskin-Robbins or causing the big throwdown at Christmas dinner because he brought a stripper named Caramel to the sacred event.

My stepmother hated when he did that.

God, I loved him.

"Okay, what's this surprise?" he asked Cookie before he realized there were other people in the room—namely, me.

He dropped the armload of files he was carrying onto a chair and opened his arms. I put down my coffee cup and hurried over to be swallowed by him.

"Charley," he said, squeezing so hard I worried my insides would become my outsides. And I loved every pounds-per-square-inch of it. "We've been so worried. Reyes has been beside himself."

"Well, he can just stay beside himself. I've been there. It's a great place to be. Warm. Lots of shade. Oh, hey, Reyes," I said to my husband when he walked in on my rant. My teasing rant since I could feel him getting nearer with every step he took.

Thankfully, we healed much faster than the average Shade-demon casualty. He wore bandages under his T-shirt. At this point, I was thankful for two things: they were actually bandages and not duct tape, and he wouldn't need them for long.

I gave the G-man—a.k.a. Garrett—a quick hug, too, and went back to my cup-o-reason-for-living.

Uncle Bob grabbed the files he'd brought and tossed them on the metal table. "Case after case after case. People going crazy. Mutilating themselves. Attacking their family members. Is this really an infection, or is it something else?"

When no one else answered, I sat at the table and said, "It's something else."

Shame warmed my cheeks as Reyes sat beside me. Cookie, Garrett, and Pari pulled up chairs on the other side of the rectangle. I looked over my shoulder. Even Gemma joined us. I smiled at her reassuringly as she sat at the farthest end.

"We opened a hell dimension, Uncle Bob." When he gaped at me, I added, "Not on purpose."

"So, it's true?" He turned away and rubbed his stubbly jaw. After a long moment, he asked, "How do I go to the captain with this?"

"Captain Eckert understands more than you think." The captain and I'd had an encounter a while back. The guy knew a lot about the supernatural realm. Certainly more than most.

"But a hell dimension?" he asked.

"I'm not sure I'd put it in those exact words," Reyes said.

I agreed. "Even if you told him, Ubie, there's nothing he can do. We're working on it. Speaking of which, what the hell, Reyes?" I offered him my angriest grimace. "Why are these things so strong?"

He opened his hands in helplessness. "I was creating the dimension to hold a god. They needed to be strong."

"Wait, what god?" Gemma asked.

Reyes and I turned to her.

"Me," I said. "He was building it for me. Kind of. Long story short, he only thought he was building it for me. His Brother tricked him." I looked up at him, unable to deny the sting of the entire situation. "You must have really hated me."

"Dutch," he said, his tone low. "I was angry and confused. I thought you'd betrayed me."

Trying to lighten the mood, I said, "Historically, we've had a rather abusive relationship."

"Don't," he said softly, averting his gaze, but not before I saw the hurt in his eyes.

I winced. If anyone knew about an abusive relationship, it was my husband. The monster that raised him had exacted every conceivable violation of mind and body humanly possible. And here I was talking about abusive relationships.

I bit back a curse. "Reyes—"

"What else do we know?" he asked, changing the subject.

He was right. We had bigger fish to fillet. "Have your guys noticed anything that would tie the victims together? Any connection other than geography?"

"Not a thing," Uncle Bob said. "Even the CDC is looking into that. They've come up empty-handed as well. At least this explains why they can't actually find a virus."

"Are they still looking in that direction?" Cookie asked.

"Yes, but they're also looking for possible environmental causes."

"Reyes," I said, veering back to my original point, "I'd really like to know if there is anything tying these victims together. Something we're not seeing."

"Anything particular in mind?" he asked.

"No, but it's happened before. On two separate occasions, the victims of our investigations could see into the supernatural realm."

He scraped a hand down his handsome face. "I guess there could be, but there are too many. Not that many humans can see past the veil."

"True, but there could still be a connection. Something completely out of left field. Something we'd never think of."

"How do you propose we find out?" Garrett asked.

And that was the question. I looked at my husband. "If you think it's safe, Reyes, I'd like to send Angel into the Shade. Will the demons go after him?"

"I don't know why they would. He can't help them cross, and that seems to be their main goal."

"I'll go in," Osh said, materializing in a chair beside Pari. He wore his signature black top hat and duster.

Pari, Cookie, and Gemma jumped, each in her own unique way.

Cookie vaulted out of her chair, then caught herself and sat back down.

Gemma lost her balance and toppled over. After dragging herself back onto her chair, she gave me a thumbs-up.

Pari grabbed her chest and cursed. It was a very Pari-like reaction to any surprising situation. "Holy shit." She fanned herself. "That was cool."

He dazzled her with his most charming lopsided grin. She reciprocated with a come-hither glance over a coy shoulder.

My gaze bounced between the two of them. "Robbing the cradle, aren't you?"

"Sorry," Pari said, snapping back to us.

"I was talking to him. He's just a teensy bit older than he looks. And the answer is no."

Osh tried out his grin on me. "It wasn't a question, sugar."

It didn't work. Well, it did, but . . . "The answer is still no."

He bristled. "Look, we have to stop this. Beep's in danger thanks to Captain Dimwit over there." He gestured toward Reyes.

"Osh, he feels bad enough."

"No, I don't think he does."

Reyes stood. Osh immediately followed. And the monthly hour-long stare-down commenced.

Seriously? We were back to this?

"Guys!" I shouted, holding up my hands. "What exactly happened while I was gone?"

"Why don't you ask your idiot husband?"

"Osh," I admonished, then turned to the man who'd abducted my heart eons ago. "Reyes, what is he talking about?"

"Shit he doesn't understand," he said cryptically.

Great. It was going to be one of those nights.

"Well, I don't care. Cut the shit, guys. We have to stick together on this."

Osh sat back down in a huff.

"For the record, Osh, this entire situation is my fault, not Reyes's."

"No, it's not," Reyes said.

I ignored him. "And we have three days. We don't have time for a pissing contest. Osh, the Shade demons did not like us invading their territory. I'm not sending you in there."

Before he could argue, I closed my eyes and summoned Angel.

"It's about time, *pendeja*," he said when he manifested beside me. "Where the fuck you been?"

I bolted out of my chair and tackle-hugged him. He hugged me back, his lanky arms locking me into his viselike grip.

Angel was a thirteen-year-old juvenile delinquent who'd died in the nineties. He wore a red bandanna low on his brow. A dirty A-line tee covered his upper half, and baggy jeans on the verge of slipping off his hips cloaked his bottom half. A gangbanger any shot caller would be proud of. I'd missed that head of thick, dark hair, cinnamon-colored skin, and glossy brown eyes with lashes any girl would give her right kidney for. So unfair.

He gave me a minute to take him in before turning into his usual self. He bent his head until his mouth was at my ear. "I saw a storeroom on the way in. *Mira*. We can check it out, yeah? Just you and me. You naked. Me watching you be naked."

I laughed and placed several tiny kisses on his peach fuzz–covered cheek. Angel wouldn't be Angel without earning demerits for inappropriate conduct of a celestial being.

"He gets more action with your wife than you do," Osh said, baiting my husband.

I rolled my eyes, then stabbed him with a warning glare.

"Sit," I said to Angel, offering him my chair while I took a seat on Reyes's lap. And, no, I didn't miss the smirk he cast Osh's way.

Angel scanned the room, greeting those who could see him and pretty much ignoring those who couldn't. After taking inventory, he looked back at me, his face full of concern.

"I'm okay," I said, shaking my head.

"What am I looking for?" he asked, dropping it. He already knew where I was sending him.

"Anything the victims might have in common. Why are the Shade demons targeting them? It could be completely random, but if it's not, we need to know."

For some in the room, I was having a one-sided conversation, but everyone there had been on the team long enough to understand.

Garrett spoke up then, addressing Ubie. "Can you get us a list of names?"

He shuffled through the files and found the one he was looking for. "It's being updated constantly, but here's what we have so far. I can send you updated lists as we get them."

"Thanks." Garrett took the file from him and read through the names.

"Anything jumping out?" I asked.

"Not offhand. I'll do some checking."

"Thanks." I turned toward the surly slave demon in the top hat. "Osh, with Angel here—"

"I'm on Beep duty."

"Yes. Thank you."

He tipped his hat and vanished.

"Seriously," Pari said, "that is the hottest thing I've ever seen."

"Cook, Pari has something she needs you to look into. A name."

"Really?" Cookie said, tearing her gaze away from where Osh had been, just as impressed as Pari.

I turned to my sister. "Gemma, I want you to get some rest."

"Does he do that a lot?" she asked, pointing to Osh's vacant chair.

I'd lost them all.

7

Coffee helps me maintain my "never killed anyone" streak.
—T-SHIRT

While the gang went to work, I walked over to Ubie. Well, I heated up my coffee, then I walked over to Ubie.

"How are you?" I asked him as he straightened the folders.

"I'm good, pumpkin. How about you?"

"Fan-freaking-tastic. Mostly tastic."

He looked away, suddenly uncomfortable. "Charley, what you did for Cookie, for Amber . . . I can never repay you."

"Sure you can. I take installments with no money down, but I'll have to run a credit check. I ain't no scrub."

He stopped and gave me his full attention. "What does that even mean?"

"No idea."

He sat down with a soft chuckle, so I took advantage of his light mood.

"I have a strange question for you."

"So, you really are back." His irises sparkled with mirth.

I swatted his hand. He surprised me and caught it, lacing my fingers into his. He'd been there for me my whole life. When no one else knew what to do with me, I could always count on Ubie.

"Okay, this might sound strange, but you were at the hospital with Gemma when I was born, right?"

His brows slid together, wondering where I was headed. "I was."

"Do you remember anything unusual?"

"Besides your mother dying?"

A pinprick of pain stung the core of my being. I ignored it. "Yes, besides that. Did anything suspicious happen?"

He lowered his head in thought. "No. Not that I can recall." He slowly removed his hands from mine and leaned back. "But you have to understand, pumpkin, all I thought about back then was becoming a detective and sex. And not necessarily in that order."

My mind was racing so hard, trying to figure out what on Earth my mother's death would have to do with the hell dimension taking over the world twenty-eight years later that I almost missed it.

Almost.

I raised my gaze back to his. "What about Dad? Did he mention anything unusual? Did he suspect foul play? Did he investigate?"

"No. Not that I know of."

I planted my shoulder blades on the back of my chair and crossed my arms. I must have misread him. Odd but not completely out of the ordinary. Emotions weren't finite. They could be tricky. Maybe he'd been more upset about my mother's death than I'd ever realized.

"What about when Gemma passed out?"

"Yeah," he said, running a hand through his thick head of hair, "I found her in the hall by the nurses' station. They checked her out, but she was fine."

"And no idea why she fainted?"

"Nope." He pressed his lips together and shook his head, and I fought with every ounce of my being to tamp down my knee-jerk reaction to

stream gesture for okay, his blue eyes shimmering in the low light. "You?"

"Better now that I'm back on Earth."

He laughed as Amber chased the little boy around the commons area.

"He's cute," Quentin said.

"He's adorable," I agreed. "Did Reyes get everyone out?"

He nodded and said, "Finally," in a dramatic gesture. It apparently took an act of God for Reyes to convince the sisters at the convent to let him fly them out of the city. The mother superior insisted that, if anything, their jobs required them to face the creatures of hell head-on.

"Not these creatures," he'd said to them. "Not this hell."

In an act of desperation, he offered to make a sizable donation for upgrades to the convent if they'd leave for a few days.

If it was sizable enough to sway the stalwart mother superior, the offer must have had several zeroes at the end. It was one thing to stick to your guns and do your perceived duty, but it was another to be stubborn to the point of ridiculousness. The convent, like all old buildings, needed a lot of TLC.

"Are you okay?" I asked him.

Giggling and panting, Amber walked up to join us.

"Yeah," he said.

She stepped close to Quentin, their arms touching, their fingers grazing against each other's. Their romance was the sweetest thing. Amber was so dedicated to him, and Quentin was head over heels. It was a perfect pairing despite the age difference of three years, which was a pretty big deal in adolescence.

But I'd glimpsed their futures. I wasn't clairvoyant by any stretch of the imagination. That was Amber's department. But I had witnessed the fact that they'd still be together when Beep faced Satan. And they'd be fighting right alongside her. I felt if there were ever a destined love, it was theirs.

But I'd sworn to Quentin, by all that was holy, if he touched her before her eighteenth birthday, I'd skin him alive.

He didn't believe me, but I swore it nonetheless.

"Have you guys learned anything that can help us out with this little guy?" I asked them, talking and signing at the same time.

I knelt down, hoping to the draw him closer, but he stared from where he stood, several feet away.

"Yes," Amber said. "He got sick. That's all he remembers. But he knows his name."

"Oh, yeah?" I gave him my best Sunday smile, but he continued to stare.

"It's your light," Amber said. "He's not sure what to think of it."

"I'm sorry, hon. I promise my light is completely harmless."

He took a step closer, casting a wary glance toward Reyes, who was hanging back, leaning against a wall, arms crossed at his chest.

He got that a lot. Looks of suspicion. And doubt. And lust. Mostly lust. Many of the glances originated from Thelma and Louise. My eyeballs.

Amber and Quentin lowered themselves onto the concrete floor and sat cross-legged, so I followed suit.

Another step.

"What's your name?" I asked him.

"Meiko," Amber answered when he didn't.

I sucked in a soft breath. "That's my favorite name ever."

One more step.

"Did you say Meiko?" Uncle Bob asked from across the room. Both he and Cookie were watching us. "That name sounds familiar."

I looked over at him. "From a case?"

"I'm not sure. Let me do some digging."

"Thanks, Uncle Bob." I looked back at Meiko. "You don't remember what happened to you?"

He shook his head and took another step. After another wary glance in Reyes's direction, he turned back to us, raised his hands, and laughed.

When I questioned Amber and Quentin with raised brows, Quentin rolled his eyes.

"Your light. It's blinding. It shoots out of you and creates these flutters of embers, like sparks floating in the air."

"Like lightning bugs," Amber added.

"Seriously?" I asked them. "It's that cool?"

Amber snorted. "Like I said, I can finally see what all the fuss is about."

"I shoot sparks. Who'd a thunk?"

"You should see her when she's angry," Reyes said from behind me. "It's like a lightning storm."

I swiveled my head to face him. "No way. No way am I that cool."

One corner of his mouth rose, his expression soft.

"Gah, I wish I could see it."

When I turned back to Meiko, he was almost upon me. He reached out, trying to capture the light particles in his hands.

I sat perfectly still, not wanting to scare him. "I'm so sorry you were sick."

He laughed again and reached above my head. "It's okay."

Thrilled that he spoke to me, I forged on. "How old are you?"

He held up five fingers.

"Wow. Do you know your mommy's and daddy's names?"

"No." He put his hand on my face as though fascinated, then his other, his small mouth widening across his handsome face. "Just my mommy. Belinda Makayla Banks."

"Oh, that's wonderful. I'd like to get in touch with her if I can."

He shook his head. "You can't find her."

"Why do you say that?"

"No one can."

"I'm pretty good at finding stuff."

He saddened. "It won't matter."

I gestured toward Cookie. "Belinda Makayla Banks."

"Belinda Banks?" She rose from her chair. "A girl with that name went missing some— How many years has it been?"

"Oh, you're right," Ubie said. He snapped his fingers trying to think back. "That was a while ago. Maybe ten years?"

"She was never found?" I asked them.

"Not that I recall," he said, looking at Cookie for confirmation. "It wasn't my case, but I don't think a body was ever recovered."

Still holding on to my face, he patted my cheeks softly. "That's because she's locked in a box."

I stilled. Quentin tapped Amber's shoulder in question. She signed what Meiko said, and then he stilled as well.

A chill slid up my spine. "Your mommy is locked in a box?" I said for the benefit of Cookie and Uncle Bob.

Cookie sucked in a sharp breath.

Meiko nodded. "It's where he keeps us. Mommy says Grandma is looking for us, but he keeps us in the box so she can't find us."

I placed my hands over his ever so softly. "Sweetheart, is there anyone else in the box with your mommy?"

"Just my sister." He poked my chin softly, as though testing me out. "She's older. She thinks she knows everything."

Without moving my head, I glanced at Cookie and Uncle Bob. "He has a sister."

Cookie's hand flattened over her mouth. Uncle Bob hadn't gotten past the stillness of his state of shock.

"Cook, I need intel."

"Sorry. Oh, my God." She ducked her head and tapped furiously on her keyboard.

Reyes had stepped closer, but so far, Meiko hadn't noticed.

Quentin touched my shoulder, his face full of concern. "His mother and sister could still be alive."

I nodded and held up a pair of crossed fingers. "Sweetheart, what's your sister's name?"

"Molly Makayla Banks the first." He rolled his eyes, and I almost cracked a smile. Only a little brother.

"Yes!" Cookie said in full eureka mode.

I put my hands on Meiko's face.

He let me.

"Belinda Makayla Banks went missing after walking home from a friend's house ten years ago this March."

When she stopped talking but kept reading, I nudged her with a "Cook."

"Right, sorry. Hon, she was fourteen years old. She didn't have any children."

I bit down but kept my expression neutral. "Are your mom and sister okay?"

Meiko shrugged, then went back to jumping for fireflies. "Yeah. They're okay. My sister's not the boss of me, though. Mommy is."

Uncle Bob walked over to us. "I'll find out whose case this was and get everything I can on it."

"Thanks, Ubie."

Meiko shouted a word with every jump. "This! Is! So! Fun!"

"Meiko," I said, trying to coax his attention back to me. "Do you know the man's name?"

"The man?" he asked, jumping for a particularly high spark of light.

"The man who took your mother? Who keeps her locked in a box?"

"Of course."

I put my hands on his face again. Forced his attention back to me. "Can you tell me what it is? The man's name?"

"I guess, but it won't matter."

"Can you try me anyway?"

Giving in, he lifted a slim shoulder. "It's Reyes Alexander Farrow."

I turned to my husband about the same time his jaw hit the floor.

8

I'm not really into the whole "rise and shine" thing.
Most days I just caffeinate and hope for the best.
—BUMPER STICKER

"You're kidnapping fourteen-year-old girls and keeping them in locked boxes?" I asked him after Amber took Meiko to her room to rest. Quentin went to his room, which was right next door to Amber's. I wasn't sure how I felt about that.

I hoped Meiko wouldn't realize he didn't need sleep and would stay with her. It was after midnight. The kids needed their z's.

Uncle Bob and Cookie were still trying to figure out what was going on as well. It's not every day one gets told her husband has been keeping a woman and a couple of children locked in a box for ten years.

Reyes had sat back at the table, in shock. "Why would he say that?"

"I have no idea, but he saw you. And while he wasn't overly fond of you, he didn't recognize you."

He did a deadpan thing.

"You know what I mean," I said, waving off his legitimate reaction. "That means this guy is, what? Going by your name? Why would someone go by your name?"

"Maybe this is a setup," Uncle Bob said. "Maybe someone wants Reyes worried about this to keep his mind off something else."

"Like a hell dimension expanding within our own?" Reyes said. "It's him."

I shook my head. "Reyes, why would Lucifer do this? More importantly, how would he do it? Meiko's a real boy who really died. Would Lucifer kill a child just to distract you?"

"Do the words *in a heartbeat* mean anything?"

"True. He would, but this would be an awfully elaborate setup. Either way, I don't care why or how. We need to find them."

"Which is exactly what he would want. Us distracted by this case instead of finding a way to close the Shade."

"I can do both," I said, offended. "I'm great at multitasking."

"Dutch, we have priorities."

"Yes, we do. I am prioritizing my need to find Rocket."

Cookie perked up. "Oh, good idea. He can tell us about your mother's death."

"Actually, I was thinking he could tell us if Meiko's mother and sister are still alive."

"Oh, yes. That, too."

"Any thoughts on where they are since someone"—I scowled at my husband—"leveled his home?"

Reyes winced. "I'll rebuild it. Once we close the hell dimension, I'll rebuild it."

I tousled his hair, expecting a glare of annoyance for my efforts. Instead, I got a sheepish shrug. He really felt bad about leveling the abandoned asylum Rocket and Blue lived in. That made me much happier than it should have.

"Do you know where they are now?" I asked him.

"Since Rocket won't have anything to do with me, Osh had to bring them here."

A gasp of delight escaped me. "They're here?"

He arched a brow in affirmation.

"They've been here the whole time?"

Another brow.

I held my fists over my heart and said, "This is so great," before taking off down the hall. I got about thirty feet before I realized I had no idea where I was going. I shouted back to him, "Where am I going?"

"All the way to the end and down the stairs."

"We have another level? I love this place!"

I hurried down the stairs to a massive and very dark basement. I had to run my hand along the walls to try to find a light switch. Two hours later, give or take, I found one and flipped it. A long line of fluorescent lights flashed on and off before taking hold and illuminating the area properly.

The room was huge. It had a few dented cabinets and a little trash here and there, but for the most part it was clean.

"Rocket?" I said, easing into the room. There was no telling what Rocket would do when summoned, which was why I rarely did it. He became disoriented easily. "It's me, sweetheart. Charley."

I looked to the right and found several markings in the wall. That's what Rocket did. Wrote the names of those who passed. Well, scratched the names of those who passed into any wall he happened to be near. I used to believe he wrote everyone's names, but I later found out he only wrote the names of Beep's army. They were all good, all deserving, save one.

Since I'd learned the truth about whose names he wrote down and how, I remembered one tiny detail that hadn't sat well. I wanted to ask him about it, but first I had to know about Belinda and her daughter.

It wasn't until I realized Meiko had followed me that I rethought my mission. He didn't need to hear if his mother and sister had also died. Or been killed.

He walked up beside me and slipped his hand in mine.

"I thought you were taking a nap," I said, teasing him.

He giggled and shook his head. Little darling. Maybe I could trick Rocket into giving me the information without actually revealing their state of existence.

"Miss Charlotte?"

I looked over and saw Rocket huddled in a shadowed corner. I hurried over to him. "Rocket!"

He sat curled into himself, his arms covering his head as though he were about to be attacked.

I knelt beside him. "Rocket, sweetheart, what happened?"

Meiko petted his shoulder, and Rocket looked from under his arms at him. His mouth formed a sad half smile. Meiko smiled and patted his face just like he had mine.

"Rocket, what's wrong? What happened?"

"Blue doesn't like it here, Miss Charlotte."

I sank to the ground, sitting beside him. "I'm sorry, hon. I know it's not home, but—"

I rarely saw his little sister, Blue, but their new BFF, Rebecca—or, as I called her, Strawberry because of the Strawberry Shortcake pajamas she'd died in when she was nine—I saw on a semi-regular basis. Yet she was nowhere to be seen, either.

"Where is Blue, sweetheart?"

He pointed to a wall with no room on the other side, so there was no telling where she was.

"What about Strawberry?"

Again, he pointed to the wall. I turned and looked. Maybe there was a room. A hidden room with a secret doorway. Now we're talking.

"I missed you," I said to him.

"You were gone one hundred seven years, two months, fourteen days, twelve hours, and thirty-three minutes."

Holy shit. I blinked and said aloud, "Holy shit."

Meiko giggled and put a hand over my mouth.

"Crap," I said from behind it, my voice muffled. "Sorry, hon. Cussing is bad."

But my sparks had caught his attention, and he was back to bouncing around, trying to catch them.

Rocket tried to catch a couple himself.

"Sweetheart," I said, grabbing his hands to get his attention, "how do you know how long I was gone?"

"Because I counted the seconds."

I leaned forward and hugged him. He hugged me back and, as usual, I had a near-death experience.

"Rocket," I said, my voice strained, "I need to give you some names."

He nodded, still holding me tight, so I whispered the first one in his ear.

"Belinda Makayla Banks."

Loosening his hold, his lashes fluttered as he thought. Or was it Blue? I'd discovered a few days before I left planet Earth that it was really Blue who knew the names of those who had passed. Every name of every person who'd ever died on Earth. It turned my world upside down. Made me doubt everything I thought I knew to be true.

He bounced back to me and shook his head. "No, no, no. Not her time."

Relief washed over me, and my shoulders sagged.

Rocket started to get up, but I kept a hand on his shoulder, leaned in, and gave him another name. "Molly Makayla Banks."

Again, he went into a trance as name after name flashed in his mind. He refocused on me and shook his head again. "Not her time. I can play now?"

Giddy with relief, I let him get up and said, "Thank you."

He offered me a cheeky grin, then looked at Meiko. "He doesn't have much time. He has to leave."

"Wait, what?" Did he mean Meiko needed to cross? To leave this plane?

When he started toward Meiko to join him in the Catch Charley's Light game, I scrambled up and stepped in front of him.

"Rocket," I began, but he picked me up by the shoulders, set me to the side, and started walking again.

My light must reach pretty far, because Meiko had chased a spark all the way down the long room, bouncing and giggling while his arms waved in the air.

I hurried after Rocket, who was chasing one himself with a singular focus.

When I stepped in front of him again, he frowned and went to grab my arms. I shifted onto the celestial plane. His arms went right through me, and he stumbled forward. This made Meiko laugh harder.

Rocket scowled at me. "No cheating, Miss Charlotte. Cheating is against the rules."

"I'm sorry, hon, but I have one more question."

Even though I knew my question was against the rules—the odds of Rocket answering were slim to nil—I had to try. I needed know when Meiko had passed. Were his mother and sister in a dire situation? Was Belinda's abductor spiraling into a homicidal state with the death of her son? If he could just tell me when he'd died, or how, it would help. Any information would help.

He drew in a deep breath, not that he needed it, and let his shoulders deflate like a petulant child.

I took advantage immediately. Rocket didn't have the longest attention span. Not that I could talk.

"Meiko Banks." I rushed it out, realizing I didn't know his middle name. Crossing my fingers there weren't two Meiko Bankses in the world, I waited.

Instead of his usual trancelike state, he just stared at me, looked at Meiko, then stared at me again.

"He's right there, Miss Charlotte."

"I know, hon, and I know this is breaking the rules, but can you tell me when he passed?"

His bewildered expression made me wonder if he thought me a tad insane. It happened to the best of us.

"He's right there."

It had been too much to hope.

He walked up to me and knocked, literally knocked, on my head. That was definitely a learned behavior, and I had to wonder who'd done that to him when he was alive. Rocket doing it to me was humorous, but the thought of someone doing it to him, taking advantage of his mental state, was not.

"He's right there, Miss Charlotte. Not his time."

"Not his . . . ?"

I pursed my lips. Realization slowly—very slowly—started to dawn, the barest hint of light peeking over the horizon of my consciousness.

I opened my mouth to speak, then closed it. I repeated this behavior two more times before asking, "Rocket, are you telling me Meiko hasn't passed away?"

"No, no, no. Not his time yet. But soon."

I whirled around and studied the boy jumping to catch invisible light.

"He's alive? Wait, soon?"

Rocket's mouth formed an upside-down *U.* Or, in this situation, a rainbow, because this was about the best news I'd had in a hundred years.

"How long does he have?"

"No breaking rules, Miss Charlotte." He frowned in annoyance. "Not when or why or how or where. Only is."

"But you said soon. You said not yet but soon."

He shrugged. "You should have hurried faster. You've been gone too long, Miss Charlotte. Too long. Now he'll find him."

Alarm closed around my throat. His mother's abductor? Was he going to kill him? Perhaps finish something he'd started earlier?

I needed more. I did need to know where, and I apparently needed to know soon.

Walking up to Meiko, I decided to take a chance. I knelt beside him. "Meiko, sweetheart, do you remember where you are? Where you woke up before you came here?"

Meiko patted my cheeks again, fascinated with my light, and shook his head.

Damn it. I'd have to put Amber on it when I wasn't around. I was too much of a distraction. Now I knew how everyone around me felt. Like Meiko, I was easily distracted by shiny things.

Meiko put his hands over my eyes, and when he took them off, his face was one of stunned surprise. He did it again and gasped.

I looked at his hands. "What?"

"It goes through me." He did it again and giggled.

Then, sadly, it was Rocket's turn. Before I knew what he was going to do, Rocket slammed a hand over my face, knocking me back and almost bloodying my nose.

Because of this, he grabbed my whole head before I could recover in a second attempt, cutting off my oxygen supply. But it made him happy. Both of them. They laughed so hard they fell on the ground.

After a moment, I swatted Rocket's hands away. "You guys have got to get a new hobby."

Still giggling, Meiko took off after more sparks. It was my chance to ask Rocket one more question.

I filled my lungs and went for it, not sure I wanted the answer. "Rocket, do you remember the walls at the asylum?"

He nodded, really wanting to put his hands over my face again. I took his hand into mine instead, hoping that would work. It did. He looked down at them, fascinated.

I went for it. I asked about the exception to the rule. "Why did you have Earl Walker's name on the wall? He can't possibly be a part of Beep's army. He's . . . he *was* a monster."

Earl Walker was the man who raised—if one could call it that—Reyes. He was the worst humanity had to offer. And yet Rocket had scratched his name on one of the walls in the asylum.

Rocket blinked, again looking at me like I was crazy. "His name was on the bad wall, Miss Charlotte. You know that."

I didn't, actually. "I wasn't aware that you had a bad wall. What did those names mean?"

"They are bad."

"Okay, I kind of figured that, but—"

"Bad people. They have to stand in the corner, but they'll be back. They'll come after her."

Alarm jolted through me so fast, the edges of my vision darkened. "They come back?"

"From the fire. They are bad. Only bad people go into the fire."

This was not happening. There were actually souls that Satan kept to . . . to what? Be in his own army when he faced my daughter?

Rocket was right. Only bad people went into the fire. Well, mostly. As with all things, there were exceptions to the rule. Garrett being one of them, but that was a long time ago. I was certain he was over the fact that Reyes had sent him to hell. Besides, it was only for a few seconds. Surely it didn't cause permanent damage.

I felt a tug on the tips of my hair and turned to see Strawberry, a tiny blonde with more attitude than a runway model, trying to brush my hair.

I lurched back. The last time she'd brushed my hair, she'd done it with a filthy, broken toilet brush. This time she had an actual hairbrush. The travel kind that folded out. Still, there was no telling where that thing had been.

She pursed her lips and jammed her tiny hands on her hips. "Rocket has been very upset," she said, chastising me thoroughly.

If I had a dollar for every time that girl chastised me, I'd have, like, thirty bucks. But still, thirty bucks was thirty bucks.

I grinned and pulled her into a hug. She fought me, but it had to be done. I got about three-quarters of a second before she wiggled out of my arms.

"He says the world doesn't feel right anymore. He's not writing names. He's giving up."

I pointed to the few names on one wall.

"He didn't do that. I did. Someone has to do it."

Well, crap on a Keebler. "I'm sorry, sweet pea. Reyes is going to build him a new place. It'll be okay."

"No, it won't. His home is gone, and Blue won't play anymore."

Now, that did send up a red flag. "Where is she?"

Strawberry pointed to the same wall that Rocket had.

"Is there another room behind that wall?"

She walked over to it and bent to peek through the concrete barrier. Straightening up, she said, "Nope."

Okay, well, the structures of the earthly realm weren't tangible in the supernatural one. Maybe Blue really was there.

Deciding to check it out, I shifted my molecules into supernatural mode and was immediately struck by the savage beauty of it all. Comparing the supernatural realm to the earthly one was like comparing a tempest of fire to a sunny spring day. Wind thrashed around me, whipping my hair about my head and scouring my skin. The abrasive texture of this realm only made it seem harsh. I'd learned to love it. The rustic colors. The fierce landscape.

I looked just past where the wall would have been and saw her sitting on a rock like she was looking out on the ocean. I walked toward her. She stiffened, so I stopped and spoke from where I stood.

I had to shout to be heard above the storm. "Blue?"

Though she didn't turn around, she lowered her head. She'd heard me.

"I'm so sorry about your place, Blue. We're going to build you another one."

"It ain't that," she said softly, and somehow I heard her over the howling winds. "I miss my mama."

My heart shattered. Blue had died in the thirties of dust pneumonia. I was surprised she still remembered her.

"Oh, sweetheart." I walked closer, and she scooted over so I could sit by her.

Her short brown bob didn't move in the wind like my hair did. Maybe that was the difference between being corporeal and incorporeal. She wore denim overalls and a dirty white shirt.

I climbed onto the rock and sat beside her.

"I miss mine, too."

"Ain't no girl don't need her mama," she said, her voice raspy.

"You are so very, very right." I thought of my mother, and then I thought of Beep. "Hon, do you know what's going on with the hell dimension?"

"Yeah." She nodded. "You don't got too long, now."

Stress cramped my stomach. "Any thoughts on how we might close it?"

Shaking her head, she said, "But you do. You got thoughts. You just gotta listen to 'em."

"I have to listen? Could you add a side of vague to that?"

She smiled up at me for the first time, and I wanted to hug her and pet her and squeeze her and possibly change her name to George.

Just when I thought we were bonding, she put a finger over her lips and said, "Shhhh, you just have to listen," seconds before her molecules separated and she flew away on the wind.

And I thought my light was cool.

I ran back up the stairs and yelled to Cookie before remembering there were sleeping children on the premises. Not that my outburst would bother Quentin, but Amber might not appreciate it.

"They're alive!" I said before catching myself. I burst into the commons and said in a loud drunk whisper, "They're alive!"

"Who?" she asked as Ubie and Reyes turned interested expressions on me.

"All of them. Everyone. Even Meiko, but not for long. We have to find them, Cook."

"Meiko is alive?"

"Yes, and so is his mother and sister. First thing tomorrow, I need Amber and Quentin grilling that boy while I'm not around. We need anything. Any tidbit of information, even if it doesn't seem important."

"Got it, hon. Who are you calling?"

I'd picked up her phone, having no idea where mine was, and searched her contacts. "Do you have Kit's number?"

She nodded, took her phone, and handed it back.

"You have her name under Special Agent Carson, FBI?"

"Yes. What do you have her name under?"

"SAC. But don't call her that. She doesn't appreciate the efficiency of it."

I pressed her number and waited. And waited. And waited.

After what would have been seventeen years back in Marmalade, Kit picked up.

"Mrs. Davidson?" she asked, her voice all scraggly and unappealing.

"SAC, you've never called me that."

"Charley?" I could see her bolting upright. Not literally, but in my mind's eye. It seemed like something she'd do. "I thought . . . Cookie said you were gone."

"I was. I'm back. Are you still in Albuquerque?"

"Where else would I be? Do you know what time it is?"

"No idea and not really. I need everything you have on Belinda Banks. And then I need you to leave town."

After a loud crash and a few scraping sounds, she groaned and asked, "Why and why?"

"As of this moment, Belinda is still alive, and she may have had children with her abductor."

Her voice went from groggy to alert in 1.2 seconds. "I'll be there in twenty."

"Perfect. Wait, how do you know where I am?"

"I'm assuming you're with your brood?"

"Yes. But how do you know where they are?"

"Davidson, I've dedicated part of my life to keeping an eye on you and yours."

"Aw, that's so sweet."

"That way, I'll know where you are when I have to arrest you."

I'd buy that.

9

*I want to be the reason you
tilt your phone away from others when you read it.*
—MEME

True to her word, Kit showed up twenty minutes later with the file on
Belinda Banks. How she managed a trip from her apartment to her office
and then all the way out here in twenty minutes was beyond me, but I
wasn't about to question her enthusiasm.

"She's been missing for ten years," she said, taking a seat at the metal
table without so much as a "Glad you're back."

Reyes, Uncle Bob, and Cook were there. Garrett swore he was onto
something, so he was still deep in research mode in his room, and what a
man did alone in his room was none of my business.

"You think she's still alive?"

"I know she is." I handed her a cup of joe and sat beside her with my
own cup of joe. Joe got around. "But I don't know for how long. She's
being kept somewhere with two children, a boy and a girl. I'm not saying they are hers, but they do call her *Mommy*."

She showed her palms in surrender. "Should I even ask where you got
this information?"

I shook my head. "No."

Reyes, Cookie, and Uncle Bob all agreed with head shakes of their own.

"I'm going to stand over here and look out the window while I drink my coffee." She slid the file over to us and walked to a large, dirty window, turning her back to us, giving us a better view of the dark mop of bedhead she had to deal with every morning. Poor kid.

Cookie grabbed the file before any of us could. Which was probably best. She'd had a lot of coffee. It brought out her competitive side.

She flipped through the pages. "Nope. Nope. Nope. Nope. Oh, this is interesting."

"What?" Uncle Bob asked, looking over her shoulder.

"They had several suspects, but none panned out."

I put my weight on my elbows and leaned closer. "Were there any named Reyes Alexander Farrow?"

Kit spared a surprised glance over her shoulder.

"No peeking," I said in warning.

She averted her gaze again.

"No Reyeses, but there was a Randy. If that helps."

I crinkled my nose in disappointment.

"Still, this gives us a starting point. Amber and Quentin can ask Meiko about these men, see if any of them go by the name of Reyes."

"That's just weird," Ubie said.

Cookie took out her phone and snapped shots of the important pages in the file. "We totally need a copier."

"Who's Meiko?" Kit asked.

"Why would someone go by your name?" Ubie continued.

Reyes shrugged.

"Who's Meiko?" she repeated.

"Maybe it's someone you know," I suggested, still on the Reyes thing.

Kit finally turned around, exasperated. It was like she didn't know us at all. "Who. Is. Meiko?"

"He may or may not be Belinda's son. We think he's sick. We know he doesn't have much time. We have to find them, Kit. We have to hunt this Reyes Alexander Farrow fucker down. We have to make him pay." When Reyes slipped me the barest hint of a glower, I added, "The other Reyes Alexander Farrow."

He continued his vigil.

"The one that's not you. And as for you," I said, focusing on Kit, "I need you to get out of town ay-sap."

"Um, no? What makes you think you can order me around? When I get to the office tomorrow—"

"Hold on right there, Little Miss Sunshine." I pointed an index finger at God to stop her. "We totally agreed on the phone you were leaving this town in your rearview mirror."

"We didn't agree to shit," she said. "You never even gave me a reason why."

I glanced at Reyes, then back to her. "It's this infection, Kit. It's not what you think. It's supernatural. All of it."

"Supernatural? How do you—? Wait, never mind." She took another sip.

"The CDC can test until the stars burn out. There is no cure. Not a medicinal one, anyway. You can't fight it."

"And you can?" she asked.

"We're the only ones who can."

"Yeah, well, that's not good enough. I can't leave, especially now. If we have a lead on this case, I need to follow up."

"Kit, we'll do everything we can to find them before anything happens. And we could do that better if we knew you were safe."

The expression lining her pretty face wasn't so much of a smile as a smirk with a dash of warmth mixed in. "Not on your life, twinkle toes. This is my case."

I narrowed my lids. "You aren't old enough to have landed this case when it happened."

"No, but my father did. It's one of the few that got away. A fourteen-year-old girl disappears without a trace? It bothered him. A lot. And to be honest, knowing there's nothing I can do about the infection will free up that stressor. I'll take this case. You take the supernatural thingama-jig."

"Is that a professional term?"

"In this situation, apparently so."

I knew when I'd been licked. Not Reyes-licked, but beaten-licked. Sadly.

She gathered the file, downed the rest of her coffee, then headed back out into the night without so much as a "Great to see you."

I really liked her.

I had to practically force Cookie to go to bed. With the help of my lying scumbag of an uncle, we accomplished what quickly turning into *Mission: Impossible.* I watched Uncle Bob escort her to their room, my heart hurting, and asked myself for the millionth time why he would lie to me.

"He must have a good reason," Reyes said behind me, guessing my thoughts.

"Maybe, but why not just tell me? He never lies to me. He's one of the few people on Earth who never lies to me."

"What's stranger," he added, "is that he knows he can't get away with it, so why try?"

I hadn't thought of that. Why would he lie when he of all people would know I'd spot it almost before it left his mouth? It made no sense.

Reyes took my hand and escorted me to the stairs to our industrial suite, letting me go first.

"Reyes," I said, halfway up, "all of this is happening because of what we did. What I did. My need to release those souls from the hell dimension has caused the deaths of innocent people."

"This isn't on you, Dutch."

"It's entirely on me. All this sickness and destruction. The threat of an apocalypse. I mean, think about it. Who could've guessed that one day little Charley Davidson, coffee addict and aspiring dog groomer, would cause the extinction of the entire human race? This is going to look so bad on my résumé."

"I'm the one who created it."

"Yes. For me!"

I'd reached the landing. I turned to Reyes, who was still on the stairs, so we stood at eye level. A level on which I very much liked to be.

I rested my arms on his shoulders and clasped my hands behind his neck, letting my fingers tangle into his hair. His heat sank into me, and my body absorbed it as though it were water and I a scorched desert.

He tightened his grip on the handrail and dropped his gaze. "I'm the one who shattered the god glass. Who opened the gate. I'm sorrier than you can imagine."

It didn't matter what he said, how much he argued; none of this was his fault. He was only trying to escape a hell dimension I'd sent him into.

After placing a tiny kiss on his cheek, I peeled his hand off the handrail and pulled him to the huge plate glass window to look at the beautiful city lights. To remind us both what was at stake.

What would happen to this beautiful city, this beautiful world, if the Shade really did take over? We simply had no way of knowing, but the fact that it was a hell dimension, emphasis on *hell,* didn't bode well.

Still, I needed to focus on what I could do, not what I couldn't. It wasn't like I could collapse the hell dimension myself. Not in a million years, much less three days. It was too strong.

Snapping out of my thoughts, I filled my lungs and hit reboot. "Okay, Cookie gave me everything she could dig up from when my mother died."

"Which was?"

"Pretty much nothing. She died in childbirth at Lovelace. Even though I can't fathom what her death has to do with any of this, I'm going to start there tomorrow. If nothing else, I'm going to find out if there was any foul play."

Reyes pressed into me from behind. "Sounds good," he said, brushing his mouth along my neck. That one act sent tiny shock waves rocketing through my body.

"Did you miss me?" he asked.

I almost wept. "More than you can possibly imagine."

"I don't know." He nipped at an earlobe, and my knees almost gave beneath my weight. Which could have been a possible side effect of being weightless for so long. "I have a pretty big imagination."

I turned in his arms and looked up at him. "Reyes, how long were you in there? It was only an hour here on Earth. How long was it there?"

"It doesn't matter."

I leaned back. "Of course it does."

He leaned forward. "No, it doesn't."

"Pretty please?"

I was so not above begging, but I had to fight the urge to whimper when he slid his hands under my sweater and unclasped my bra. Then, with exquisite tenderness, he tested the weight of Danger and Will.

"With cherries on top?" I added, my voice suddenly hoarse.

His thumbs brushed over my nipples, and a spasm of pleasure rippled through to my core. The muscles between my legs tightened in response.

"I lost count," he said at my ear.

"How high did you get before you lost count?"

Absently, as though his mind were barely on the subject at all, as though it were a paltry thing, he said, "Seventeen hundred."

I snapped to attention. "Seventeen hundred?"

He took his tongue off the rim of my ear and said, "Yes," before replacing it with his teeth.

Despite the tingle of delight his ministrations were causing, I leaned away from him again. "Seventeen hundred what?"

He let out a frustrated sigh but didn't look up. He was too busy study-ing my mouth, his intense gaze heating me from the inside out.

"Please tell me hours," I said. "Seventeen hundred hours. No! Better yet, minutes. Say minutes."

The barest hint of a grin broke through, but his attention seemed to have been hijacked by Danger and Will. He lifted the sweater and bra over my head and let them fall to the floor.

Then he spent an inordinate amount of time memorizing their exact shapes before saying, "Let's go with that."

"Let's go with what?" I asked.

He pressed into me again, his hands caressing the girls like they were the treasures of a king and he'd just been crowned. "Minutes."

"But it wasn't really minutes?"

"No, Dutch." He wrapped a hand around my throat, the movement way sexier than it should have been, and pushed me into the glass. "It wasn't really minutes."

The glass, ice cold against my back, was in direct contrast to the scorch-ing heat pressing into me. With one skillful jerk, he had my pants around my ankles. The cool air hit me first, followed quickly by his blistering heat.

But it was my turn. He could seduce me with that Cheshire grin of his alone, but it was high time I did a little seducing of my own.

I pushed him back, unzipped my boots, and stepped out of my pants. He waited, his expression hungry, but when he started forward again, I held up a hand to stop him.

"Off," I said, instructing him with an index finger to remove his cloth-ing as well.

He complied, a wolfish smile on his handsome face. He peeled off his shirt, his muscles bunching with each movement, the effect mesmeriz-ing.

When he removed his pants, his erection showed just how much he appreciated the fact that I was back. The valley between hip and abdomen caught my attention while he finished undressing. Then he straightened and allowed me a long, lingering look at what I'd missed.

My gaze traveled from the top of his gorgeous head to the tips of his perfect toes. I took in every line. Every curvature. Every shadow. I watched as the low light caressed his muscles, highlighting their existence with spectacular devotion, as though it loved them as much as I did.

He'd filled out in the time I'd known him the way men do. He'd gained mass without even trying. His shoulders had actually widened, making the tapering to his lean hips even more pronounced. My great-grandmother could have done her laundry on his abs. And she would have enjoyed every second of it.

I tilted my head to worship a whole other part of him. His ass, with the deep dips on the sides, was the stuff of legend.

"Are you finished?" he asked, the humor in his voice unmistakable.

"Not even close."

"Sucks to be you, then."

He started forward, but I held up my hand again. He stopped and crossed his arms, looking like Adonis, Aphrodite's favorite in the flesh. But he remained in place, albeit with a slightly annoyed look on his face.

I ignored his impudence. Instead, I laid my head back against the glass and closed my eyes. One by one, I dismissed the objects in the world around us. There was no glass at my back or tile at my feet. Then there was no room. No warehouse. No city. I focused until the only thing left was the man I loved.

"Dutch," he said, his voice edged with a warning, but I only concentrated all the harder.

I sent out my energy. To caress him. To explore. I searched out his erogenous zones. Warmed them. Stroked them. I felt him tense and then weaken beneath my touch. When I brushed my energy over his cock, he sucked in a sharp breath.

I finally opened my eyes. He'd thrown his head back, basking in the sensations I was causing, and I fought the urge to raise my arms in triumph. But I'd lost my concentration and bounced back quickly.

He lowered his head and lifted his lids, taking me in from beneath his thick lashes. His gaze glistened with hunger and, if I didn't know better, the exhilaration of challenge.

"Are you finished now?" he asked.

My mouth formed an unattractive pout. "I guess."

He was in front of me at once, his hands braced against the glass on either side of my head, one corner of his mouth tilted up in a grin that defined bloodthirsty. But he didn't touch me. He didn't have to. Apparently it was his turn to show off, and in the span of a heartbeat, he proved just what an amateur he'd married.

Electricity arced off him and over me. It wrapped around my throat and the wrists at my side, locking me against the glass.

He bent forward and whispered softly into my ear, "Didn't anyone ever tell you not to play with electricity?"

And then, with the skill of a surgeon, he sent electrical currents in soft waves over my skin. He spread my legs with it, just enough to give him easier access. Then he sent tiny, stinging waves feathering over my clit. A combination of pleasure and pain rocketed through me and settled in my abdomen.

I gasped as the tendrils burrowed farther inside, ebbing and flowing, coaxing me ever closer to the edge. A second pulse of currents rushed up my stomach and over Danger and Will, hardening their nipples and causing a flood tide of sensation to wash over me.

"Reyes," I said, suddenly wanting nothing more than for him to bury himself between my legs.

Clearly having too much fun, he tsked softly but didn't release his hold. He did, however, close the distance between us. His heavy erection pressed against my clit, stroking the tender flesh there, and if he hadn't been holding me up, I might have lost my ability to stand.

"Reyes, please."

He closed his mouth over Danger's peak and sucked softly, buckling my knees at last. When he released my wrists, I grabbed a handful of hair and forced his mouth to mine. My other hand sought out his thick cock, and I stroked it from base to tip.

He had me on the floor in the next instant, wedging his hips between my legs, driving his cock deep inside of me. The immediate spike of ecstasy caused the embers that resided in every molecule in my body to explode. They crashed into each other as an orgasm burst free and spilled over me in decadent hot waves.

I whimpered into his mouth. The sound seemed to drive him over the edge as his own orgasm racked his body. He tensed, his muscles the consistency of solid marble, then shuddered and collapsed next to me.

I turned onto my side to look at him. He had an arm thrown over his half his face, his dark hair hanging in wet clumps beneath it. But he wore a grin as wolfish as any I'd seen.

"Fine," I said after taking a long moment to catch my breath. "You win."

He laughed softly, and I marveled at the spectacular being next to me. Stunning and clever and brave, he never ceased to amaze me.

"If you keep doing that," he said, his lids closed, his voice sleepy, "I'm going to have to show you what else a god is capable of."

I giggled, turned his face to mine, and kissed him. "I think I'm safe for now."

With a grin worthy of a seasoned hustler, he said, "Then you don't know me at all."

10

One would think, since we only had cots to sleep on, we would've made use of them both, one body per bunk. Instead, we both occupied one, Reyes on bottom with me draped over him like a rag doll and Artemis draped over me like a Rottie doll. I could only pray I didn't drool as much as she did.

Reyes's arms encircled us both, and despite the paw partially blocking my airway, I fell into a sleep that bordered on cadaverous. It was positively euphoric until someone poked me in the ribs. Three times.

I jerked awake and peered into the darkness, trying to make out the accoster's identity. Not because it was dark. The departed practically glowed. But because it was insanely early and I hadn't slept in a hundred years.

Literally. I never slept in Marmalade, which sounded worse than it actually was. It just never occurred to me to get any z's while there. Or eat. Or make pee-pee. Thank God, because there wasn't a shred of toilet paper in the entire realm.

"Aunt Lil?" I asked, repositioning Artemis's paw and rubbing my eyes.

"Hey, pumpkin head. What's going on?"

When I tried to rise, Artemis groaned and Reyes tightened his hold. I looked back at him to ascertain his state of alertness.

Eyes closed? Check.

Breathing deep? Check.

Serene expression of slumber? Nope.

In its place, he wore an agonizingly adorable smirk.

"We have company," I said, running a finger down the perfect bridge of his nose.

"No."

I giggled. "That wasn't really a question."

"No, anyway."

"Are you still with that hottie from hell?" Aunt Lil asked.

"Yep."

"Damn. I've seen that boy naked." She wiggled her brows. "He's a keeper."

Reyes threw an arm over his face, embarrassed, and rolled over, taking me with him and almost ejecting Artemis from her throne, but she shifted her weight and settled it crossways over both of us.

I disentangled myself from Reyes's hold, which was harder than it sounded since he was fighting to keep me close. Then I wiggled out from under Artemis and jumped up before embarking on a *Lord of the Rings*–like quest for my underwear.

"Have you seen a pair of undies?" I asked Aunt Lil.

"Nope. I don't wear the things. I prefer things au naturel, if you know what I mean. Get some air down there."

I had a fight another giggle. "Thanks, Aunt Lil, I do."

Aunt Lillian—an elderly great-aunt, to be exact—died in the sixties at a hippie commune, wearing a floral muumuu and a killer set of love beads. Her bluish hair, combined with her departed state of well-being, practically glowed.

Because she died before I was born, I hadn't known her when she was alive, but she'd been there for me growing up. She never failed to offer colorful, if not overly sage, advice. And I could definitely use some now.

"What's with all the demons in your apartment?"

"You went to our apartment?" I asked, alarmed. "Ah. Found a pair." I pulled on Reyes's boxers. They slipped low on my hips, but they'd work for the time being. Now to salvage the reputations of Danger and Will. I began the quest anew. If I were a bra . . .

"Sure did."

"Did they bother you? The demons?" I was worried about Angel. He hadn't checked in. I didn't know if the Shade demons would go after a departed or not. Either way, I shouldn't have risked him.

"Not me, pumpkin. They know better."

I chuckled. "I'm sure they do. Where have you been, anyway?"

"Took a little vacay. Decided to visit the churches in Britain and met this vicar with killer abs."

"Aunt Lil!" I gaped at her. "A vicar?" Giving up on the bra, I pulled on Reyes's T-shirt and sat back on the cot next to him. He snaked an arm around my waist and buried his face against my hip.

"With killer abs," she repeated as though I were daft.

"Oh, right. Okay, then."

"You gonna get to the part where you tell me why you have a crap ton of demons living it up in your apartment?"

"We accidently opened a hell dimension."

"Oh. I once accidently opened a god dose of LSD. Two words: *never again*. Still, I don't think you should have done that."

"I agree. Do you know anything about how my mother died?"

"Died in childbirth. Can you blame her? Giving birth to a god and the grim reaper in one shot?"

I sucked in a soft breath as the thinly disguised truth of her statement sank in. "Was that it, Aunt Lil? Was that what killed her?"

"Heavens, no. God wouldn't have sent you to her if you were going to kill her."

"Then she didn't die because of me?"

"Well, now, I didn't say that. I just said He knew your mother could handle it. Sometimes these things just happen. Childbirth is never a for-sure thing, sweet cheeks."

I bit back my uncertainty and changed direction. "What about Uncle Bob?"

She cackled in delight. "I always liked that boy."

"I know, but do you think he would know anything about Mom's death? Do you think he could've covered something up?"

The astonishment on her face pretty much said it all. "Pumpkin, where is this coming from?"

"I was told to find out what happened to Mom. That somehow it will help us close this hell dimension."

Her face brightened. "That's exciting, eh?"

"I suppose."

"All right, I just wanted to check up on you. The vicar's waiting."

So much for the sage-ish advice. "You're meeting him now?"

"No time like the present. I'm not getting any younger. Neither are you." She gestured toward Reyes and wriggled her brows again.

"Thanks for stopping by, Aunt Lil."

She leaned in so I could hug her, her cool essence a stark contrast to Reyes's warmth. "Aw, pumpkin butt, don't be so down in the dumps." She straightened and winked. "You just have to listen."

"What?" I asked, but she'd vanished.

I could've summoned her back, but I knew beyond a shadow of a doubt she'd only get more cryptic the longer we talked. The departed did that.

"She's a character," Reyes said into my hip.

"Yes, she—" I stilled when felt a ripple in the air around me. A dissonance. "Do you feel that?"

He stopped breathing for a moment, and then we both jumped off the cot, leaving poor Artemis to fend for herself.

I rushed downstairs, but since I'd stolen Reyes's underwear and

T-shirt, it took him a few seconds to throw something on. Still, by the time I got to the front door, he was right on my heels, barefoot but in jeans and a black tee.

The visitor only knocked once before throwing open the door. Three men stood on the threshold of our humble abode. Three bikers. Each more handsome every time I saw them, but only two of them were standing. The other one was more slumped over the other two, the demon inside him weighing him down.

"Eric," I said, surprised as Donovan and the non-archangel Michael carried their fellow bike lover inside. "Here." I showed them to the sofa.

They eased him onto it, his legs hanging over the arm of the couch, then turned to me.

"Charley Davidson," Donovan said, giving me his full attention, a sensuous grin on his face, "as I live and breathe."

Donovan, Michael, and Eric had been members of the Bandits, a motorcycle club here in Albuquerque. We'd become acquainted through a little mishap that might have involved me breaking and entering into Rocket's abandoned asylum, which they owned at the time, and their Rottweilers who guarded said asylum.

After a few insults were thrown around for good measure, I'd grown to love the boys and, more importantly, their Rottweiler, Artemis. She died soon after I met her. Someone had poisoned her, and Donovan had insisted—with the threat of violence, of course—that I find out who had done such a despicable deed.

But what he didn't know was that Artemis, to my surprise and ever-lasting joy, became my guardian. She'd been by my side through countless confrontations, and Donovan never knew.

Even crazier was the fact that the boys became guardians of Beep. They were now part of her human crew, which begged the question, why were they here when they should be guarding my daughter?

Donovan, scruffy as ever and sexy as hell, pulled me into a warm embrace. "How have you been, love?"

"Good." I squeezed hard and breathed in the scent of motor oil and aftershave. "Better now."

He chuckled and let Michael give me a hug. I always thought of Michael as the mafioso of the group. A little heavier than the other two, and he had a gait that encompassed all things *swagger* and a mischievous grin that kept me wondering exactly what was going on behind those killer blues.

I knelt next to Eric. The prince, I called him. Tall, dark, with Grecian good looks and a slim, muscular frame, he was the stuff of romance-novel dreams.

Donovan came to stand beside me. "We think he's infected."

I pushed back of lock of his dark hair. "He is."

"Son of a bitch." He sank into a chair. "This is a supernatural thing, right? Your area of expertise? So, you can cure him."

I glanced at Reyes, pleaded without saying a word. There had to be something we could do.

Reyes frowned in thought.

"What are you guys doing here?" I asked, changing the subject while Reyes came up with a plan. "I thought you were with Beep."

Donovan gestured toward my husband. "Your ball and chain was going to fly us out yesterday, but Eric wanted to get his grandmother. It took a little more convincing than he thought it would, and by the time we got her packed, he just—"

"—went crazy," Michael finished for him.

I turned back to the topic of conversation. "He's out cold. Did you give him something?"

"Rohypnol."

"You roofied him?"

One corner of his mouth twitched, unapologetic.

"Wait, why do you even have Rohypnol?"

The other corner joined in.

"What is this?" Michael asked, growing agitated. "What's going on?"

I couldn't bring myself to go into detail again, so I gave them the Cliffs-Notes and let that sink in for a bit while I pulled Reyes aside.

"We changed something," I said, whispering as we stood in a corner. "This isn't supposed to happen."

"What do you mean?"

"I saw them. At the convent, I saw Beep's army. The vastness. The devotion. And I saw the major players, these three guys being among them. They're destined to be her guardians."

"It doesn't mean it won't still happen."

"The last time we tried to get one of these things out of a human—"

"It ended badly, I know. But that one had been nesting awhile. I think there are stages to this and Eric is still in an early stage."

That sounded promising. "Okay. So what do we do?"

"What we've always done. Maybe it's early enough that it'll work this time."

I tried to force my heart, a.k.a. Betty White, to slow her erratic beating. If Betty panicked, I panicked. Or vice versa. Either way. "We have to try. I know my light won't kill them, but maybe it'll weaken it enough to help with the extraction."

He raised his brows in agreement. "It's worth a shot."

After Reyes and I formulated a plan, we sat the boys down and gave them the facts. "Like we said, he has a demon inside of him. Normally, getting one out is not that big a deal, but these demons? They're different."

"Different how?" Donovan asked.

"They were created for a specific purpose with certain safeguards weaved into their DNA."

"What kind of safeguards?" he asked, growing warier.

"They were made to withstand the effects of my light, for one."

Michael quirked a brow because that's what Michael did. "Your light?"

Surprising me with his careful concern, Reyes sank to his knees in front of them, his powerful legs easily balancing his weight. With a gentle edge in his voice, he said, "We can try to get it out, but it could kill him. You have to decide."

After a long pause, Donovan asked, "What will happen if we don't get it out?"

Reyes pressed his lips together. "It will kill him. Eventually. We're not certain how long it takes, but there have already been a handful of deaths with dozens more on the way if we don't stop this."

Donovan and Michael exchanged worried glances. After a moment, Donovan nodded. "Do it."

Reyes stood, and I took my turn to kneel in front of them. I put my elbows on Donovan's knees and gazed up at him. "There's something I never told you," I said to Donovan.

He flashed me that sensuous grin of his. "You want to run away with me?"

I shook my head, squelching a grin. Only he could turn such a dire situation into a reason to flirt. "Besides that."

"Then I'm sure you had good reason."

He had no idea. "I have a guardian. Kind of like you guys watch over Beep? She watches over me."

"Okay," he said, his glistening gaze studying my mouth. He was such a rascal.

I swallowed and charged forward. "I want you to see her."

He lifted one corner of his mouth. "Absolutely."

"In order for that to happen, I need to peel back the veil that separates the earthly plane from the supernatural one."

"Sweetheart," he said, leaning down until we were nose to nose, "I trust you completely."

"Thank you. What about you, Michael?"

"I think I'll just stick to this plane. I was never one for flying, anyway."

I laughed softly, took Donovan's hand, and led him closer to the sofa. We sat on a makeshift coffee table together.

"Let me know when you're ready," I said to Reyes.

He offered a curt nod, ready to go, so I tightened my hold on Donovan's hand and pulled him into the celestial realm. He filled his lungs with nonexistent air, his eyes wide, full of wonder and a bit of horror as he scanned the volatile realm.

"This is another plane, a celestial plane. Reyes and I can exist on a trillion different planes, but we exist mainly on our worldly plane and this one." Knowing what was about to happen, I couldn't hold back the barest remnant of a smile. "As does someone else you know."

When he finally wrenched his gaze away and looked at me, I lowered my palm toward the ground and summoned her. Artemis rose from the earth, her big head pushing up into my hand.

I rubbed her ears, but Artemis's first mission took precedence. She growled viciously at the demon, snarling and snapping her teeth. Then, as if she'd felt him beside her, she turned and saw Donovan.

And she attacked.

Her tiny tail wagged at the speed of light as she whimpered and clawed at her former owner, trying to coerce him to pet her.

Donovan, shocked to the core, gaped at her a solid minute before finally reaching out and putting his hand on her head. She leaped into his lap, knocking him off balance, but he recovered quickly.

Her jubilance infected all three of us. Even Reyes cracked a grin, something he didn't do that often in Donovan's presence.

"I can pet her," he said, astonished. "She's real."

"She's most definitely real. She's saved my ass enough times for me to know that."

He buried his face in her fur, and she yelped with excitement. Then, just as suddenly, she let loose a low, guttural growl, her primary assignment coming to the forefront when the demon inside Eric started to writhe. As though it sensed what we were about to do, Artemis jumped off Donovan and crouched low to the floor, every muscle at the ready, waiting to pounce.

Reyes signaled with a nod.

I placed my hand on Eric's torso, steadied my nerves, and pushed my light inside him.

It didn't take long for Donovan to see the monster that had taken up residence inside one of his best friends. He jerked back, and I almost lost my grip on his hand.

Thankfully, I managed to keep hold of him and keep my other on Eric's chest. I knew if I lost Donovan now, he'd only want back on this plane. He'd want to see what was happening to the man who was like a brother to him.

The demon didn't like what I was doing. It bucked and kicked and clawed, not weakening in the least. I shook my head at Reyes. "It's not working."

"Then it's the old-fashioned way."

I pulled back my hand and whispered, "Artemis."

She shot forward and attacked. Sinking her teeth into the demon's head, she locked her jaws and dragged it out of Eric with a ferocious growl. As though it were a rag doll, she shook it, mauling it violently.

This demon, like the last one, was strong. It clamped a hand around her throat and squeezed. But she astonished all of us when she simply de-materialized out of its grip and went back for more. Every time the demon got ahold of her, she did the same thing, slipping through its grasp over and over, then going back with canines bared.

After a few moments, she went for its body, tearing into its stomach. Reyes grabbed its head and, just like before, he twisted and jerked, ripping the head clean off.

Like a mental patient with multiple personalities, Artemis switched from vicious protector to affectionate friend in the time it took for my heart to beat. Her stubby tail practically vibrated as she pranced back to Donovan with the tattered remnants of a Shade demon in her mouth. An offering only a celestial guardian could appreciate.

He sat stunned, not sure what to think, not sure what to believe. Finally, he reached over and drew her to him, cradling her head, Shade demon or not. But the battle hadn't been won yet. We had to see about Eric.

I gave Donovan a few more seconds with her, then let go. He shifted back onto the earthly plane, as did I. She could still see him, but he couldn't see her. He sat in a state of shock while I checked Eric for a pulse.

Feeling the faintest whisper of a heartbeat, I beamed at Reyes. "He's alive. He made it."

He let out the breath he'd been holding. "Let's hope he's still sane."

"He wasn't that sane to begin with," Michael said. He now stood at the far end of the room. Far, far away from us.

I could hardly blame him. I'd stand as far away from me as I could, too.

Donovan turned to him, his face still the picture of astonishment. "I feel like I just dropped acid."

"Which is why I stayed over here. I did acid once. That is a trip I never want to take again."

11

Reyes made breakfast as Eric slowly regained consciousness. Very slowly.

After placing a warm cloth on his forehead, I patted his cheek and asked Donovan, "How much Rohypnol did you give him?"

"I looked up the legal dose and gave him that."

"Donovan, it's Rohypnol. There is no legal dose."

"I looked it up. It said LD."

My mouth dropped open. "The LD is the lethal dose. Please tell me you didn't—"

He chuckled and dismissed my question with a wave of his hand. "He'll be fine. Unless the thing inside him ate his brain. Do they do that?"

"No," I said with a light chuckle. "Never."

His expression morphed into one of concern. "You are the worst liar."

"I hear that so often. So, is this what we do?" I asked Reyes. "Do we go to each and every infected and rip the demons out of them?"

He flipped a three-egg omelet. "How? There's no way they'll allow that in the hospital. And I think many are already too far gone. The demon too strong."

Eric moaned and rubbed his thick head of dark hair, dislodging the cloth. One long leg was draped over the edge of the sofa. The other dangled off the side.

Despite the infection not really being an infection, Cookie walked over to him and felt for a fever. He let her, going still until she was finished, then he opened his eyes and tried to focus.

I sat on the coffee table next to him. "How are you, Eric?"

He frowned and fought to keep his gaze on me. "How many of you are there supposed to be?"

"Just one, thank the Maker. How many of you are there supposed to be?"

"You only wish there were two of me, gorgeous," he said, a wicked grin spreading across his face.

"Damn, you caught me." I knelt next to him and gave his head a hug. "How do you feel?"

"Fucked up."

"That would be the Rohypnol. At least, I hope it's the Rohypnol."

He leaned away from me in shock. "You roofied me?"

That time I grinned. "You wish. Do you remember anything?"

"Only that the flu sucks. I feel like I've been hit by a truck."

"You were. In a way. But I'll let your fearless leader explain."

When I tried to stand, he took my hand and held it to his chest. They always were the biggest flirts. "You're leaving me already?"

"Making breakfast. Well, I'm watching breakfast being made. Can you eat?"

He put a hand on his stomach. "You know, I think I can."

"That kid could eat a Chevy if he were hungry enough," Donovan said. "Nothing bothers him." He looked from me to Reyes and back. "I don't know how to thank you guys."

"I need my laundry done," I offered.

He laughed. "Laundry it is."

Eric put the back of my hand to his lips, closed his eyes, and whispered, "You were wrong."

I leaned closer. "Oh, yeah? About what?"

"Your light. It did help. It did weaken it."

"Eric," I said, my voice cracking when I realized what he was saying. "You remember?"

He shook his head. "Only parts. Only you. Your light. It . . . I don't know . . . it got weaker. The weaker it got, the better I felt."

"So you knew something was inside you?"

"Not at first. But after a while, I could . . . I could hear it breathing. Like it was using my lungs to get air and my eyes to see and my ears to hear."

"I'm so sorry," I said, and I was. I was sorry for every person going through that same thing as we spoke.

"It's not your fault."

"Yes, unfortunately, it is."

"No. I don't think it is." He tried to sit up but gave in and fell back onto the sofa. "It's all a smoke screen."

Reyes walked over. "What do you mean? How do you know that?"

He rubbed his face with his free hand. "I'm sorry. That's all I remembered. Something about it being a smoke screen."

"You could understand it?" I asked.

"Its thoughts. I could make out what it was thinking. Just bits and pieces, and I remember something about all of it being a part of a bigger picture."

I looked over at Reyes. "This just gets better and better."

Frustrated, his free hand curled into a fist. I walked over to him, uncurled it, and laced my fingers through his. His gaze finally met mine, sad and knowing, before he planted a knee-dissolving kiss on me and went back to cooking. So I went back to watching; I just did it from the vantage point of the floor next to Eric as I knelt beside him again.

"Hey, pumpkin," I said when Meiko walked in.

He ignored me and began the jump-for-sparks game.

"He's adorable," Eric said. "Yours?"

I snorted. "No. Wait." When I gaped at him, he graced me with a lopsided grin. "You can see him?"

He shrugged. "Can't everyone?"

"No, everyone can't," I said, offended. "What the hell?"

"Sorry."

"No, you aren't." I stood up and stomped over to Cookie. "Everyone can see the departed now. Pretty soon, I'm not going to be that special."

Cookie reached up and patted my hair. "Don't you worry, hon. You take special to a whole new level."

"Really?" I sank into the chair next to her and put my head on her shoulder. "You aren't just saying that?"

"Of course not."

I raised my head. "You know I can tell when people are lying."

She forced my head back onto her shoulder. "Just go with it, sweetheart."

"Okay." I snuggled closer. "Can you tell me I'm pretty?"

"You're very pretty."

I sighed, certain my light glowed just a little brighter than it had before, sad that I couldn't see it for myself.

Eric was up and eating in no time. Garrett, Pari, Amber, and Quentin joined us for breakfast, too. Gemma wasn't hungry. I couldn't blame her.

While Pari talked tattoos with the guys, Garrett showed Reyes and me what he'd found.

"It's only one passage, a quatrain, but it talks about a world within a world."

I perked up. "That sounds promising."

"The problem with prophecies is that they're much clearer after the fact, when specific events can point to what was written instead of vice versa. So as far as gleaning anything useful from it, I deciphered one section that talks about finding the heart and destroying it."

"The heart?" I asked. "The heart of what? A demon?"

He reread the passage, probably for the hundredth time. I could feel the frustration radiating out of him. "It doesn't say."

"Well, does it say how?"

"Not that I can tell, but I'll keep working on it. Sometimes it just takes one word, one connection, to make all the pieces of the puzzle fit together."

"So, that's it?" I asked, trying not to sound too disappointed.

"That's it. That's all I've found so far."

I sat back and crossed my arms. "Who writes all these stupid prophecies, anyway? They're stupid."

"This one was written by Nostradamus himself."

"Wow. Nostradamus?" I straightened in my chair. "Okay, I feel special again."

"And pretty?" Pari asked.

"And pretty. But only because last night Reyes was doing that thing he does with his tongue—"

"Charley!" Cookie screeched, her voice discovering new octaves that were as yet unknown to mankind. "There are children present."

"What? He can do things with his tongue that most people—"

"Charley!" she repeated.

"What? He can make the shape of a clover with his tongue." I turned to Reyes and ordered him to show her the tongue thing with a point and a nudge.

He stuck out his tongue and curled the end into a clover.

Cookie's face became infused with a bright pink hue.

I giggled, looked right at her, and said, "Perv."

"You did that on purpose."

"It's like you don't know me at all."

The main door opened, and my lying scumbag of an uncle whom I adored despite the decades of deceit and betrayal walked in.

I brightened. "Hey, Uncle Bob."

"Hey, pumpkin. Honey one and honey two." He gave both his girls a peck. Amber grinned. Cookie was still busy blushing. "What'd I miss?"

"We dragged a Shade demon out of Eric, only this time the host survived."

"This time?" Eric asked, horrified.

I dismissed his concern with a wave of my hand.

"That's great, pumpkin." Ubie took out his laptop and opened it. "I knew I'd heard that name before."

"Eric?" Amber asked.

"Meiko. Is he here?"

She nodded and pointed to the little guy sitting in her lap. Kind of. While the departed were solid to Reyes and me, even though Quentin and Amber could see them, they were still incorporeal. So he was actually just levitating in and around the area of her lap. But he didn't know that, so it was all good.

He cleared his throat. "Can you take him to another room, smidgeon?"

"I guess, but you have to tell me everything when I come back."

"Don't I always?"

She deadpanned him, then added, "Everything," the way only a thirteen-year-old girl could. With the skill of a seasoned nanny, she convinced Meiko they should go watch the sunrise.

"Okay," Ubie said when they were gone. "A custodian found a boy in a Dumpster at North Valley High last Saturday."

"Oh, my goodness," Cookie said, but I had more of a knee-jerk reaction.

"No! It can't be Meiko." I stood and walked around the table to see what he was looking at, which was nothing yet. "He's still alive. Rocket said."

Ubie patted the air. "Let me finish."

I eased into a seat beside him.

"The school had cameras. It's hard to see, but it caught this guy carrying what could be the boy in a white sheet."

We all gathered around his laptop as he played a grainy video. A man, barely visible in the far corner of the camera's lens, walked past carrying something wrapped in a white sheet. He wore a baseball cap, so it would be impossible to identify him from that footage.

"We figure maybe this guy thought he was dead when he dumped him? Or maybe he thought he would die. We don't know for sure."

I leaned closer, trying to get a detail, any detail, from the rough footage. "How did the custodian find him?"

"Taking out the trash. He saw the sheet and immediately suspected something. He jumped into the Dumpster and found the boy."

"Wait, how do you know that's Meiko?"

"Because it's an unusual name. It was weaved into a braided bracelet he was wearing."

"He is wearing a bracelet," I said.

Ubie showed me a picture of an unconscious boy in a hospital gown.

"That's him," Quentin said, pointing to the picture, his soft, deep voice almost pronouncing the words coherently. He didn't use his voice often, and I loved it when he did.

Ubie gave him a grateful nod. "Then you're right, Charley. He is still alive, but he's in a coma."

"A coma?" A vise tightened around my chest.

Quentin tapped me on the shoulder. I explained, and his face fell.

"He threw him away like a piece of garbage," he said, the abruptness of his signs showing his distress. "He's just a little boy."

"I know, hon." I rubbed his shoulder, then turned to Ubie. "Uncle Bob, we have to find his mother and sister. I need a full canvass—traffic cam footage and cell tower records to check for pings at the time Meiko was left in the Dumpster."

He raked a hand down his face, and I realized he'd been up all night. "Hon, this isn't New York."

"Well, what *do* we have? He will have stuck close to home, right? That school is in Los Ranchos just off Fourth. What do we know about that custodian?"

"He's been cleared. We can canvass the area, talk to the school staff and neighbors, see if they saw anything unusual. But with everything going on, the whole town is in an uproar. I wouldn't get my hopes up."

"I'll revisit the missing persons report," Cookie said. "If only I knew someone on the police force who could get it for me."

Uncle Bob held up his hands in surrender. "I'll have it to you in an hour."

"And, Uncle Bob, we need a guard on Meiko. If Belinda's abductor finds out he's still alive, he'll finish the job. I've been assured of that."

"Already on it. Because they admitted him as a John Doe, his name won't be on any of his charts. I'll make sure it stays that way, just in case this guy figures out his mistake."

I studied Ubie's profile. The one I loved so much. The one I trusted more than just about anyone else's. Reyes was right. He must've had a good reason to lie to me. I just could not fathom what that might be.

Normally, I would've asked for his help with the inquiries into my mother's death. I missed Team Davidson. We worked well together. Not this time, however. I'd have to go it alone. Well, alone-ish. At least until I could figure out what he was lying about and why.

He turned a questioning gaze on me. I snapped back to attention and refocused on the screen, taking note of every detail I could make out.

Even though nothing struck me as important, I kept watching it over and over as we ate. By the time we'd fed and clothed ourselves, Albuquerque featured heavily on news channels across the nation. People were evacuating the city in droves, and looting had grown to epidemic levels.

In total, however, even with the now hundreds of patients in hospitals across the city, there had only been seven deaths linked to the disease.

The mass publicity partly stemmed from the bizarre nature of the infection. The strange symptoms and behaviors of those infected. Another twist that whipped the press into a frenzy was the fact that the CDC couldn't identify, or even find, a virus. That mystery upped the epidemic's appeal a hundredfold. Was it environmental? Was it a mass poisoning? Was it a biological weapon?

While the press had christened the perceived virus Delirium, civilians were calling it a full-blown zombie apocalypse. If I hadn't played such an integral part in causing it, I probably would have gone with the latter as well.

I sat pondering the zombie angle while I drove us to the state office in Santa Fe. Then my thoughts strayed to another battle on the horizon. One our daughter was destined to fight. I'd thought about her future trials and tribulations a lot while in Marmalade, but there was one thing I hadn't thought of until one of the wraiths pointed it out in the odd way they pointed out many things.

That's what was so strange about them. About the whole dimension. We didn't have actual conversations, the wraiths and me. They could simply read my thoughts, and whenever they had something to offer, a suggestion to make, or a smart-ass opinion to throw in, they spoke to me. But they were voiceless. Instead, their thoughts were injected into my head.

Good thing, because along with the perpetual night of Marmalade came a complete absence of sound. Any sound. It was a vacuum, eliminating sight, sound, scent, touch, and taste.

It was a punishment.

But I did have tons of time to do that deep thinking thing that was so popular with the kids these days. Having absolutely zero data coming in and zero going out tended to shift one's perspective. And raise one's odds of successfully entering an insanity plea should the need arise.

So, one day, sometime about halfway through my coffin-esque vacay, I was thinking about Beep's army, the Sentry. I contemplated the key players. The hordes of departed that stand at her side. The hellhounds that surround her and protect her with their lives. And one of the wraiths said something that struck a dissonant chord. Why I hadn't thought of it before, I'd never know, but if a wraith brought it up, it was important.

Since I'd finally gotten my land legs back, I opted to drive us to the state capital. I looked over at my contemplative husband, his profile outlined beautifully by the vivid colors of the Sandia Mountains. He rested his right hand at his mouth, his long fingers brushing against his lips, a soft line between his brows as he thought.

He kept his gaze locked on the landscape, but he grinned and said, "It's usually better for the driver to watch the road."

"*Usually* being the operative word."

He let his dark irises drift toward me.

I patted Misery's dash. "She missed me. Poor girl."

"I guarantee you, Mrs. Davidson, I missed you more."

My stomach flip-flopped with that information, but I opted to address another segment of his statement. "Mrs. Davidson. I never changed my name."

"I'm not sure Farrow suits you."

I gaped at him, appalled. "You don't want me to take your name. You're ashamed of me."

He didn't take the bait. "Something's eating at you."

"Ya think?" God, I was good at comebacks. Prolly why I was named Most Likely to Be Jailed for Sassing a Cop. I still had the sash and crown to prove it. "Do you remember that one sparkling moment of clairvoyance I had way back when you ripped Beep out of my arms and gave her to your biological human parents to raise because she'd be safer?"

He shifted in his seat. "Yes."

"Well, during my stint in Marmalade, I was floating there, minding my own business, when a wraith brought up a super good point."

"And that was?"

"I saw everyone around our daughter on her big debut. You know, when she kicks your father's ass."

His jaw tightened. "He's not my father."

"Either way, so I saw everyone from her great army to the Twelve, her pack of hellhounds."

"Yeah, I remember who the Twelve are."

"I saw Amber and Quentin, Angel and Mr. Wong. Everyone. But do you know who I didn't see?"

He planted a curious expression on me.

I took a deep breath and said, "Us."

His soft frown reappeared, and he turned to look out the window again. He did that when he was thinking. He was a thinker.

"Reyes, I'm not sure we're going to make it."

"That's not necessarily what that means. Those who prophesize rarely see themselves in their visions."

"Really? Well, okay, then wouldn't I have at least seen you? I mean, think about it. Why would our daughter have to face Lucifer without us? All these prophecies, all these predictions, they all say the same thing. Our daughter is going to face Satan in a battle for humanity. Not you. Not me. Not the three of us. Beep. Just Beep. Why is that?"

Unable to answer, he worked his jaw, his lids at half-mast as something that resembled resentment flashed across his face.

"What was that?" I asked, not able to read his emotions clearly, as usual. "Why resentment?"

He shook his head. "We're gods, Dutch. You're right. What could stop us from being there for her? We're immortal. The only way we can die, the *only* way, is if another god kills us. So you kill me, right?"

"Wrong," I said, alarmed.

"And then what? Who kills you? Because I know you, and short of death, nothing would keep you from being at our daughter's side. And you don't seem particularly suicidal."

He had me there.

"So who kills you?"

12

You never know what I'll have up my sleeve.
Today, for example, it was a dryer sheet.
—TRUE FACT

Reyes and I were sitting stock-still on I-25, the commuters and the evac-uators merging into one mass exodus.

"Nobody kills me," I said, answering his question. "And I certainly don't kill you. Maybe it's something else. Maybe, I don't know, we get stuck in traffic. Like now."

Reyes growled.

I ignored.

I looked in the rearview at Meiko instead as he bounced up and down to catch sparkles in the air. "Seat belt, mister." I laughed out loud when he toppled over the seat and devolved into a fit of giggles. "He's never been in a car," I said to Reyes. "He wanted to try it out."

Reyes took my hand, drawing my attention back to him. "You know, you can grieve."

We both knew he wasn't talking about Meiko. I dipped my head. "No, I can't. Not yet. There'll be plenty of time for that later."

"Take this exit," he said, pointing. "Let's take an alternate route."

The exit was only about fifty feet in front of us. "Okay, but it's going to take a while." Total gridlock sucked.

"Or not," he said, a challenging grin on his handsome face.

"Point taken."

There was just enough room for Misery to squeeze by on the right and veer wildly onto the exit. God, I loved veering.

I tightened my hold on her steering wheel. "If there are any cops up here, you're paying the ticket."

"Deal."

We exited off I-25 about a half mile from where we merged onto it and drove back to HQ since the alternate route passed right by it.

"That was fast," Cookie said when we walked in.

"Just the opposite, actually. Where's Amber?"

She pointed down the hall in the opposite direction of my and Reyes's suite. "In the TV room."

I stilled and turned back to her. "There's a TV room? Why didn't anyone tell me we had a TV room?"

Cook shrugged, completely uninterested, her eyes glued to her computer screen.

After releasing a long sigh of utter annoyance, I started for the TV room. "No one tells me anything."

Having given Meiko a taste of life in Misery, I took him back to Amber and Quentin and once again set them on the task of garnering any info they could. Then Reyes and I headed out to the state office for a second time, this time with Gemma in tow.

Just under an hour later, we pulled up outside the Official Building that Houses the Office Where One Acquires Certificates of Life and Death. It wasn't actually called that, but it sounded much cooler than *the Santa Fe State Office*.

"We'll be right back," I said to Gemma as Reyes and I hopped out.

Well, I hopped. He was way too cool to hop. He, like, glided.

"Can't I come?" she asked, just as I slammed the door.

I pointed to my ear and shook my head. "Sorry! I can't hear you!"

She'd been talking nonstop on the way up, and there was only so much Gemma a girl could take, especially when humanity was on the brink of extinction.

She sat back and crossed her arms in disappointment.

Getting my mother's death certificate proved easier than I'd assumed. I had all the necessary documentation, so I filled out a quick form, and voilà.

We sat on a bench outside to look it over.

"There was an autopsy," I said in surprise. "Her doctor ordered it."

Gemma leaned closer to get a better look. "Why would he order an autopsy if she died of natural causes, as it says right there," she said, pointing, "and her death wasn't suspicious?"

Reyes looked at her. "Maybe we should ask him."

I dug my brand-new phone, a.k.a. Donovan's burner, out of my bag and called Cookie. It barely began to ring when she picked up.

"I have three words for you," she said, using way more than three words.

"Male pattern baldness?" I asked, taking a stab.

"No."

"Stop following me?"

"Um, no."

"Be the change?" I could do this all day.

"Thaniel Lee Just."

"Just what?"

"That's his last name."

"Just?"

"Yes. It's Pari's guy."

"I forgot she was seeing someone. Is he cute?"

"Well, she is seeing someone, who is a *she*. This is not her. This is the cutter. The possible serial killer?"

"Oh, right." I didn't really have time to deal with a possible serial killer, but then those three little words played over again in my mind: *possible serial killer.* "That was fast. How'd you find him?"

"Thankfully, there aren't many truck drivers in New Mexico named Thaniel. I narrowed it down from the list—"

"How many were on it?"

"On what?"

"The list? How many guys named Thaniel?"

She hesitated a long moment, then said, "One."

"So it pretty much narrowed itself down."

"You could say that, but I still did the work."

"Yes, you did."

"I earn my keep."

"Yes, you do."

"Now you're just humoring me."

"What? I would never humor you. I'm not that humorous. You totally earn your keep. And pretty much mine as well. And probably a little of Reyes's, too. He's a bit of a slacker."

"As I was saying, I hunted down a picture."

"See? Hunting is hard work. I'm more of a gatherer."

"And I showed it to Pari. It's him. He drives for a company called Sundial Shipping. I called pretending to be an aunt from out of town who wanted to surprise him."

"Did you use your toothless elderly man voice? I love it when you use your toothless elderly man voice."

"Charley, that was one time. And I had a cold. And why was he toothless?"

"Because you were slurring your words."

"I couldn't breathe."

"And it worked beautifully."

"Besides, I was trying to be a stripper named Tiffany."

"Oh, right." I cringed. "Yeah, don't ever do that again. What'd you get on this guy?"

"Address. Phone number. The amount of sick days he's taken lately. He's either really sick or something's up. Do you think he's infected?"

I thought back to the timeline. "It would make sense except for the fact that he went to see Pari two weeks ago. That was right around the time we accidently released the Shade, and Pari said most of the names he'd carved into his skin had been there a while."

"True."

I heard her typing in the background along with the sound of a child's voice asking where babies come from. Poor Amber.

"Okay, it doesn't look like he's been admitted to any hospitals, so that's a good sign."

"It is. Text me his info. I'll swing by and ask him if he's taken any lives lately. But first, can you find out where a Dr. Scott Clarke hangs his hat? He was my mother's ob-gyn. I want to go see him after I get a look at the autopsy report."

"They did an autopsy on your mother?"

"They did. Do you find that as odd as we do?"

"It's not completely unheard of, but if she died in childbirth, they usually chalk it up to natural causes."

"Exactly."

"Okay, I'm on it."

"Thanks, Cook. You might want to check on Amber."

"Oh, okay. Any particular reason?"

"I think she's about to tell Meiko where babies come from."

"Good lord."

Reyes and I pulled into the parking lot for the Office of the Medical Investigator in Albuquerque. We ordered Gemma to stay in the Jeep again, much to her chagrin, and started inside when Reyes took hold of my arm and pulled me to a stop.

"There are a lot of bodies in here," he said, like that was supposed to mean something.

It took me a sec, but I caught on, rolled my eyes, and held up my right hand. "I promise not to bring anyone back from the dead."

"And we all know how good you are at keeping promises."

Beyond offended, I pursed my lips and held up an index finger. "One person. I brought one person back from the dead."

"Lie."

"I brought one person back from the dead whose soul had already left her body."

"And?"

"And are you ever going to let me live that down?"

"No. I need something to hold over your head for all eternity. And?"

"And." I stepped closer, staring him down. Or up. Either way. "I would do it again in a heartbeat. I would bring her back."

"I know you would. And?"

Now I really was confused. "And what?"

"And you're sorry and you'll never bring anyone else back from the dead."

"And," I started, but I stopped and lowered my gaze. "And I can't make that promise."

"Dutch," he said, his tone warning.

"We don't know what the future holds, Reyes. Would you rather I lie to you?"

"No."

"Then I'm sorry, but I can't promise I'll never bring anyone else back." Ignoring the heat of his wrath, I strode past him and into the building.

We walked to the receptionist's desk and asked for my buddy Wade, the chief medical investigator. She gestured toward a row of chairs and picked up her phone, so I had to sit next to a grouchy god while we waited for Wade. After an eternity of sulking, I heard footsteps.

"Sup, Powers?" I asked, jumping up as Wade walked down the hall toward us.

"Davidson." He took my hand in a firm shake. "What's your uncle up to?"

"Lying. I need an autopsy report, and you seem like the kind of guy who cuts up dead people. Wait, that came out wrong."

He tamped down a smile and turned to Reyes.

"Oh, this is my husband, Reyes."

"Yes, I remember you."

Surprised, I asked, "You two know each other?"

"No," Wade quickly corrected. "Just, you know." He cleared his throat. "From the news."

Reyes held out his hand.

Wade took it and said, "Glad all that was straightened out."

Reyes had been convicted for a murder he didn't commit. He did ten years in a super max before they figured out the man he was convicted of killing was, in fact, still alive.

"Me, too," Reyes said, releasing the tension in Wade's shoulders with a disarming grin.

He let Wade off the hook for what could have been a very awkward situation, earning himself a crap-ton of brownie points.

God, I loved brownies.

Wade refocused on me. "So, this autopsy report, is it for a case you're working on with your uncle?"

"Yes."

He waved to get the receptionist's attention. "Okay, I'll need a case number."

"I mean, no."

He crinkled his forehead. "Charley, I can't just—"

"It was performed on my mother."

Wade drew in a breath of understanding. "Ah, well, in that case, we'd better go to my office."

We followed him back to his office, and thirty minutes later—apparently, someone had to go to records to get it—we had a hard copy of my mother's autopsy report.

I quickly read over it. "It doesn't look like there was anything unusual."

He shook his head. "No."

"According to the autopsy, she died of cardiac arrest." I frowned at him. "Doesn't everyone on the planet technically die from cardiac arrest?"

"Well, yes, but here at the Office of the Medical Investigator, we like to look for extenuating circumstances. What might have caused said cardiac arrest. Like a double gunshot wound to the head. For example."

"That would do it."

Reyes skimmed the paper. "But there's nothing like that here?"

"No, sir. I knew the medical examiner. He was very good. If there had been anything of note, he would have found it."

"Knew?" I asked him.

"Yes. I'm sorry to say he died a couple of weeks ago."

Damn it. I wanted to talk to him.

I cast a sideways glance at Reyes, then back to Wade. "Interesting timing. Was he sick?"

"Not that I know of, but many people keep stuff like that a secret."

"True dat, Wade. Thanks for this. Oh, hey, how's the old ball and chain?"

"Good. Still hates to be called the ball and chain."

I rolled my eyes. "Still? I was hoping she'd gotten over that."

He gifted me with a mischievous smirk. "Trust me, the stars will burn out first."

I leaned in and whispered, "Best not tell her I said hi, then."

"Good idea."

We started to walk out when I turned back and asked, "Is the coffee still free here?"

13

The doctor called today.
Apparently my blood type has changed from
"O Positive" to "Mountain Roast."
—MEME

"This is so frustrating. We're looking into her death with no idea why. No idea what we're looking for. It's like searching for a needle in a haystack the size of Kansas."

We walked out of the OMI with nothing more than what we went in with. Besides a cup of coffee. I stuffed the report into my bag and took another swig, feeling the burn as the bitter liquid scorched my throat. Reyes had scorched places even more sensitive, so I was good.

"I'm beginning to wonder if this isn't a wild-goose chase," he said.

"I would too if not for Mocha Cappuccino."

He stopped and turned to me. "I know I'm going to regret this, but what does a caffeinated beverage have to do with any of this?"

I put a hand on his shoulder and chuckled. "A caffeinated beverage. You kill me. Mocha Cappuccino, or MoCap for short, was my BFF in Marmalade. She's the one who told me to look into my mother's death. She said I'd find the answers there. And she never steered me wrong, not in a hundred years."

He crossed his arms. "So, this wraith was female?"

"Oh, I have no idea. I did worry about that. I didn't want to offend any of them by giving them a name linked to a gender they didn't identify with."

He pinched the bridge of his perfect nose. "How many were there?"

"Genders?"

"Wraiths."

"Dozens. I think. It was hard to tell. I only associated with a few." I bent closer. "I don't want to brag, but we were kind of the cool clique, if you know what I mean."

He bit down, and I couldn't tell if it was from mirth or frustration or both. Quite possibly both. "What did you name the others?"

"Oh." I looked up in thought and counted off with my fingers. "Okay, there was Salted Caramel Macchiato, Pumpkin Spice Latte, Iced Café Americano—he was the edgy one of the group—Peppermint Mocha Frappuccino, Chai Latte, London Fog, and Hot Chocolate. And trust me when I say that boy was hot." I snorted and elbowed him in the ribs. "Who am I forgetting?"

"It's okay. I'm not sure why I asked."

I figured I'd annoyed him, but when I looked up, he had an affectionate expression on his face. Tender. Almost amorous. Amorous enough for the pitter-pats of my heartbeats to trip and pile into one another.

Rising onto my tiptoes, I eased close until we were nose to nose. "If you're going to look at me like that, Mister Man, we may have to go back to HQ and try out that other cot."

A wall of heat crashed into me. He backed me against the stone exterior of the building and pressed his lean body against mine. "You like playing with fire," he said, stating the obvious.

"If that's not clear by now, gorgeous, I'm not sure what else I can do to convince you."

He grinned and went for the jugular, his mouth searing a trail from my throat to my ear.

My phone chimed with Cookie's special ringtone, shouting out, "Yeah, baby, yeah!" Reyes sighed and leaned back just enough for me to pull my phone out of my bag.

"Cookie sent the address of the ob-gyn."

"I guess we should go. Since MoCap said to."

A grin stole across my face. "MoCap's not the boss of me," I said, imitating my favorite five-year-old.

When I climbed into Misery's passenger seat, Gemma frowned at me.

"What?" I asked, the picture of innocence.

"I can't take you guys anywhere."

She really couldn't.

"It's embarrassing."

It really was.

Reyes climbed in, and she glared at him, too. He ignored her as he drove us to Dr. Clarke's house. Misery liked him, the way he handled her, the way he pushed her into drive and then slid her into park, so it was cool. We found the house with ease and pulled to a stop in front.

"Can you two try to behave?" Gemma asked.

Reyes turned and flashed one of those killer smiles at her. Her expression took on a dreamlike quality, and I knew all was forgiven.

"How do you do that?" I asked as we walked up the path. It probably helped that he was all kinds of smexy, but still.

He grinned and took my hand. A warmth spread through me, the act so sweet, so endearing. Then I realized why he took my hand.

He gestured to our right. "It's been following us all day."

A Shade demon, one that had crossed through what was surely now a departed human. It stuck to the shadows, hovering in all its gray glory. How am I always the last to know these things?

"Will it do anything?" Before he could answer, I asked, "*Can* it do anything?"

"Your guess is as good as mine."

We walked to Dr. Clarke's door and knocked. His house, a one-story sandstone with a neat lawn and a row of rosebushes bordering the front walk, spoke of a man with both reserved tastes and a green thumb.

A woman in her late sixties answered. She gave me a quick once-over, but when her gaze landed on Reyes, apprehension rushed through her. He did that.

"Hi," I said, thrilled that she even answered the door, "I was wondering if Dr. Clarke was in."

She glanced over her shoulder and hesitated. "He's fallen asleep in the recliner again." She focused on Reyes. "With a Smith & Wesson on his lap." Back to me. "Can I ask what this is about?"

"Yes," I said, my admiration soaring. "I'm sorry. My mother was a patient of his, and I wanted to ask him a couple of questions."

"He's been retired for twenty-eight years."

"Really?" I asked, the surprise in my voice evident. "Then my mother might have been one of his last patients."

"Ah, I see. Well, let me check."

She all but slammed the door in our faces. I gave Reyes an admonishing glare. "Stop looking so sketchy. You scare people."

Without taking his eyes off the door, he raised a middle finger in response.

Stealthy.

"That's funny. Clearly, your life means little to you."

"Is that a threat?"

"It's a promise."

A lopsided grin tugged at his full mouth as the door opened.

"Come in," Mrs. Clarke said.

"Thank you."

She showed us to a bright, only slightly outdated living room, and indeed the good doctor was sitting in a recliner with a blanket over his legs. And either he was really happy to see us or he actually had a Smith & Wesson in his lap.

We introduced ourselves while Mrs. Clarke went for some lemonade.

"So," he said, giving us a once-over and gesturing toward the sofa that catty-cornered his recliner, "your mother was a patient of mine. How old are you?"

We sat on the sofa, my knees almost touching his. "Twenty-eight. You delivered me."

"From sin?" he asked with a deep belly laugh.

Mrs. Clarke shouted from the kitchen, "Scott Clarke, I told you that joke is offensive!"

He dismissed her with a wave. "What can I do for you?"

"Well, I don't want to upset you, but my mother died in childbirth, and I wondered if you might remember what happened."

His expression changed to one of recognition. "You're Charlotte Davidson."

"I—I am."

"I remember your mother. Beautiful girl, that one."

I beamed at him. "Thank you. I thought so." When she crossed through me, I remembered thinking that very thing. "I think so," I corrected when he gave me an odd look. "From pictures."

"Of course."

"Can you tell me about the delivery? Was there anything unusual?"

He shifted in his chair. "Not that I can remember."

Mrs. Clarke brought in glasses of lemonade. I took mine and offered a thanks while wondering what to do next. He was lying. Just like Uncle Bob. Was this some sort of conspiracy?

I studied my lemonade before venturing further. "Dr. Clarke, I understand why you might not want to tell me if something went wrong."

"That's just it. Nothing went wrong. There was no reason for her to die. She carried to full term. Her blood pressure wasn't elevated. Her vitals were strong. Her heart rate was within normal range. She began seizing as you were being born. Then she just stopped breathing, and all attempts to bring her back failed. Thus, I suspect, explains your presence here. You have questions you want answered."

He didn't lie that time. Not a bit.

"I do have questions, but probably not the ones you think."

"What do you mean, sweetheart?" Mrs. Clarke asked, sitting in a matching recliner beside her husband.

I drew in a deep breath. "I was just told something else went wrong. Something . . . unusual. *More* unusual," I added.

The doctor exchanged glances with his wife, and I exchanged a glance with Reyes, wondering what could have happened that he wouldn't, or couldn't, tell me. So I chose another tack.

"Why did you retire so young?" I asked him. He must have been in his late forties, early fifties when he accepted the gold watch.

After another round of glances, he acquiesced and said, "The way I see it, when you start hallucinating in the delivery room, it's time to call it a day."

My spine shot straight up. "Hallucinating. What did you see?"

"Oh, I can't say for sure. And it isn't worth mentioning, anyway, being a hallucination and all. Truth be told, I'd been looking to retire and make my wife my sugar mama. She comes from money." He added a conspiratorial wink.

I laughed softly, leaned forward, and put my hand on his knee.

We'd ruffled him. I felt the emotion as clearly as I felt Mrs. Clarke's anxiety. She didn't want us upsetting her husband. I didn't want that, either, but the entire human race needed to know what happened in that delivery room.

"Dr. Clarke, nothing you can say would surprise me."

"Want to make a wager on that?"

I held out my hand, ready and waiting for a handshake to seal the deal.

He shook his head and gave up. "I could've sworn I saw . . . something. Just for an instant. Just for a split second. I'm not afraid to say it. It scared me, it was so real."

Reyes's pulse sped up. He'd been in the delivery room that day. It was the first time we saw each other. In this life, anyway.

"Dr. Clarke, what did you see?"

"You promise not to have me thrown into the loony bin?"

After a quiet giggle, I held up my right hand and made an X with the index finger of my left. "Cross my heart."

He hesitated a moment longer, then acquiesced. "A demon. I saw a demon."

In a reflexive move that ranked right up there with Betamax and New Coke, I whirled around and ogled my husband. Then, coming to my senses, I gathered myself, turned back, and asked, "Can you describe it?"

"Dutch," Reyes said from behind me. "Is that necessary?"

I knew what he was thinking. He'd caused a good doctor to retire. Not that I knew for certain he was a good doctor. He could've sucked, but I doubted it. If nothing else, he probably had great bedside manners. Something he and Reyes had in common.

"Your mother was pushing and, like I said, I only saw it for a second, but it was huge."

Check.

"And black."

Check. The robe Reyes used to wear when he appeared to me was a huge black mass of undulating waves. He'd had a flair for dramatics in his younger years. And later. He'd been appearing to me as the Big Bad up until a little over a year ago, before we'd been officially introduced.

Dr. Clarke continued. "And it was shiny with these scales and claws and sharp, pointed teeth."

Uncheck. Uncheck. Uncheck. Uncheck.

"Scott," Mrs. Clarke said, bringing him back to us with a pat on his hand.

But I sat there stunned. He most definitely was not talking about my husband.

"Like I said, a hallucination, but it looked so real." His eyes watered at the memory. "Especially when it tore into her flesh."

I dropped my glass and toppled the coffee table over when I bolted off the sofa. Then I quickly recovered and knelt to pick up the glass. Reyes took a knee beside me to help, but his face had paled. It struck him as hard as it did me.

"I'll get a towel," Mrs. Clarke said, hurrying to the kitchen.

"Dr. Clarke, have you seen things like that before?"

"Not like that."

I stopped and looked up at him. "But other things?"

He lifted a noncommittal shoulder. "When I was a kid."

He could see into the supernatural realm when he was a kid and had grown out of it. I'd heard of that.

"But you can't believe that was real, honey," he said to me.

Mrs. Clarke handed me a towel.

I dabbed at the carpet and said to her, "I'm sorry."

"Don't be silly. He scares me with his stories, too."

Reyes took the towel to the kitchen, and I sat back down, my head reeling. "You only saw it for a second?"

"Yes, thank God. But it wasn't real. Your mother didn't have a mark on her. I'd imagined the whole thing." He offered his wife a weak smile, but I could feel his emotions. He was lying, probably for her benefit. He knew it was real.

"Thankfully, I haven't seen anything like it since, except that one time Gayle got one of those mud masks from Sri Lanka. 'Bout gave me a heart attack. I kinda think that was her plan, though. Knock me off for the insurance money."

She reached over and swatted his arm, the love in her eyes crystal clear.

"Why their mud is better than ours I'll never know."

Reyes came back but remained standing. Apparently, that was his subtle hint that we were done here. I was so bad at that whole subtly thing.

"Is that why you ordered the autopsy?" I asked him. "Because of what you saw?"

"Actually, your father insisted."

"Really?" Pride sprouted inside me. I knew he loved my mother. How could he not? I couldn't imagine what he'd gone through when she'd died and left him with two children, one a newborn.

"He was grieving. He wanted answers. And he was a cop."

"Yes, he was. Thank you. And thank you for your time, Doctor."

I leaned forward and shook his hand.

"Mrs. Clarke."

"You take care, honey," she said.

"I will."

We hurried outside. The second the door closed, I bent at the waist and gulped huge rations of cool air.

Reyes put a hand on my back and rubbed.

"A demon attacked her," I said, astonished beyond belief. Nothing in this world could have prepared me for that scenario. "That was the last thing I expected to hear."

"You and me both."

I stood and scrubbed my face with my fingers. "How? Why?"

"It doesn't matter."

"No, it does." I stalked off to get away from the Clarkes' house. "Did a demon kill my mother?"

"I don't know. But I wouldn't put it past him."

"Him?" When he didn't answer, realization hit home. "Lucifer."

"If I had to guess, I would say he was trying to stop you from being born. Or kill you before you could defend yourself."

"No wonder Gemma and Uncle Bob didn't notice anything unusual. They couldn't have. But you were there, too. You didn't see it?"

"I arrived just as you were being born. Your light had summoned me. Maybe your light killed it before I got there."

"This is just too much."

He closed the distance between us. "Let's go back and regroup."

"Okay, but I need to make a pit stop on the way. Cookie texted the address of a possible serial killer. I need to go check him out."

"What is it with you and serial killers?"

"Right? I'm like a serial-killer magnet."

"No, you're an all-things-great-and-fucked-up magnet."

He had me there.

Because I wasn't quite as good at following directions as Reyes, I parked about half a block from our desired destination, a.k.a. Thaniel Just's house. Once I realized my mistake, I seriously, and I mean seriously, considered getting back in Misery and driving the rest of the way to the house, but the walk would do me good. After one hundred years cooped up inside the vacuum of space, I needed to get out. Stretch my legs. See the world. Or well, half a block of Elm Street.

"So, this guy's name? Thaniel Lee Just. How serial killer is that?"

Gemma tsked at me, her disappointment evident. "Charlotte Jean Davidson, you can't decide a guy is a serial killer based on his name."

"Gemma, he lives on Elm Street. That can't be a coincidence."

She crossed her arms and sat back. "I give up."

She was so fun.

We found Thaniel's house, a small A-frame with a half-built Harley in front and a red Ford Raptor parked in back.

I walked up to a large window and peeked inside while Reyes pulled out his phone and checked the news outlets.

"No lights on. I don't think anyone's home. But . . ."

"But what?" He walked up beside me.

"Look at that workbench."

A workbench sat in the middle of what should have been his living room, complete with a welder, grinder, and other tools used in metalwork. He even had his own smelting pot and blacksmithing station.

"He makes his own weapons."

"That's it," Reyes said, lifting his phone again. "We're calling the police."

I deadpanned him and went around the house to see what else I could see. "Darn it!" I yelled to the son of Satan. "He has blinds. You know, we could always just kind of hop inside." I walked back to the front.

"I've done worse. But how about we give him a chance to answer for his crimes before we sentence him to death by lethal injection?"

"You seem to think there's nothing to this."

"Pari saw him one time and made an assumption."

"Yeah, but Pari's assumptions are pretty dead-on."

"Like the time she told you one of her clients was going to rob a bank and you showed up to stop him with your uncle and twenty cops in tow only to find out he was the janitor? And that he was going to mop the bank, not rob it? Like that time?"

"That was completely different. She misunderstood him. This guy has dozens of names carved into his body."

"And I have the map to the gates of hell on mine."

I crossed my arms and sat on the half-built Harley. "All right, what gives, Farrow? You sure are going to a lot of trouble to defend this guy."

"I've been there, in his shoes. People judge you before they get to know you, and maybe no matter how bad what you did sounds on the surface, you still did it for the right reasons."

"Are we talking about Thaniel? Because I'm not sure there is ever a right reason to serial kill."

He tilted his head in a noncommittal gesture.

"Okay, what are you not telling me? Are you still mad about Amber?"

"I'm still mad you did that without even consulting me first. You're not the only one who's affected by your rash decisions."

"And what were the odds you would've let me do it?"

He clenched his teeth, his jaw muscles tensing.

"My point exactly."

A male voice wafted to us from inside the house. "You know that chair you're sitting on is kind of expensive."

Startled, I jumped off the Harley and whirled around to see a guy around my age with sandy hair and light blue eyes scrutinizing me from the door of the A-frame.

I brushed off where I'd been sitting and showed him my teeth. "Sorry about that. Are you Thaniel?"

He popped open an energy drink and tipped the can to his lips before answering with, "Who wants to know?" He was younger than I was expecting, with one of those baby faces that made it hard to pinpoint his age exactly but was part adorable and part smexy as fuck. Not that I'd noticed.

"I was just wondering if I could ask you a couple of questions."

He gave Reyes a once-over, then studied me a good thirty seconds before saying, "Shoot."

I stepped back onto the porch to get closer to him, to be able to read his emotions better, then hit him with my best shot.

"Okay, first, have you killed anyone lately?" I was busy. I didn't have time to beat around the bush. But the only emotion I could detect was annoyance. And possibly mild curiosity.

"Damn," he said, turning to go back inside his humble abode. "What gave me away?"

I followed him. There was something familiar about him. Something that tugged at my insides the second my gaze landed on his.

Reyes hung back while I walked into the lair of a killer. Or not. Either way.

"You make your own knives," I said, impressed with the array of sharp, finely crafted instruments on display.

"Among other things."

He kept his back turned to me, thus I couldn't see his face, but his emotions were all over the place. Not worry, however. Or panic. If my side hobby were killing people and someone had asked me about it, I'd have been a little taken aback.

Then again, wasn't that one of the traits of many a serial killer? Arrogance? Maybe he thought he was untouchable.

Well, I had two words for him: *Al Capone.*

He wore a long-sleeved T-shirt, so I couldn't see the markings Pari talked about.

"Who told you I'd killed someone?" he asked.

"No one. Just a guess."

He turned to me at last. "You should get a new hobby."

"Probably. You don't seem too worried about me. Maybe I'm a cop."

"You're not a cop." He gestured toward Reyes outside. "He damned sure isn't a cop. So, what, then? Did Merry's mother send you?"

Awareness prickled up my spine. "You know Merry?"

"I did, yeah."

The prickling turned to sharp stabs of apprehension. "It's funny, you speaking about her in the past tense like that."

He finished his energy drink in one gulp. "Oh, yeah? Why?"

"Since she has yet to be found."

"You're awfully trusting, coming inside when you think I had something to do with her death."

"So, she is dead?"

Reyes stood at the doorway, watching our exchange.

Thaniel glanced at him, then asked, "How would I know?"

"That's a good question. How about I ask you another?"

"Nah." He tossed the can into the trash and went to the fridge for round two. "I think I'm done answering questions."

"You haven't actually answered anything I've asked."

"Not true. If you consider all the half answers I gave you, you have almost three whole answers."

There was something about him. Something so . . . not completely human.

He was studying me when his eyes began to water. As though they stung. Or . . . as though he were looking at a very bright light.

He turned away before any wetness slipped from between his lashes, but the evidence was still there no matter how hard he tried to hide it.

Holy shit, could all of Albuquerque see into the supernatural realm? I was feeling less and less special by the minute.

Whatever his story, he clearly wasn't a serial killer. "Look, you need to get out of Albuquerque."

"You worried about me?"

I ran my fingers over a beautifully carved knife. "The infected zone is expanding."

"I have an incredible immune system."

"So did Typhoid Mary. I hear you have a high tolerance for pain, as well."

He appraised me with wariness and suspicion, then asked so softly I almost didn't hear him, "What are you?"

At last. "Why do you ask?"

He cracked open his second energy drink. "No reason."

Oh, but there was. Very few people could actually see my light. Well, more could now than, like, two days ago, but still. He knew I was something other. Something not completely human. Rather like him.

"I guess the real question is," he continued, taking another swig mid-sentence before finishing with, "what the fuck is he?"

He gestured toward Reyes with a nod.

Reyes's mouth formed an easy smile, completely unconcerned.

14

Trust me. You can dance.
—VODKA

Thaniel claimed he had to go to work. He was lying, but he wanted away from the likes of us. I could hardly blame him. Besides, I had the only real answer I'd needed from him. He wasn't a serial killer. What he was exactly was still up for debate, but that was the only answer that mattered at the moment.

The sun had started to set, so we headed back to HQ, avoiding the Shade like it was the plague. Mostly because it was.

"We have two days left," I said as we pulled into the warehouse's gated lot, and just saying that aloud caused a spike of apprehension.

"I know. I just can't figure out what your mother's death has to do with anything."

"Join Club Clueless. Fifty percent off today only. At least we lost our shadow."

"I'm right here," Gemma said.

"Not you, hon. The other—"

Reyes cleared his throat and gestured ahead.

"Son of a bitch."

The Shade demon was still following us. Still hovering. Still being icky. Hopefully it'd stay outside. Keep its stalking relegated to an outdoor activity.

With everything that was happening, we were worried about the team's morale. I thought about setting up counseling sessions for everyone with Gemma, but she probably needed them worse than any of us. We hadn't been attacked.

To our surprise, however, the team seemed to be working through their frustrations. We walked in to find a tableful of people with jobs to do eating pizza, drinking beer, and playing strip poker.

Score!

Then I realized nobody was stripping. I hated when that happened. Still, one should always look on the bright side of eternal damnation should the Shade win.

I leaned toward Reyes. "I'm going to call this my homecoming party."

He raised a brow. "I'm going to call this your bankruptcy proceedings." His smirk grew wolfish. He went to join the illicit festivities and added, "Hope you brought cash."

"Hope you brought a pretty box for your ass, because I'm about to own it."

His shimmering gaze captured mine. "In your dreams, Davidson."

I almost laughed out loud. He only called me Davidson during competitive activities. He took that shit seriously. My mutilated Monopoly board proved that.

And there was this Twister mat a while back, but that was destroyed for an entirely different reason.

Before I sat down to join the other slackers, I strolled over to Gemma to make sure she was okay.

"Are you going to play?" I asked her, taking a seat at her side.

"No. I'll just watch."

"Not as much fun as playing." I elbowed her but got no response. "Gem, I know you're worried about Wyatt."

She nodded. "I can't get ahold of him."

"How about we ask Uncle Bob?"

"Okay." Gemma had always been moody growing up, but this time I understood. Fear for a loved one's life was rarely a walk in the park. Unless it was Jurassic Park. Then maybe.

The rectangular table on which they'd played would never win the "Best Table to Play Poker On" award, but not all tables sought that kind of attention. That kind of validation. Sitting around the large chunk of metal were some of the best people I'd ever had the pleasure of meeting.

Reyes sat down between Cookie and Amber. On either side of them, Ubie and Quentin, with Meiko sitting on his lap, kept their cards hidden from straying eyes. The rest of the table accommodated the likes of Garrett, Osh, Pari, Donovan, Michael, and Eric. The whole team.

Almost.

My dad would have loved this, and not because he was a gambling addict in his youth. No, he would have cherished this moment as much as I did.

I savored the scene as long as I could, memorizing each face. Each smile. Each laugh. This was a room filled with greatness. With gifts and talents that were unmatched the world over. A god, a warrior, a spiritualist, a healer, a scholar, a magician, a caregiver, a ruler, and a handful of guardians.

This was my world. These were my people. True, they were the same people I was about to wipe the floor with, but they were my people nonetheless.

Gemma and I walked up behind Ubie, partly to ask him about Wyatt, but mostly to freak him out. I'd seen him play cards too many times to let this opportunity slip by.

I bent down until I was right over his shoulder and said, "Uncle Bob, have you heard anything about Wyatt?"

He panicked and hunched over to cover his cards, his lids forming narrow slits of distrust. Leery was a good look for him.

"What?" he growled.

"Wyatt. Gemma wants to know if you've heard anything about him."

He relaxed, but only a little. Wise man. "No. And that's good. Means he's fine." Without looking up, he asked, "Are you okay, Gemma?"

She nodded. "Good as gold-plated plasticware."

"That's the spirit," I said, slapping her on the back. "Uncle Bob, do those two queens make that a good hand considering you only have non-matching, single-digit numbers on the other cards?"

His jaw tightened, and he let loose a long, heavy sigh before throwing his cards on the table. "I fold."

"So, no?"

Blowing off steam. That's what this was. We'd faced so much together over the last year, we deserved this and more. Like more coffee. And more Oreos. Both of which I planned to partake.

My problem with poker was twofold. First, I had a slight problem remembering what beat what. My question to Ubie earlier had been genuine. Sure, I knew my timing sucked, but the question was totally legit.

Second, and I saw this as both a blessing and a curse, I tended to bet big. That meant I also lost big. But, hey, it was Reyes's money. My investigations business was apparently broke. I made a mental note to accuse Cookie of embezzlement later.

Amber had Quentin cut the deck, then spouted off the rules for the hand, speaking an unfamiliar language—and I knew them all—as she dealt the cards. "Texas Hold'em. Jokers wild. Buy-in is ten."

I had no idea what she was saying. That girl had many sides. Deep sides. Scary sides.

When she finished, she signed everything she'd just said to Quentin, who gave her the universal gesture for *rock and roll*. Kid was born to play poker. He could spot a tell from a mile away. A mile and a half on a clear night.

Meiko hadn't quite caught on to the fact that Quentin was deaf. He asked him question after question, pointing here and waving there, which could be why he was sitting, a.k.a. hovering, in Quentin's lap as opposed to anyone else's. Q was the only person with the ability to see him who could also completely ignore him.

Meiko flashed Amber the rock-and-roll symbol as well, and then he and Quentin high-fived, Q's blue eyes sparkling with mirth as the boy's tiny hand slipped through his. I had a serious premonition that kid was going to make a great dad someday. And if it happened to be with Amber, it'd better be far, far in the future. Like a decade. Or two.

Several hours later, I hadn't mopped the floor with anyone so much as scraped a push broom across it, irritating one and all.

Uncle Bob was about to kill the lot of us, screaming about how unfair it was to play poker with a bunch of mutants with supernatural gifts. I felt the name-calling was a not-so-silent cry for help, but he refused to agree to therapy. Donovan offered to roofie him, so that was nice. I shook my head, though. He'd totally arrest us all. Especially me.

"You're the worst of them all," he said, jabbing a finger in my direction.

I didn't argue. Mostly because he'd nailed it. But could he really blame me? Cheating was easier to swallow than losing.

Cookie, however, was proving to be a bit of a badass. Who knew? And Osh, well, he'd decided it was Pick on Charley Night. I could've sworn that was last week.

He pinched the bridge of his nose. "How is it you can remember every single language ever spoken on Earth, not to mention a shitload of celestial languages, but you can't remember that a full house beats a flush? And you have so many tells, it's impossible to learn which one means what."

I smirked. "Where I'm from, that's called *strategy*."

"Where I'm from, that's called *a motive to kill*."

"Oh, yeah?" I leaned forward. Gave him my best Mona Lisa. Lowered my voice and said, "I can remember that a queen of gods beats a joker of demons every time. Did I have a tell that time?"

Cook and I high-fived as she dealt the cards. Apparently, we were taking turns. Nobody told me we had to shuffle. I was really bad at shuffling, which the entire room found out when it took me twenty minutes to get the cards to form a riffle, then bridge together. So much harder than it looked.

We played way too late into the night until the entire event devolved into Reyes and I strategizing less and flirting more.

Every scorching gaze sent shivers down my spine. Every time he licked his lips, I warmed in places tucked into unmentionables.

Osh told us to get a room.

Garrett offered the use of his if we'd just leave.

And Ubie suggested we get a hotel room somewhere far away. Like China.

After a few begs and pleads for mercy, I developed the distinct impression they were trying to get rid of us.

Jealousy was so unbecoming.

But we did accomplish one thing throughout the game: a plan.

Considering we had a world to save, one would think sleep a good option in downtime like this. A benefit, even, but not Team Beep. Hell no. We stayed up all night, the lot of us, betting away our children's futures and brainstorming ideas on how to stop a hell dimension from taking over the world. And the longer we played, the better the ideas got.

For example, I had the idea of having Reyes create another dimension, one not quite so hellish, and moving everyone on Earth there. Sadly, he was a little rusty on the dimension-building front. Which was sad, because I really wanted red clouds, purple oceans, and little creatures called latte-lites that pooped coffee beans.

I totally needed to get into the dimension-designing biz.

Garrett wanted to nuke it. The dimension, not my idea.

Pari wanted to upload a computer virus. She loved *Independence Day*. And Will Smith. Mostly Will Smith.

Quentin wanted to send it through a portal, like, say, me. But sending a hell dimension through me and into the heart of heaven wasn't any way to win friends and influence people. Especially celestial people. Godly people—namely, God.

Reyes was a portal, too. The darkness inside of him led straight to Lucifer's hell. But, while a bitch to get to, it was still in this dimension. In this celestial realm. Kind of like two cities in the same county.

Uncle Bob wanted to call in reinforcements. He couldn't understand how Reyes's Brother could just sit back and let this happen. We were riding the same wavelength there, and I had to wonder what the Big Guy was thinking. If nothing else, He could've sent His angels to stop the demons from possessing people.

Cookie thought it'd be super fun to send her ex. Not that he could do anything to stop the hell dimension or the Shade demons, just that it would be super fun to send him.

The biker gang, Donovan, Michael, and Eric, wanted me to summon Beep's hellhounds, the Twelve, to eviscerate all the demons inside it, thereby rendering the dimension harmless. But I wasn't sure all the hellhounds in all the gin joints in all the world would even make a dent. We had no idea how many demons existed. There could've have been millions for all we knew.

And so the ideas went, one after another, until they deteriorated into things like, "Maybe we could bind the Shade demons with Silly String," and "What if they're allergic to strawberries? We could feed all the infected strawberries."

On and on until Amber, God bless her, stopped all of us in our tracks when she asked, "Why can't you just put it back into another piece of glass?"

And that was what I sat there thinking about when the first rays of sunlight crested Nine Mile Hill.

"How did you do that?" I asked Reyes before raising him $100 million. Only three of us were still actually playing: Reyes, Osh, and me.

Gemma had gone to bed hours earlier.

Having lost his house and his motorcycle to Quentin in a daring yet somehow moronic bet, Garrett went back to his translations.

Amber and Quentin had fallen asleep on the table, forcing us to play around them while Meiko braided Amber's hair. Or tried to, since he was incorporeal and couldn't actually get ahold of it.

The biker boys were drinking bourbon and watching reruns of *Buffy the Vampire Slayer,* saying if the world was about to end, they were going to go out watching Sarah Michelle Gellar kick demon ass.

And Cookie and Uncle Bob were snuggling in a dark corner, talking quietly about everything they were going to do when all of this was over. But apparently not quietly enough, because I really didn't need to know how heavenly Ubie's massages were and how Cookie wanted one every day for a year to do that thing he liked with her—

"How did I do that?" Reyes asked, interrupting my thoughts. "Well, first I looked at my cards and then I didn't make a $100 million bet with a pair of twos."

I gasped, indignant. "I don't have a pair of twos. How do you know I have a pair of twos? Have you been cheating all night?"

"Duh," he said, ripping the cards out of my hand with a wicked grin.

Osh groaned and tossed down his cards. "Dude, I could've won that hand. I'd be so rich right now."

"With what? A pair of threes."

He lifted a shoulder, pouting.

I set my jaw, rising above. "But, since you're asking, no. I meant, how did you put a hell dimension in the god glass?" Originally, the hell dimension resided in an opalescent piece of jewelry called god glass. When

Reyes escaped, it shattered. But how did it get inside the glass in the first place?

"I didn't put it there. I built it inside of it."

Fascinated, I leaned forward as he dealt another hand. "How?"

He lifted a single brow.

"C'mon, Reyes. How did you do it? How do you build an entire dimension, and inside a piece of glass, no less?"

He stopped what he was doing and gave me his full attention, albeit with a frown. "It's just what I do."

When my mouth stretched into a thin line, he continued, trying his best to explain something that was so mystical, so magical, I couldn't wrap my head around it.

"How do you breathe? How does your heart beat? You just do. It just does, and building a dimension is just what I did."

"Right." I straightened in my chair. "Okay, but how?"

A helpless grin softened his features, his five-o'clock shadow framing them to perfection. "I could tell you, but then I'd have to kill you."

"You could try."

"Oh, my God, not this again." Osh sank lower in his chair. "I can't take it."

"Jelly?" I asked.

Still, I couldn't stop thinking about what Amber had said. The god glass had supposedly been forged by a god, a.k.a. Reyes, and was unbreakable. But Reyes broke it. Maybe he was the only one who could. Maybe that connection he had as its creator gave him a certain amount of control over it. A power.

I looked at the three of us, the three most powerful beings on this plane, and I knew somehow that it would come down to us. That the outcome of this entire ordeal would boil down to us three.

"I do have another idea," I said, narrowing my lids in thought.

Reyes and Osh gave me their attention.

"I'm going to see Pandu."

Osh frowned. "Pandu? The kid who wrote those books?"

I nodded. "He's a prophet. He might have seen something in our pasts or even our futures that could help."

"What's this about your mother's death?" Osh asked.

"One of the wraiths told me that in order to stop the dimension, I needed to figure out what really happened to her."

"And have you?"

Reyes stood and strode to the coffeepot to make more coffee. "We're getting there. Why?" He turned back to him. "Is there something you're not telling us?"

Osh smirked. "I didn't sup on her soul, if that's what you mean."

Still, Osh had been on this plane for centuries. "Do you know something, Osh?" I asked, getting excited. "Did you hear anything?"

A look of sympathy settled over his features. "No, sugar. I knew you were coming. Hell, who didn't? But I've never heard anything other than your mother died in childbirth."

"You knew I was coming?"

"Yes. And if I'd known you were going to be such a pain in the ass, I'd have stopped it myself."

I dropped my gaze.

"I'm kidding, sugar."

"No, it's just, we think someone did try to stop it. We think a demon attacked her while I was being born."

His expression turned to stone, and he stared at me for a good thirty seconds before asking, "Why do you think that?"

"A human who could see into the supernatural realm when he was a kid saw it, but only for a second."

Osh stood, his brows knitting as though trying to grasp what I'd just said. "You're sure?"

"No. But I know something went horribly wrong that day. I know she wasn't supposed to die."

"Let me see what I can dig up."

"And just what are you going to do?" Reyes asked.

Osh tossed him a glare over his shoulder. "I'll get back to you."

And he was gone.

15

Your clothes would look nicer on my bedroom floor.
—T-SHIRT

A half hour later, I stood in a steam-filled bathroom wrapped in a towel and gazing at the dark circles under my eyes, while Reyes showered beside me.

"Where do you think Osh ran off to?"

He turned off the water, seriously disappointing the departed Rottweiler chasing the streams bouncing off the floor. But she soon found another calling. She charged out the door, and a few seconds later, we heard giggling as Artemis found Meiko, her new best friend.

"You know," he said, not bothering with a towel as he walked to stand behind me, water dripping off him and pooling at our feet, "for some reason, Osh isn't on my mind as much as he's on yours."

I grinned. "Jelly?"

He didn't respond. Instead, he reached down, lifted my right leg, and braced my knee on the sink. Then he pushed me over said sink as his fingers found the sensitive flesh at my core.

I gasped when he parted the folds there and rubbed softly. So softly I wanted to help, to push into him and against him and over him. But he'd wedged me between the sink and his hip, denying me a single inch of wiggle room.

Grasping the edge of the sink, I closed my eyes and let the feel of him wash over me. His deft fingers. His hard abdomen. His even harder cock as it rested against the folds of my cunt, the tip pressing into me.

I considered begging. I considered offering him money or a foot massage or my soul. Then I remembered he'd already won all three last night.

No, that wasn't true. He'd won all three, but that last one he'd won long ago.

He slid his fingers inside me and massaged my clit with his thumb, the sensation heavenly. But I wanted more of him. I wanted to taste him and tease him and make him come in my mouth.

"Oh, wait," I said, rubbing my hip. "I have a cramp."

"Liar."

Fuck. How did he know? "No, I do. I swear," I added, trying not to giggle.

"Fine," he said, acquiescing at last. "Let me just do this one thing."

"What one thing?"

He leaned over me and brushed back a wet strand of hair to whisper, "Fuck you until you can't stand up straight."

"That's cheating," I said, but he entered me in one, long, exquisite thrust.

And the rest of the morning was spent with him doing his darnedest to meet, and/or exceed his goal. And what an admirable goal it was.

Given we had so little time before the world ended should we fail, we couldn't seem to get enough of each other. I focused on his touch. Memorized it. Savored it. Hoping it would last me the next hundred years. Praying it wouldn't have to.

———

By the time we emerged from our penthouse suite, I could still walk. Barely.

Cookie had showered and was already at her computer.

Ubie had gone in to work despite my insistence that he take a horrible-itchy-rash-in-his-groin day. That shit always worked.

And Garrett was still in his room, scouring the prophecies. Guy was dedicated, I'd give him that.

I gave Cook her latest assignment, adding to her already toppling pile, and told her I wanted to know everything about our self-mutilating truck driver, Thaniel Just. While not important in the grand scheme of things, there was something about him. Something familiar. Something I couldn't quite put my finger on.

"I want to know everything about him, Cook. His family. His education. His work history. Any criminal activity."

"Yeah, yeah," Cookie said, impatient. She put a gentle hand on my shoulder. "Look, you need to go check on your sister. Amber and Quentin said she seems upset."

"Really?" Concern sent needles prickling over my skin. "Okay."

Moments later, I found Gemma in her room, gazing out a dust-covered window.

"Hey, Gem," I said a little too lightheartedly.

She turned, her eyes filled with tears.

"Gem, what's wrong?" I walked to stand beside her, biting my lip in apprehension.

"It's about when you were born."

"Oh," I said, surprised. "Did you remember something?" A part of me hoped she hadn't. She'd never seen into the supernatural realm, and after talking to Dr. Clarke yesterday, I wanted it to stay that way.

She swallowed hard, then nodded. "I remember Uncle Bob had fallen asleep."

"Was this before or after the vending machine love fest?"

"After. We were in the waiting room, and something woke me up."

Dread slid up my spine, cold and wet.

"I don't know how I didn't remember it until now. I heard strange sounds coming from the hall."

No.

"I walked toward them."

No, no, no, no, no.

"I could've sworn I saw"—she stopped and turned away as though embarrassed—"I couldn't sworn I saw a monster."

My lids closed. I'd wanted this information so badly the day before, but now . . . Would it be worth it? Would it break the thread holding Gemma together? She'd always had this perfect ideal of the world. No, she'd always needed it. And then there I was at every turn, challenging her ideals and her need to feel safe in a very unsafe world.

What would knowing that a monster could've been responsible for our mother's death do to her?

She placed a pleading look on me, and my chest tightened. "Charley, I could swear I saw Mom fighting it. The monster."

Doubt mixed with a hefty dose of denial slammed into me. "She fought it?"

"I think . . . this is going to sound crazy, but I think it threw her against a wall, only she didn't hit it. The wall. She . . . she went through it. The monster dragged her back out and—" She covered her mouth with a shaking hand. "It pounced on her."

I felt Reyes at the door, his heat blistering, his wariness palpable.

"The next thing I remember is waking up in Uncle Bob's arms."

I couldn't speak.

"He told me that I'd fainted, but he was really upset. I remember him being really upset, and I felt bad. I thought that he was mad because I'd fainted. By that point, I didn't remember anything about the monster. Just that Uncle Bob was agitated."

I couldn't move.

"He didn't tell me until we got home that Mom had died, and he only told me because he was crying and I kept asking him why. He didn't want to tell me, but I knew something was wrong."

I couldn't breathe.

"Charley," she said, tears running down her face, "am I infected?"

Her question shocked me out of my stupor. "What?"

I pulled her into my arms, and she crumbled, sobs racking her body.

"No. You are most definitely not infected."

"Then how do you explain it?" she said between hitches of breath. "How am I remembering things that couldn't possibly have happened?" She drew back. "I get it. You're the grim reaper. I've known for years, but how could Mom—our mother—fight a demon? It's impossible. She wasn't . . . she wasn't like you. And I'm not like you."

"Gem, I think what you saw might have really transpired."

"No." She shook her head and sat on the cot. "No, that's not possible. I can't see into your world, Charley. You know that. I've never been able to see into your world."

I thought about Dr. Clarke, about his ability and how it waned as he grew older, but clearly it didn't dissipate entirely. "Are you sure you can't? Have you ever seen a ghost or—"

"Everyone has seen a ghost, Charley. I'm a psychiatrist. Everyone has seen a ghost, and 99 percent of the time there is a perfectly reasonable explanation."

"Okay, what about the other 1 percent?"

"I may be Miss Logical, but I've seen far too much to dismiss the otherworld entirely."

"Thank you," I said, sarcasm dripping from both syllables.

She sniffed. "You know what I mean."

"And you know enough about the human psyche to realize you've been blocking this for a very long time."

"You think so?"

"I do."

"So, you really don't think I'm crazy?"

"I didn't say that," I teased.

Her experience could explain a lot more than just what happened to our mother. It could explain that why, if she was sensitive to the supernatural realm, she blocked it growing up. Even knowing I was the grim reaper, she blocked out the things she could clearly see. I had always blamed Gemma's disinterest on our stepmother, but clearly, there was more to it than that. Clearly, it was a survival mechanism.

"Think about it, Gem. If we were talking about one of your patients, and that patient had seen a monster attack her mother as a child but had no memory of it, what would you say to her?"

"That she had blocked a traumatic event from her childhood."

"And if she'd blocked that event, maybe she blocked the tool that allowed her to see that event. Like hysterical blindness, of a sort. It's possible, right?"

She wrapped her arms around herself. "It's very possible." The next time she looked at me, her expression screamed desperation, sprinkled with the hope of skepticism. "I don't know, Charley. Do you really think I had the ability to see into your world all this time?"

"I do."

"I just . . . I can't think anymore."

"I know, sweetheart. But that is exactly what you need to do. I need to know if you remember anything else. Anything at all."

After a moment where courage warred with the comfort of denial, she lifted her chin and nodded. "I'll try."

"Thanks, Gem. I know it's asking a lot."

"Charley, is that thing, that monster . . . is that what you deal with every day?"

"Well, not *every* day."

"Then you're not asking anything of me but to step up and stop being a child, stop pretending monsters don't exist when I've known all along that they do."

"No, Gemma." I pulled her into my arms. "It's how anyone in your position would have coped."

"Not you," she argued.

"Gem, this wasn't your burden to carry."

"Charley." She leaned away from me and stabbed me with her best look of admonition. "I don't care what you say, you are the bravest person I've ever known."

I fought a tightening in my chest. Now was not the time to argue with her, so I simply thanked her and hugged her for as long as time would allow, wishing we'd had this conversation years ago. I think we could've been great friends growing up. We'd wasted so much time.

Once Gem and I calmed enough to stop clinging to each other, Reyes and I went to check on Garrett. But my head was reeling. Her account certainly validated the doctor's, and the fact that she saw that at four years old crushed the ribs around my heart.

We found Garrett in his room, books and papers with chicken scratches strewn about the small box.

"Anything new?" Reyes asked.

Garrett's frustrated sigh spoke volumes. He threw a book against a wall. An old book. Probably an irreplaceable one. I crossed my fingers he didn't get it from the library. They were pretty serious about book abuse. Librarians may come across as meek and docile, but do not ruin a book. Or three. By spilling coffee on them.

"The prophecies all focus on you two and Beep and the ensuing battle with Lucifer. Nothing about a rogue hell dimension trying to take over the world except that one tiny excerpt, and I can't even be certain about it."

"But it talked about a world within a world," I said, arguing.

"Yes, and Nostradamus could've been talking about the McDonald's franchise taking over the world for all I know."

"But it talked about finding the heart and destroying it."

"Again, it could've been telling us to bomb the McDonald's headquarters to stop it from taking over said world. Did you know they are in over 120 countries now?"

"That's a lot of Big Macs."

"On the bright side," he continued, "the city is being quarantined. No flights in or out."

"You're kidding," Reyes said.

"The CDC has declared a state of emergency. They don't know what this is, so even though there hasn't been that many deaths compared to the number of infected, the infected aren't getting better. Not a single case has been released from the hospitals, which are officially overrun. But because of the quarantine, they can't bring in outside help or shuttle the infected out of the city."

I braced myself for the news and asked, "How many deaths?"

"Nine total."

I sank against the doorframe. Nine. Nine people had died because of something I did.

Reyes wrapped his hand around my jaw and tilted my face up to his, his expression both reproachful and cautioning. "Now's not the time." He held me there a long moment, keeping his gaze locked on mine, until I nodded.

And then I felt every molecule in my body separating as we shifted onto the celestial plane. Yet he held my gaze steady, his thick lashes creating shadows on his cheeks as his attention dropped to my mouth.

A thumb brushed across my mouth, parting my lips just enough for his tongue to gain entrance. Just as it did, just as the warmth of his kiss infiltrated the sensitive tissue, we materialized in Jakarta.

I pulled back to look around. The street we stood on was dark. Though it was barely 7:00 A.M. in Albuquerque, it was a little after 9:00 P.M. here. The noise from a local market wafted toward us, but we'd materialized on a side street so we could make our way to Pandu's house without being seen.

Pandu Yoso, a deaf, blind seven-year-old prophet, had written a set of children's books that detailed my and Reyes's journey from when we were merely gods in the celestial realm to when we were born on Earth all the way to when we had Beep. Only he chronicled them as though we were stars.

The books were quite beautiful. Pandu told the stories to his parents, and they wrote them down. And even though he was deaf and blind, Pandu had illustrated them. The thought of meeting this kid made me giddy.

Garrett had discovered the books and made the connection. In them, Pandu called me the First Star, Reyes the Dark Star, and Beep Stardust, and I needed to know one thing: If he could see that far into the past, literally millions of years, could he see into the future as well?

Though Pandu's books were international bestsellers, his parents didn't want to leave their family and friends, so they had built a small house at the edge of their old neighborhood. They could have afforded something much nicer in a more affluent part of town, but they had chosen to stay close. In cities like this, one's neighbors often became one's family. It was something that didn't happen enough in the United States.

We knocked on a freshly painted wood door. A young man answered, a crease between his brows.

"*Selamat Sore,*" I said, dipping my head and wishing him a good night. I quickly added in Bahasa Indonesia, "We are very sorry to disturb you so late."

A woman walked up behind him, carrying a small child. She had the same crease of concern lining her brow line. They looked from me to Reyes then back again.

"*Selamat Sore,*" the man said at last.

"If it is no trouble, we would greatly appreciate it if we could speak to your son, *Mas* Pandu." They exchanged wary glances, so I continued to plead my case. "I am the First Star." It was a cheap shot, but I needed to see their kid. Tonight.

Their lids formed saucers, and they studied us with a renewed sense of awe.

"You are the First Star?" the woman asked. "The Star Eater?"

I dipped my head in acknowledgment.

"And you are the Dark Star?" she asked Reyes. "The Hellmaker?"

He gave the barest hint of a nod, confirming his identity.

Her hand rose softly to cover her mouth. The man motioned us inside, almost as though he were relieved to see us.

"You are *Pak* Surya," I said to Pandu's father, using the customary title to show respect as they led us into a small sitting room.

He nodded and gestured to his wife. "This is Kasih."

Having been given permission to use her name as opposed to her husband's, I dipped my head again and said, "*Bu* Kasih. I am Charley, and this is Reyes."

They followed suit, calling us *Pak* Reyes and *Bu* Charley.

"Pandu is writing the fourth book, but it is not going well," Kasih said.

Surya offered a worried smile.

"Why?" Reyes asked. He had to duck to get into the room.

"He will not eat," Surya said, concern written clearly on his face. "The visions have become violent. They are of a lightless realm that is taking over the earth."

I tried not to react. If their sudden focus on me was any indication, I failed.

"Please continue," I said.

"He goes into a rage, throwing things and screaming."

"He even had a seizure," Kasih added. "I am worried he is being punished for seeing into their realm. I am worried the demons stole him from me."

"That hasn't happened," I assured her, hoping like hell I wasn't lying.

She relaxed, but only a little. "He says we are all going to die, for this is the realm the Dark Star created for the Star Eater. It holds the feasters of souls."

Reyes stood far above everyone else in the room, so when they turned their attention to him, they had to crane their necks.

"Like Osh?" I asked him, keeping with their language.

"Osh'ekiel?" Kasih said, surprised.

I inclined my head. "You know about him?"

Her voice was soft when she spoke. "The soul eater, yes. But these are different. Osh'ekiel was born into slavery. He lives off the souls of others, siphoning and swallowing only what he needs for nourishment. The feasters gorge upon them. They rip them apart and grind them to dust with their teeth until there is nothing left."

They damned sure nailed it.

"They do indeed. May we see him?"

She nodded and took me to a small room at the back of the house. For the area, their home was a mansion, but to me, it was warm and filled with love and respect for their families and traditions.

They pulled back a curtain. The room was lit with only a single candle with Pandu's gaze glued to it as though he were in a trance. But the minute I entered the room, he turned toward me.

A tiny child, he looked no older than five-year-old Meiko. His slender build did nothing to take away from the chubbiness of his cheeks and huge, dark eyes. He wore a pair of white pajamas and blue sandals.

He held up a hand, beckoning me.

I knelt in front of him and placed my hand into his. With a smile, he held up the other. I repeated the action, letting him drape his hands over mine before making the introductions.

"Hello," I said in Bahasa Isyarat Indonesia, Indonesian sign language.

An epic smile swallowed his face. He let go of my hands and said, "I knew who you were when you came inside my father's house. I waited." His signs were fluid and complete, not like a child's at all.

When he draped his hands over mine again, I asked, "How did you know?"

He laughed, throwing his head back, and it made me laugh in return. "I saw your light. You are the First Star. The Star Eater."

I hesitated, unable to believe how amazing this kid was. "Can you see the light from the candle?"

He shook his head. "I can only feel its warmth on my face."

My heart grew. Just a little. "But you can see my light."

"All can see your light eventually."

He had a point. "Your parents said you are not eating. You are upset."

"You are, too."

"You see more than most."

His grin widened, the shimmer in his irises mesmerizing.

"*Mas* Pandu, how do I stop it?"

"I only see what has come to pass, but long ago, when the world was much younger, I saw what you seek placed beside the dead. It was placed there for you and lies inside the tombs. You must find the heart."

I blinked in confusion. "For me? When was it placed there?"

"Centuries ago. It is deep in the earth and is protected by the house of the pontiff. It is guarded by man and guarded by beast, and only the pure can enter."

"The house of the pontiff. Do you mean the house of the pope? The Vatican?" I asked, surprised.

"Yes, below the city. But only you can go." He turned and looked straight at Reyes and yet didn't see him directly. It was as though he saw through him. "He cannot go."

"Reyes? Why not?"

"He is the darkness. Only the light can enter."

I felt a wave of shame spike within my husband.

So did Pandu. "Your darkness is not born of malevolence, but of void, one that waits for light to fill it. The light from the First Star. When it does, you will become more than you ever imagined. I cannot see this, but I have read it in the prophecies."

He needed to get together with Garrett. "Can I ask you a question?" I said, asking him a question.

He dipped his head.

"How are you only seven years old?"

"Because my body was born seven years ago."

I laughed softly. "But your soul?"

"It was born with the stars."

With his fingers draped over mine, I brought them to my mouth and kissed them. He put a hand on my face and closed his eyes.

When he opened them again, he said softly, "You must hurry. Time slips like sand through my fingers."

I started to rise, but something stopped me. "*Mas* Pandu, would you like me to heal you? I'm not sure I can, but I can try."

"If you heal me, I will not be able to hear. I will not be able to see."

For a second time, I kissed his fingers.

When his mouth widened and his eyes crinkled, the candlelight washed over his face just so, and I saw deeper into his eyes. I saw planets and moons and nebulae. I saw stars being born and supernovas exploding. I saw galaxy upon galaxy as far as space and time would allow. A celestial realm. I saw an entire celestial realm within him.

I blinked back to the Milky Way and gaped, and I could've sworn he saw me. His smile, knowing and wise, tuned mischievous.

"Can we see each other again?" I asked when he'd draped his hands over mine.

"You are the First Star. I will see you always."

16

If history repeats itself, I am so getting a dinosaur.
—T-SHIRT

We said our good-byes to Pandu and his family.

"Did you see that?" I asked Reyes when we stepped outside.

"I did."

"It was . . . he was . . . I didn't know that was possible."

"We've seen it before."

"True." We'd seen something similar in Beep's eyes, but she was a portal to any dimension in any realm that existed. The dimension didn't live inside her; she simply had access to them. "Reyes, we need to stop this. We can't let it get to Beep or Pandu."

"I know." With time running out, he wrapped me in his arms and shifted. We materialized . . . in Paris.

"I think we missed the mark."

"I thought we could grab something to eat. We need to wait until the museum closes. Which gives us two hours."

I gasped. For like a minute. "We need to see the Eiffel Tower."

"We can do that."

"You're not going to throw me off it, are you?"

The corners of his eyes crinkled with mirth. He was mirthy. I loved making him mirthy. "I wasn't planning on it, but if that's what you want . . ."

"No, I'm good. Thrilling as it is, I've been thrown off enough buildings to last a lifetime."

"I threw you off one."

"Which was more than enough."

We ate at an outside café on Rue d'Arcole, close enough to Notre Dame for me to see its spires. The food was as delectable as the scenery. We heard over a dozen languages as we ate, the street crowded with tourists from all over the world, as our waiter, having found out we were from the States—New Mexico, to be precise—sang a made-up song about our home state. Even Reyes chuckled at him, but once he brought the crème brûlée, shit got real. Reyes tried to sneak a bite and almost lost an arm.

What no one tells you is not to materialize on the top of the Eiffel Tower—the very top, not inside the observation deck—during high winds. After almost falling to my death three times, and nearly causing an international incident when alarms started blaring, we hightailed it out of there.

Two seconds later, we found ourselves outside Vatican City in Rome. Mostly because we couldn't materialize inside Vatican City in Rome. Something was stopping us. A force field of some kind. A spell, maybe?

Reyes held out his hand, testing the invisible barrier. "You'll have to go without me from here."

"You mean, Pandu was right? You can't go into the city?"

"I doubt Pandu is ever wrong."

"But I don't understand. You've been on sacred ground before. Hell, we lived in an abandoned convent for eight months."

"It's not about that. It's protected."

I scanned the area, trying to see the barrier, too. "From what?"

"From me."

"You mean, beings like you."

He looked me up and down with a dark expression I couldn't decipher. Not harsh. Not angry. Just curious. "There are no beings like me. I thought you'd figured that out by now."

"I just meant, you know, a part of you is demon. Is that what you're talking about?"

"No. It's protected against me specifically."

"How do you—? Never mind. Freaking Vatican people."

We recently found out they'd been watching us for years. Sending their sheep over to keep an eye on us. To spy. And who knew how many they'd sent?

"Do you know how to get in?" he asked.

I began to question Cookie's presence in our lives.

"You can't materialize inside the tombs."

Yep. She was one of them. I was certain of it.

"You'll have to get a ticket and go in like a tourist."

She was a little too understanding.

"Once you get in, you need to concentrate."

A little too forgiving.

"If it was really placed there for you, the heart will call to you."

I was so outing her when we got back. And I thought she was my best friend.

"Are you listening?"

"What? Of course. The heart will call me." I started toward the gardens, then turned back. "Like, on my cell?"

His jaw tightened, that muscle jumping under the perfectly sculpted planes of his face.

Mission.

Accomplished.

I got another two feet and turned back again. "You don't think it's a real heart, do you? He meant that metaphorically, right?"

His only answer was a slight shrug of his right shoulder.

Great.

I might not have been able to materialize in the necropolis itself, but I could materialize at the entrance. I popped in next to an older woman with a poodle in a pink sweater. She was oblivious, but the poodle went berserk.

As she scolded it in Italian, I sought the entrance to the tombs. The beauty of the area struck me first. The Vatican Gardens lay spread before me. Lush greens punctuated with vivid florals took my breath away.

After a short walk, I found the entrance to the catacombs. Several stragglers were just now leaving them under the annoyed glare of a guard ready to close up for the day.

The Vatican Necropolis of the Via Triumphalis sat directly under the gardens. They held over one thousand tombs, mostly common people, and they dated back as far as the first century BC.

The guards hadn't closed the entrance just yet, as there were a few more stragglers coming out, so I shifted and straddled two planes at once, rendering me invisible in the earthly one.

I didn't know how long I could stay dematerialized. Apparently, the protection spell—which, again, who knew that was possible—wouldn't allow me to materialize inside the necropolis itself. The farther inside I walked, the more resistance I felt. And it wouldn't allow me to dematerialize to get out, either. I could only pray I wouldn't be stuck inside the necropolis all night. We didn't have that kind of time.

I just made it past the guards when I couldn't fight it anymore. The resistance. I materialized and hurried inside before a guard saw me.

The burial chambers were amazing, the walls carved out of the stone and graves of all shapes and sizes filling the rooms.

They'd set up catwalks for tourists to see the excavations, but I hid out behind a stone chair—or the tomb of a very short person, I wasn't sure which. I waited to see if any guards would pass by. One did. I hoped he was just checking to make sure all the visitors left. If he did regular sweeps, I could be in trouble.

Once he was out of earshot, I hopped up and walked deeper inside, passing various chambers, some more elaborate than others but all incredible. The cool underground caverns could have kept me occupied for hours, but I had a job to do and a man waiting outside who would freak if I took too long.

I hadn't missed the fact that he'd barely let me out of his sight since I'd gotten back. Fine with me since in his sight was where I'd dreamed of being for dozens of years in Marmalade time. It was endearing, though. His attention. His—

Wait a minute. Maybe it had nothing to do with him wanting to be near me. Maybe he'd been sent by the Vatican to keep an eye on me. If I discounted the fact that he was the one they were most worried about and he was, in fact, the son of Satan, it made perfect sense. I was so calling him out when I got back.

As I strode through the place like I owned it, I noticed the fact that one of the chambers looked just like my first apartment. If all the tombs had been furniture, that is.

This was getting me nowhere. Reyes said to concentrate. I was totally concentrating, but perhaps I was concentrating on the wrong things. Like conspiracies and my first apartment.

I stopped at the refrigerator in my apartment, closed my eyes, and concentrated on concentrating. *Come on, Davidson. You can do this. Think really hard and try to get past the fact that you haven't had coffee in, like, an hour.* How was I supposed to concentrate when my caffeine dipstick was registering low?

Maybe I should go get coffee then come—

It hit me. A magnetic pull, tugging at my insides. Surprised, I lifted my lids and walked toward it.

I'd felt it before. That same power. That same pulsing strength. But I couldn't place where.

To get to it, I'd have to leave the catwalk. I prayed for forgiveness as I climbed the rail and eased into the stone chamber. The magnet pulled me along an unlit passageway. I used the flashlight on my phone and weaved tighter and tighter into the tunnel.

This section hadn't been opened to the public yet, and might never be. It was narrow with a low ceiling, as though earmarked, perhaps, for a poorer sect of the population. Just when I thought I couldn't squeeze any farther, it opened up to a small chamber that was clearly still being excavated.

Ancient mud clung to one wall while the mud on the other had been removed. The wall had been cleaned to reveal four open tombs, the arches in perfect symmetry to each other. And between two of the arches was a carving of a massive lion. It faced forward, its paw extended, its claws elongated as though taking a swipe at the artist.

In the middle of the room was a pillar about three feet tall with similar arches around its four sides.

Kneeling down beside it, I held my flashlight on the words carved on the side. The language I could've spoken. Didn't mean I could read it. It was most likely written in Latin, since most official documents of ancient Rome were. And the words were written in Latin, the letters anything but English.

I did recognize a couple of words. One, *tonna,* meant *cask* or *jar.* The other, *Livia,* was a name, and I wondered if it belonged to the tiny, dark-haired girl sitting atop the pillar. She wore a sleeveless dress with a sheer shawl thrown over her shoulders. Her hair lay in curls around her head secured with a tiara of flowers. And she was absolutely beautiful.

This could have been her family's crypt.

"Hi," I said softly, not sure what era she was from or what language she would speak, but she didn't. Speak. She swung her legs, then jumped off the pillar and pointed back at it.

It had more writing that I couldn't read.

"Do you know what this says?"

She smiled and pointed again.

"Okay. This has to be important, right?"

I looked again and tried sounding out what I could. Which made no sense whatsoever. Not until I stumbled across one word: *Cor.* Heart.

Pandu had said to find the heart.

I sagged against the millennia-old pillar. It wasn't a real heart. It was only the word *heart.* I could handle the word. Sticks and stones may break my bones, but words will never harm me. As insanely untrue as that was, in that moment, I took it to *cor.*

Turning to the little girl, I asked, "Any thoughts on how to open this?"

But Little Miss Roman Princess just pointed again. Bossy little thing.

This room had been partially excavated, including the pillar. If there had been anything inside, someone might have found it already. Just in case, I searched the whole thing for a latch of some kind or a hidey-hole. None that I could see.

"Okay, if I were a weapon hidden in an ancient pillar . . ."

The moment I walked into the chamber, the magnetic pull I'd felt before increased tenfold. But as I sat there, it grew even stronger by the minute.

The girl patted the pillar, right by where the word *cor* was.

I shook my head. "I can't break it. It's over two thousand years old."

She patted again and then put her hand over my heart.

Son of a bitch.

I was about to break a two-thousand-year-old monument that might have belonged to a little girl who might or might not have been named Livia.

The pillar was all one piece except for a recessed panel that served as the backdrop for the writing. I held my breath and pushed, trying to break it, as much as it shattered me to do so, while causing the least amount of damage possible.

Instead, I heard a click. I pushed harder, and the panel dropped down to reveal a cubicle. A wall of energy hit me, sending waves of electricity arcing over my skin and pulsing through my body.

Which was cool. No, it was super cool. But what had me closing my eyes, basking in the moment, was not the fact that I'd found the heart. It was the fact that in the past ten minutes, I'd become Indiana Jones.

My coolness factor totally skyrocketed. I couldn't wait to tell everyone.

A box sat inside. An ornate cube about three inches square. As though it were a living entity, it vibrated with power and strength. I'd felt that power before. It surged and breathed and wrapped its tentacles around me. But what I was remembering couldn't possibly have anything to do with that box.

I reached in to get it when a flashback hit me. A flashback of all the times characters had to reach inside a dark, scary place in movies only to pull back their hands to find them covered in spiders. Or snakes. Or stinging beetles.

I braced myself and wrapped my fingers around the box, praying the panel wouldn't shoot up and cut off my hand when I picked it up.

Only then did I remember I should have brought a counterweight to replace the box so I wouldn't trigger a springing mechanism that led to my ultimate death and dismemberment. Hopefully in that order. Not that doing so worked for Indiana.

With shaking fingers, I lifted the box and eased it out, breathing a sigh of relief when I cleared the opening. I examined the ornate box. The stone matched the surroundings, a light powdery gray, but it was solid. Heavy. The weight would suggest that it was simply a carved cube without a hollow interior. If that were the case, we'd come a long way for nothing.

But the box had called to me, just like Pandu said it would. Surely it opened somehow. Or perhaps the writings on the outside meant something.

This looked like a job for Garrett.

A few seconds after I took the box out of the cubicle, the panel slid back into place. A tremor of sheer panic shot up my spine. I stopped and listened, not that I was nervous or anything, but according to the Indy franchise, if something unfortunate were to happen, it would be right about now.

I looked at the little girl. "Do you hear anything?"

She stood beside me, watching my every move, her dark eyes curious.

I reached up and twisted a curl around my finger. "Are you Livia?"

She didn't answer. Instead, she reached forward, took a strand of my hair, and wrapped it around her fingers. At least we were communicating on some level. Hair was a universal language.

"I'm going to call you Livia for now, okay?"

Before I stood to leave, I studied the box, trying to hold my phone for the light and turn the box this way and that, looking for some kind of release latch. Though I couldn't find one, I hadn't seen one on the pillar, either. Maybe, like the pillar, there wasn't a visible mechanism on the box.

I poked and pushed and pulled, testing every side, trying to spring a lock or slide a section. Nothing worked until I pressed on a sharp corner. It pricked my skin and drew blood. I pulled back and shook my hand, but it had loosened one edge of the box and let me swing it to the side.

Again, power pulsated out. I closed my eyes and chanted, "Please don't be a heart. Please don't be a heart."

I cracked my lids to narrow slits and peeked inside. If it had been a heart at one time, it had turned to powder, but I didn't think so. I had a feeling this was something else. Blinking back to reality, I turned the box over and watched as a fine white dust filled my palm.

This was most definitely not a weapon. What on Earth could I do with this besides throw it in my enemy's eyes? Oh, wait, Shade demons didn't have eyes.

Then I looked closer. Sprinkled throughout the powder were tiny flakes of gold. They sparkled in the light, and with each twinkle of metal, realization took hold.

The box couldn't have held more than a cup of the powder, and the flakes were less than a tenth of that, but I knew what they were, and an icy dread curled inside my chest.

"Why would Pandu want me to have this?" I asked Livia as I returned the powder to the box and closed the lid. I stuffed it in my jacket pocket.

She giggled.

I took a stab and asked in ancient Greek, "Would you like to come home with me?" Because that didn't sound creepy at all.

Livia giggled again and pointed to something behind me.

I turned just in time to see a massive black lion take a swipe at my face.

I stumbled back, tripping over own feet, and fell on my ass. His two-inch claws missed me by a centimeter at most.

What the fuck? Where did a black lion come from? The chamber dead-ended, and he'd come from the end that died. And were black lions even a thing?

He hunched down on all fours, readying to pounce, his massive size cluing me in to the fact that he might have been a supernatural entity. One I'd certainly never seen before, but I was beginning to realize there was a lot I hadn't seen, especially when considering the fact that there were as many dimensions as there were stars in the heavens.

Scrambling to my feet, I grabbed Livia and took off through the narrow passageway. No way could he fit. Then again, no way could he have emerged out of a wall.

"Artemis!" I yelled, running through the passage. Then I remembered. If I couldn't materialize in here, maybe she couldn't, either.

Livia clung to me, but every time the lion drew close, she giggled and held out her hand to pet him. Maybe they were old friends. Maybe he belonged to her and he didn't like the fact that I was basically abducting his owner, but I didn't want to leave her down there. She'd been there for centuries.

I had a feeling, though, and this could be the movies talking, that the lion's sudden and inevitable appearance was due to the fact that I'd raided the tomb.

Then it hit me. I was the raider of the lost pillar. I was the tomb raider!

Oh, my God, I was so cool. I had to tell people. If I died in these catacombs, they'd never know how nifty I'd become in my last seconds of existence.

After making it back to the catwalks—thank goodness, because I was so bad at directions—I vaulted off the metal grate and took a shortcut through one of the ancient chambers, knocking off a couple of rocks that formed a tomb while climbing up a wall of stone steps.

The lion roared, shaking the metal grating I was trying to climb back onto. Running with a little girl in my arms and climbing with one arm was not helping the situation at all. Just as I got a leg up over the grating, the lion took another swipe.

Its claws made contact, ripping through my jacket and sweater and into the sensitive flesh of my back. I bit back a scream, conserving my energy to get me up and over the edge, but it stung like fire. And its claws had hooked into my jacket.

It jerked me back to the ground and pounced to maul me. I flipped Livia and covered her with my body while the lion went to town.

I'd never been mauled by a lion. Especially one the size of a small house. But I decided right then and there, as it tore into my shoulder and clamped down on my head, that it was an experience I never wanted to repeat.

Livia held on to me. She wasn't scared until the lion's claws caught her arm. They cut into her and left three gashes for their effort. That's when she became afraid.

She'd been here for centuries with no incidents. I'm here for five minutes and I bring hellfire down on her head and everything else in my path. 'Cause that's how I rolled, apparently.

I pulled her closer as she sobbed into my chest. The lion swatted us into a corner. We hit the stone with a loud thud, the force knocking the wind out of me and filling my vision with stars.

Since we were all but subdued, the lion now took its time. Walking forward with purpose. Its gait slow and steady.

That was when I saw a small tunnel in the shape of one of the tombs: flat on the bottom and arched on top. But unlike the other burial plots, this one went all the way under the stone walkway on which they'd built the catwalks.

I figured it had been a drainage tunnel of some kind. Either way, it was our chance.

I reached into my pocket and grabbed my pepper spray. Even though it was a million-to-one shot, I had to try. I pointed it at the lion as he knelt in front of us, ready to chow down, and sprayed it into its face.

It reared back, sniffing and snorting, and I ran for it. Or, well, hobbled for it.

It caught on quickly and took another swipe, but I ducked and dove into the tunnel.

I dragged us through it, careful of her arm, and emerged on the other side. Which was only about ten feet away from the original side, but hopefully the lion wouldn't figure that out for a while. It was still trying to swat my feet, to hook its claws and wrench us out.

As quietly as I could, I got to my feet. The girl had her arms in a vise grip around my neck. I went as far across the chamber we were in as I could before having to climb back onto the catwalk.

Stealing onto another tomb, I looked over the catwalk. I could see the lion's back on the other side, its hindquarters in the air as it still tried to get us out of the tunnel. But it wouldn't take long for him to figure out we were no longer in there.

A wave of dizziness washed over me. Probably because the lion had just had my head in its jaws. My brains in its teeth. I got the feeling he was trying to make up for every time a lion forced to perform in a circus had wanted to do that to its trainer.

Aware of every sound I made, I eased onto the catwalk and backed away, waiting for the lion to look up. Waiting for my luck to end. Naturally, it did.

The moment I saw the pitch blackness of its eyes, I turned and sprinted. It tore after us, both it and a massive dump of adrenaline spurring me on.

With the sharp twists and turns of the catwalk and the narrow passages, the lion's enormous body had difficulty catching us a second time.

Blood ran in rivulets down my right leg and soaked the back of my jacket, but the shot of raw adrenaline kept the pain at bay. I wiped blood out of my eyes and prayed we were getting close to the exit. We had to be. No matter what Reyes had told me in the past, in this place the alternative was death. And if I couldn't die like he'd said, an hour with the grumpy lion would've surely made me wish that I could.

With every step I took, I tried to dematerialize. It didn't work. Whatever they'd protected this place with was powerful. Almost as powerful as the gold flakes I had in my jacket pocket.

The girl sobbed again, and I knew another attempt on our lives was imminent.

It was too fast. The lion. I could feel its breath on the back of my neck just as the exit came into view. It was gated and locked, of course, but the closer I got, the less resistance to dematerializing I felt.

The girl buried her face in the crook of my neck, and I dove forward just as the lion's claws hooked into the side of my head, piercing my scalp and whipping my head back.

But we'd reached the outer edges of the protected haven. I dematerialized, and its claws lost their hold and slipped through me.

I landed on the greens outside the entrance to the necropolis and stumbled, taking the girl down with me. The sun was about two inches from settling on the horizon when a man in a black suit and tie blocked the view.

"Mrs. Davidson," he said, casual as you please, "I need you to come with me."

17

You had me at, "We'll make it look like an accident."
—T-SHIRT

I lay back, not sure I could even move much less go with Mr. Man in Black. But he had several friends to help him out should I refuse.

I'm not ashamed to say I'd considered dematerializing just to spite them, but I really wanted to know how he knew my name. Almost as though he'd been expecting me.

The thing about dematerializing was it did wonders for the flesh when it'd been shredded by a ginormous—yet, admittedly, beautiful—lion beast. But seriously? A lion?

Still holding Livia, I clamored to my feet. I didn't have a graceful bone in my body, but right now I was more worried about their bones.

"What the fuck?" I yelled, glaring at them. "What's with the fucking lion?"

Yes. I knew I was on holy ground, but sometimes a girl had to use profanity to get her point across.

They exchanged glances, and then one of them spoke into a radio at his wrist. It was all very Secret-Servicey.

"Can you walk?" the first one asked me. Medium height and blond, he had a foreign accent, definitely not Italian. South American, I just couldn't pinpoint the precise location. If I had to guess, I'd say Colombia.

"I'm fine," I said, jerking out of his grip when he tried to take my arm.

"You don't look fine."

My clothes had been shredded and were soaked with my blood. Reyes was going to flip.

They escorted us—or me since I doubted they knew I was carrying a centuries-old departed child—to a waiting car.

"Look, no offense, but I have somewhere else to be."

"This won't take long, Mrs. Davidson."

"I hope not. There's a shower calling my name."

He just stood there, his expression stone.

"Fine." I climbed in and leaned back against the dark interior.

Blondie got in on the other side, and the rest of the rat pack followed in another car. We pulled up to an official-looking building and walked in, passing through a security checkpoint without being stopped or searched.

Blondie sat me down in what I assumed was his office.

"As you know, we've been keeping an eye on you for some time."

I couldn't help an indelicate snort. "Since I was born."

"Before, actually."

"Look, I need to get back. Someone is expecting me, and he does not like being kept waiting."

He turned on a wall of screens from dozens of security cameras and pointed to one outside the gardens. It was focused on Reyes. He paced back and forth like a caged animal, stopping every once in a while to glare up at the camera.

"You need to send someone out there and tell him I'm okay."

Blondie smiled. "We did. He's on his way to the hospital."

I nodded. At least he knew. "Are those what I think they are?"

He had a stack of files on his desk. I only knew they were about our gang because the top file had the name *Charlotte Jean Davidson* in bold letters across the label. I wanted to ask them what font they used but felt now wasn't the time to make chummy with the enemy.

"Would you like some fresh clothes?"

"I'll be back to my place in no time," I said, picking up the file, "so no worries."

He let me. I balanced it in one hand and, reaching around Livia, thumbed through it, a little surprised at everything they knew. This was going above and beyond, and privacy was something I was quite fond of.

The next file in the stack was Reyes's. I picked it up as well as I rubbed Livia's back with my other hand. They had all of Reyes's names. All of them. *Rey'aziel. Rey'azikeen. First son of Lucifer.* Even *the Hellmaker.* But one that surprised me most was *the Dark Star.* That's what Pandu called him in his books. A children's book.

I didn't question it, though. They were boys with too much time on their hands.

I picked up another folder. "So, what am I doing here?" I asked, tamping down the sudden spike of ire when I read the name. *Elwyn Alexandra Loehr. Beep.* And, yes, even *Stardust.*

"We didn't see what was coming."

Inside, someone had written under her name, *The perfect balance of light and darkness. The boundary between heaven and hell.*

"Do you usually?"

"Yes. We know about the coming war with Lucifer and his army. But the disturbances in your hometown are, well, disturbing."

He'd taken me aback with the words *his army.* The term tightened around my throat like a noose. Beep had an army, too, but his would be ruthless. Cruel. I wondered if, when the time came, Beep could sink to his level to win humanity.

"We've been waiting a long time for someone to find the Tonna."

The stone box in my pocket. They'd probably had cameras down there as well.

"I suppose you're going to try to take it from me."

"Not at all, but we would like it back when you're finished."

"Finished with what?"

The smile he graced me with had absolutely no sincerity whatsoever.

I plucked the next file off his desk and stilled. *Amber Olivia Kowalski.* Trying again not to react, I opened the jacket. They knew everything from the premonitions she'd had at a school carnival to her two-hour death and the fact that she could now see the departed.

Quentin was next. Then Pari and Nicolette and even a file on Garrett, who had no supernatural abilities at all. And the stack just kept going.

But I'd had enough. I raised my gaze back to his.

"As you can see, we're keeping an eye on you and yours. Just in case."

"In case of what?"

"There are times when even a beloved dog needs to be put down."

And just when I thought we were bonding.

I raised my chin and said in my softest voice, "You watch us from your ivory towers like you know us. Like you could control us. Like you have dominion over us." I stood and leaned across the desk until my nose was barely centimeters from his.

No matter how hard he tried to hide it, concern spiked within him. Probably because all the papers he had on us, all the files, were now swirling around us.

It was a cheap trick, but I needed to get his attention. I knew the entire thing was being filmed, which was fine. It would give the archdiocese something to talk about.

Then, one by one, the papers caught fire, every record they had on us reduced to ashes in seconds. Of course, I didn't think for a moment those were the only copies. They'd almost certainly transferred everything to digital years ago, but it was fun to watch them burn, anyway.

"Let me assure you, Mr. Barilla," I said, hoping this really was his office and the nameplate I referenced belonged to him, "the only thing you have dominion over in this world is what you put in your coffee in the morning."

And we were gone.

Livia and I materialized outside the city limits. Reyes whirled around, his predatory instincts spiking his adrenaline.

"At least you're not foaming at the mouth," I said, looking on the bright side.

But he took in the state of my clothes, as did several passersby.

"I'm fine," I said to stop any tantrum he might have been contemplating, but he was on me at once. Well, on Livia and me. Thankfully, she was busy napping.

He wrapped an arm around my neck and pulled us close. "What happened?"

"Dude," I said, still astonished, "a lion. A black lion. Seriously, what the fuck?"

He ran his hands under my jacket and over my body. The blood was drying and my clothes were stiffening, which was even grosser than before.

I put a hand on his face. "I'm okay, handsome."

He looked at the dried blood in my hair and, I assumed, on my face, and set his jaw. He'd felt helpless, and he didn't like that feeling. Who did? But for Reyes, it was like an affront to his masculinity. Guys.

"But I really need to get out of these clothes."

"I see you've picked up another stray."

"Can we keep her? Please, please, please, please, please?"

He tried to stop the lopsided grin from forming on his face. He failed. Hard. Because that thing was stunning, if the three girls who walked by us were any indication. Two gaped at Reyes, one at me.

"You have fans," I said.

"So do you."

I shrugged. "It's probably my ass. I mean, have you seen my ass?"

———

We made it back to HQ in one piece. Which was not unexpected. I took Livia down to meet the other kids. It was like she'd found heaven. But a bigger reason I went downstairs was to empty the box into a zip-top bag. I needed to know more before sharing that with the group. I didn't want to jump to conclusions, and I didn't want to start an all-out brawl between the boys. It'd happened before.

I stuffed the bag in the pocket opposite the box and went back upstairs for a shower, but trying to sneak past an entire room full of people when you looked like you'd barely survived hostile takeover of the planet by aliens was not easy.

Cookie's reaction was the loudest. "Charley!" she shouted, making sure everyone in the room heard her. All heads turned my way.

I held up a hand. "I'm fine. I just need a shower and a change, then I'll explain."

"But—"

"No. Shower first."

Cookie sank back into her chair, and the others let me leave even though more than one jaw had fallen off its hinges.

When I got downstairs after my shower, the gang was just now sitting down for lunch. Reyes and I sat with them to catch up on the news.

Garrett filled us in. "The looting and vandalism is getting worse. The governor has declared martial law." He placed a patient yet strangely sarcastic smile on me. "How'd you guys do?"

"I'm not sure." I dragged out the box and put it on the table. "Pandu sent us to Rome."

Cookie gasped. "You guys went to Rome? That's lovely. I want to go to Rome."

"A huge black lion played shred-the-human with me."

"Oh. But still."

"I found this box in a secret compartment in one of the crypts in the Vatican Necropolis."

Everyone blinked in surprise.

"It has to mean something, Garrett."

He picked it up and turned it over. "Does it open?"

"Yes, but there wasn't anything inside," I said, lying through my freshly brushed teeth. I didn't dare spare Reyes a glance. That would've been a dead giveaway, and I was bad enough about giving away too much without killing it. "What do you think?"

"I think it's fascinating."

"That's what I like. Positivity in the face of certain annihilation."

Garrett smiled proudly. "You know what?"

"Chicken butt?"

"I could swear I've seen writing like this."

He rose. I followed while Reyes told the gang about the Vatican. While he broke the news to Cookie that they had a file on her daughter, not to mention one on herself.

We went into Garrett's room. I sat while he tore through a few books until he found what he was looking for.

"How are you doing?" I asked him.

Preoccupied, he said, "Fine. Here it is. It's Latin, obviously."

I snorted. "Obviously."

"But I don't recognize any of the words. The writing is strange."

"Then you two should get along."

"Yeah. So, how old was the chamber this was found in?"

He was totally ignoring me. I couldn't blame him. I ignored myself sometimes just to get a few minutes' respite.

"First century BC, I believe."

"Wow. How does it open?"

I showed him, drawing blood again. "See? Nothing. So, how's your love life?"

He finally gave me his full attention. "Why you asking?"

"Just curious. You know, in case the world ends tomorrow."

"Ah." He went back to the box. "I'm thinking about asking Marika to marry me."

I didn't see that coming. "Marika? The woman who tricked you into getting her pregtastic because of your ancestry?"

He lifted a shoulder.

"I thought you were with Zoe?"

"No, Pari is."

"Are you serious?"

"As the silent killer."

"Aw, they make a cute couple, don't you think?"

He did the deadpan thing.

"Hey, you have Marika. What are you so grumpy about?"

"I'm not. It's just that . . . I want what you and Reyes have."

"The strong possibility of an STD?"

"No, a love that spans the life of a million stars. All I get is betrayal and tricks."

"Oh, that." I dismissed the idea with a wave. "If you're worried about betrayal, hon, you've come to the right place. I was sent to kill Reyes, remember? To swallow him whole."

"Somehow I don't think he would've minded."

"And he built a hell dimension just for little ol' me."

"What are you saying?"

"That all relationships are tricky. Maybe not quite as tricky as ours has been, but it took a lot to get where we are. Give her a chance. Marika loves you."

"Yeah?"

"I felt it when she looked at you."

"She used me for my sperm count."

"Which is clearly excellent." When he didn't respond, I said, "I've seen amazing relationships based on worse. Ours, for one."

"Yours and Reyes's?"

"Yours and mine. We didn't always see eyeball to eyeball."

He lifted a shoulder. "I guess."

"I'm going to assume you got her outta Dodge."

"Yeah. She and Zaire were on the first plane out."

"That speaks volumes right there. I think you care more for her than you think."

"Okay," he said, crossing out of the dangerous territory of heartfelt honesty and into his comfort zone, "let me study this a bit."

"The Vatican wants it back."

"And you care why?"

"Oh, I don't. Not in the least. But if we do give it back, let me state for the record, they can put it back in the pillar themselves, because holy hell. Getting attacked by a lion sucks ass, dude. I do *not* recommend it."

A frown flashed across his face, so I sat back down. Something was clearly bothering him.

"Garrett, what is it?"

"I saw your clothes, Charles."

"That? It was either come back in my shredded and bloody clothes or come back in my birthday suit."

A sexy brow shot up.

"Don't even." I started to leave, but I turned around and asked, "Can I see your abs? You know, in case the world ends tomorrow?"

"No. Make sure it doesn't, and I'll show them to you all you want."

"Damn it."

I turned to see Reyes standing in the door. "He won't show me his abs."

"He won't show them to me, either. I asked earlier. Angel is looking for you."

"Oh, good. I've been worried about him."

I started to walk out the door, but he braced an arm across it. "What happened in there, Dutch?"

I looked at Garrett. "Nothing. I swear. We're just friends."

Garrett came up behind me. "Sweetheart, you have to be trauma-tized."

"Oh, honey, you're good but you're not that good."

"Charles," he said, his expression encouraging me to share.

Sharing was not caring in my book, so I turned back to my husband.

Reyes stared me down for a solid minute before exchanging glances with Garrett the Betrayer and moving his arm.

"Thank you." I strutted past to search out my little Angel.

"What the fuck happened?" he asked when I found him in Quentin's room with Amber lounging on the cot.

I didn't even think about the fact that they could all be friends now that Amber could see the departed. It did my heart good to see them chatting. Meiko was sitting on Angel's lap while Quentin taught Meiko how to finger-spell his own name.

"Hey, watch your language."

He winced. "Sorry."

Whew. Interrogation averted. If only they were all that easy. "Reyes said you wanted to see me."

"Oh, yeah." He handed Meiko to Amber, who sat up so it would at least look like Meiko was sitting in her lap.

"Hey, Aunt Charley," Amber said, her smile bright.

Quentin followed suit, offering me a wave and a smile that would melt the polar ice caps. Meiko would have waved, but he was busy forming a *K* with his hand. *K*s were hard for both kids and adults—mostly adults—but he was getting it.

When we got clear of their room, Angel stopped and backed me against a wall with his index finger on my chest. Ballsy.

"What happened? I'm not kidding."

Damn it. "It was kind of like *The Lion, the Witch, and the Wardrobe,* only without the witch or the wardrobe."

"Something attacked you?"

"Dude," I said, using my word of the day, "it used me as its plaything.

I feel so dirty now. Then it sat down to dine on my innards. But that's neither here nor there. How did it go?"

He'd braced a hand against the wall next to my head, his thirteen-year-old face, only just shedding the baby fat of youth when he died, full of concern. The bandanna he wore low on his brows covered the top halves of his eyes, but it couldn't hide the shimmering depths of his dark irises.

"I don't understand. Why didn't you just phase out?"

"Phase out? Interesting way to put it. I couldn't, actually. The whole place had some kind of shield around it. It was bizarre. They even had one around Vatican City that kept Reyes out. And only Reyes."

"So, it attacked and you couldn't get out?"

"It did and I couldn't."

He bit down and drew closer. "Why didn't you summon me?"

I let out a soft laugh. "I tried to summon Artemis and couldn't. I knew it wouldn't work with you either."

He shook his head.

"Angel?" I said when he got even closer. "I'm going to hug on you if you invade my space bubble any more than you already have."

He inched even closer, a challenging look on his face.

Left with little choice, I wrapped him in my arms. He wrapped back, burying his face in the crook of my neck. It seemed to be a popular place lately.

We hugged for a long time. This was more than just today. His embrace held a myriad of pent-up emotion. He'd probably been worried about me when I was cast out of the realm.

I brushed a hand over his hair and pulled him tighter. He raised his face, his mouth at my ear. "In case we die tomorrow, can I see you naked?"

"No."

"What if I let you see me naked?"

"Ew." I shoved him off me. "You are thirteen, Angel."

He brushed his T-shirt where I pushed him. "No, I died at thirteen. You've never taken me seriously."

"I take you seriously. Just not often."

"Oh!" he said, changing directions on a dime. "I found something out. They're all crazy!"

Trying not to giggle, I reached up and ran my fingers over his peach fuzz. "It's a mad, mad world."

"No, really, they're all crazy."

"Who, sweet pea?"

He winced at the term of endearment. "The infected. They're all crazy."

"Yes, that's part of the problem."

"No, I mean before they were possessed." He whirled around and began pacing the hallway. "I was listening to the chick from the CDC—"

"I'm sure you meant to say the *doctor*."

"—and she was talking about how they might have found a connection between the infected that are making them more acceptable."

"Susceptible?"

He nodded.

That perked my ass right up. "What is it? What's the connection?"

"I already told you. They're all crazy."

"What do you mean?"

"She said that they have found an indignant amount—"

"Significant?"

"—of the people they've admitted so far have some kind of history of mental illness, like skit friends or polar bears or old-timers."

In his defense, he died before any of those words were terribly commonplace with the in-crowd. "So, schizophrenia, bipolar disorder, and Alzheimer's."

"Right. They're crazy!"

"Angel, we don't use the C-word here."

"Cunt?"

"No, the other C-word. *Crazy.* They have a mental illness. But, wait, not all of them?"

He shrugged. "The other guy said that for all they know, the rest could have a mental illness and might not have been formerly diagnosed."

"Formally. Wow, Angel, that's excellent work."

"Thanks. Now can I see you n—"

"No."

"Oh, I wanted to say, if this really hinges on something that happened to your mother, maybe you could, you know"—he hedged by kicking an invisible rock—"help your sister remember. I mean, you've done it before."

I had. Several times. "I may do that," I said, thoughtful. "I was hoping she would remember more, but what if that's really all she saw?"

"Then no harm, no foul."

He had a point. "Thanks, sweetheart. I'm glad you're safe."

"Enough to show me—"

"No."

18

I'm not on the crazy train.
Trains go fast.
It's more like a wagon.
A long, slow ride on the crazy wagon.
—MEME

I searched out a formerly possessed biker dude named Eric and found him watching the news in the TV room. The same one no one told me about. "Hey, you."

"Hey, yourself. Have you seen the latest? It's crazy."

"Funny you should mention the C-word."

"Cunt?"

"No, the other C— Never mind. Can I ask you a super-sensitive question?"

"You pulled a demon feeding off my brains out of me. You can ask me anything you want to, gorgeous."

"Thanks. I don't mean for this to sound bad, but have you ever been diagnosed with a mental illness?"

"Not that I know of, unless you count clinical depression, ADHD, and bipolar disorder."

I blinked and nodded slowly. "Yeah, I think those would count."

"Sweet. Then, yeah. Why?"

"The CDC thinks those with a mental illness are the ones most susceptible when the demons scope out a host."

"I've always felt susceptible. In a strange, uncomfortable sort of way. Like when your uncle wants to play find-the-bunny with you but he always hides it in the same place: the pocket of his jeans."

"You're fucking with me, right?"

A stunning grin spread across his face. "Only a little."

I hurried back to Garrett's room and found him and Reyes in a bit of a heated discussion. The only thing I heard was Garrett saying, "This is crazy, Reyes, but of course you can count on me."

"Hey, boys," I said, totally interrupting.

They jerked to attention, surprised.

"Hey, Charles," Garrett said before turning back to his books.

"They found a commonality among the infected."

"They're all crazy!" Angel said behind me.

So, the C-word talk didn't quite sink in.

I let Angel explain. He was pouring all his energy into his retelling when Amber and Quentin came rushing at us with Meiko in tow.

Meiko ran up to me and said, "Amber and Quentin have been practicing bondage with me."

I gaped at them.

"No, sweetheart," Amber said, rushing to their defense. "We've been practicing *bonding* with you so that you feel comfortable with us and can open up. Remember?" She looked back at me. "There's a book. We were practicing."

"You know, it usually works best if you don't tell the victim you are practicing bonding with them and, you know, just bond."

"Right, well, I thought the truth might help him trust us even more."

"This is what he described," Quentin said, holding up a picture.

Amber pointed out a bird on a platform of some kind. "This is what Meiko could see out of a line of glass block at the top of the box."

Quentin gave Meiko a thumbs-up, then added, "He said it's white like it's made out of snow."

Reyes and Garrett joined us, examining the drawing themselves. It was of an eagle in flight.

"And we thought someone might recognize it," Amber added. "We thought—"

"I know where she is," I said, a chill of recognition sweeping through me. "I know where Belinda is."

They all gaped in surprise.

"You know where this is?" Reyes asked.

Garrett pointed to it. "I do, too. Los Ranchos."

"The school where they found Meiko is in Los Ranchos." I looked from one to the other. "Then what are we waiting for?"

Cookie came up just as we took off toward the front door. "Call Uncle Bob!" I shouted to her. "Tell him to meet us at the Village Hall in Los Ranchos."

"Now, wait just a minute," she said in full mommy mode.

We all stopped and circled around toward her.

"I am tired of you gallivanting across the country and leaving me here only to have to watch you come back shredded and covered in blood."

I walked back to her. "I'm sorry, Cook. Sometimes I forget."

"What? How much I care about you? How much you mean to me?"

I'd traumatized her by walking into the warehouse after a lion attack. I should've been more considerate. "Yeah, I guess."

She filled her lungs, then asked, "Now, where are you going, and why? And will there be lions?"

I laughed softly. "Meiko described the view from where they are keeping his mother and sister." I showed her the picture.

"That's in Los Ranchos."

"Exactly."

"Oh, good heavens, what are you waiting for? Get out there."

"Thank you. Can you call Ubie and let him know? Oh, and Kit. She is the agent on the case. She's been looking for a reason to arrest me. I'd rather not give her one."

"Yes, yes, I'll take care of it. Go." She shoved me toward the door.

"Wait," I said, stopping everyone again. "What if the abductor sees the troops file in? He might do something."

"Like kill them?" Quentin asked. Luckily, Meiko didn't know much sign language.

Cookie nodded. "No, you're right. Okay, text me when you want me to call in the troops."

"Thanks, Cook." She could've totally taken her husband's side, but she trusted me enough to hold off. Also, I signed her paychecks.

We took Misery while Garrett followed in his truck, hopping onto Coors and then over Alameda to the North Valley. Thankfully, traffic had died down a bit.

Los Ranchos was a very old, very prestigious part of Albuquerque that sat on the east side of the Rio Grande. It had beautiful established houses and stunning new ones, and surprisingly, the area from Meiko's vantage was in one of the more affluent neighborhoods.

The abductor must be keeping them in a basement or a shed in a backyard, perhaps.

We pulled up to the Village Hall. I turned to Meiko, who sat in the backseat with Amber and Quentin. "Is that the bird you saw?"

His eyes lit up. "That's it. It's snow, but it doesn't melt. Is Mommy here?"

"We're going to look for her, sweetheart. Does anything else look familiar?"

He looked around then shook his head. "I could only see the bird when the car was gone. Sometimes I couldn't see the bird at all. The wood was in the way."

"The car?" I scanned the area. "What kind of car, sweet pea?"

"A big one. Big and square."

"Do you remember what color it was?"

"White."

Since the day was cool enough to leave the kids in the car, ordering them to lock it and stay inside, Reyes, Garrett, and I got out and started searching the area. Meiko's vantage could have been from the residential area to the north of Village Hall, or it could've been across the street.

While the guys looked for a square, white vehicle, I studied the picture and worked my way backwards, checking out the statue from different angles.

Once I had a good idea which direction to look, I headed that way, ignoring the Shade demons that stood watching us from the middle of Rio Grande Avenue. As cars drove through them, I focused on a small area across the street.

Garrett and Reyes walked back to me, unable to find what we'd suspected was a white van.

"Do you feel anything?" Reyes asked.

I closed my eyes and reached out but was mostly met with the mundane, everyday lives of the residents. Then I felt a spike of grief, of utter devastation, as though from a woman who thought she'd lost her child.

Lifting my lids, I pointed. "There."

One corner house, older than most of its neighbors but well maintained, had a beautiful floating patio out front with a pergola and a fire pit.

We began walking toward it cautiously, checking the house for anyone watching us from the inside.

I gestured toward the patio. "Look underneath the wood floor."

"Glass block," Garrett said.

Reyes took my hand. "Someone's watching."

A curtain moved inside the house.

"That's okay. We're just interested in who built their pergola."

Garrett kept pace but scanned the area, admiring it. "We've got this if you want to get a closer look at it."

"Oddly enough, I do."

While they walked to the front door, I went to inspect the pergola. Most of the yards on this block were fenced off, but this one wasn't. Thank God for that. If it'd had a fence, Meiko wouldn't have been able to see the bird.

The guys knocked on the door, and an elderly woman answered. While they chatted, I sat on the patio and glanced around. When I was sure no one was watching, I shifted onto the supernatural plane, just for a peek.

The patio sat on top of a buried shipping container. It had a door with several locks on the end closest to the house. The only light filtering in was from the glass blocks, and if one were to climb up on the tiny counter—Meiko, for example—he could've seen out them.

A woman lay on a mattress on the floor, curled into a ball, while a little girl ate oatmeal and colored. Belinda's pain stole my breath, the depressive state she sank into dark and perilous, and I worried just as much for her daughter as herself. If something were to happen to Belinda, Molly could be her abductor's next target. If she hadn't been already.

The locks jiggled, and seven-year-old Molly ran to hide in a cabinet under the sink. Consumed with grief, Belinda didn't move.

It was the woman. She opened the door to check on them. No, to warn them, a broom handle in her hand. "Reyes'll be back soon," she said, her voice full of vehemence. "Don't you make a sound or I'll tell him."

She walked to the cabinet where she knew the girl hid and slammed the broomstick against it.

The girl, God bless her, didn't make a sound.

Tears slid down Belinda's cheeks, wetting her tangled hair. She'd given up.

The nasty woman turned to Belinda then and hit her leg with the stick. Belinda just tightened the ball she'd curled into, falling into herself. Into darkness.

I wondered why Belinda wouldn't try to overpower the older woman and get out. Then I saw the chain on her ankle, thick scars underneath attesting to how long it had been there and how many times it had very likely become infected.

Reyes, my Reyes, stood beside me, both of us straddling the tangible and intangible worlds.

"We can't materialize here," I said. "Belinda's psyche is already fractured."

"I think it's time to call in the reinforcements."

I agreed just as a vehicle pulled up outside.

"Let them know," Reyes said before rematerializing outside.

I ran through the acidic wind of the supernatural realm until I spotted Quentin. Even straddling the two planes as I was, Quentin saw me, his blue eyes sparkling with hope.

I gave him the signal to call the cavalry, offering a quick nod before slipping back into the small room that contained Belinda and her daughter. A microsecond before I evaporated from Quentin's sight, I watched him nudge Amber with his elbow, excitement evident on his handsome face.

And then I was back with Belinda. I could just make out the voices of my husband and Garrett, the box expertly soundproofed, as the two men walked around the patio in faux admiration.

But I felt another emotion I hadn't expected. Excitement. Not from Reyes or Garrett, but from the driver.

Staying incorporeal, I hurried to Reyes's side, not sure why. He would've known the driver recognized him immediately. He would've felt the rush of adrenaline. The prickle of elation.

Reyes's gaze narrowed when the man got out of the van and walked up to them. "I went to school with you."

He smiled. "You did. Not for very long, though." The man, chubby with shaggy blond hair, thick glasses, and a creep factor somewhere between hair-raising and terrifying, held out his hand.

Reyes took it, then introduced Garrett. "We were just admiring your patio. My wife and I bought a house down the road and were wanting something like this built. Do you have the contractor's name?"

"Really? Well, I—I did it myself."

"Oh, damn. Nice job." He turned to Garrett, eyebrows raised expectantly.

"Look," Garrett said, "we're good friends and all, but I'm not building you a patio."

"Where did you say you bought a house?" Fake Reyes asked.

Reyes pointed north. "Down the road about half a mile."

"Oh, you bought Pearsons' house."

He was lying. Testing Reyes. "No. The McNallys'? Devon and Angela?"

"Ah, yeah, that's right," he said, lying again, which was fine since I doubted Reyes had ever met a Devon and Angela McNally in his life.

Fake Reyes had slipped a hand into his pocket.

"It's been a long time," Reyes said, trying to keep him busy until Ubie and/or Kit showed up, but the man was growing more suspicious by the moment.

The woman, whom I could only assume was his mother, walked out then. "Everything okay?"

Fake Reyes nodded. "Sure, this is Reyes Farrow. I told you about him. We went to school together."

"Oh, yes. My son told me a lot about you."

"It's all lies," Reyes said, turning into quite the charmer. "Your son is really talented."

"It was mostly a kit," Fake Reyes said.

Garrett patted one of the wood beams. "Don't sell yourself short. You did a great job."

Reyes pointed to the van. "What are you doing now?"

"Oh, you know. Little of this. Little of that."

"Well, don't let us keep you." Garrett patted Reyes on the back.

"Okay, then." Fake Reyes—or FR as I liked to call him in casual situations—pulled his hand out of this pocket and shook both of theirs. "Maybe I'll see you at the market."

The farmers' market they had every Saturday a few months out of the year. But I didn't know if Reyes knew about it.

"Sure," he said, going along either way.

I didn't get it. FR didn't seem particularly obsessed with Reyes. Why take his name? What on earth had he hoped to accomplish by it?

"Wasn't there a woman?" the old biddy asked. This was like a horror movie. A mother who indulged her son anything. I couldn't imagine what Belinda had been through.

"My wife. Yes." Reyes gestured down the road. "She wanted to get some air, so she walked home."

"That way?" FR asked, pointing south.

Reyes let a slow smile spread across his face. He'd implied earlier the house was in the other direction. He knew he was busted.

And, sadly, FR knew *he* was busted as well. He put his hand back in his pocket.

"Something's not right," I said to Reyes from the supernatural plane. He nodded.

I whirled toward the patio and then whispered, "Reyes."

He turned and saw it, too. Smoke coming from below the patio.

I materialized inside. Fake Reyes had some kind of incendiary device set up. He was torching the place.

"Reyes!" I yelled. The smoke already hung thick in the air.

I heard Molly coughing from the cabinet.

Reyes burst through the door, splintering the frame.

"She's chained up," I told him before opening the cabinet door to find Molly curled up much the same way her mother had been. "Come with me, sweetheart. It's okay. I'm going to get you out of here."

She jumped into my arms, her eyes wild with fear as the smoke roiled around us.

I made the mistake of breathing it in and almost vomited for my effort. "It's not just smoke," I said through a series of coughs.

"I know." Belinda fought Reyes, trying to get to her daughter.

"I have her. Belinda, I have Molly." I wrapped a towel around the girl's nose and mouth and hurried through the hall, but the smoke was just as thick there.

Frantic, Belinda didn't calm. She couldn't. She tore at Reyes's shirt trying to get past him to her daughter.

Garrett charged in, but the smoke was so thick I didn't see him. We collided. He helped me up, ripped the girl out of my arms, and rushed up a set of stairs.

Sirens wailed in the distance, but I was beginning to black out. Whatever the abductor had ignited was powerful.

I stumbled back into the room just as Reyes wrenched the chain out of the wall. "I don't want to risk breaking her leg," he said by way of explanation, but he needn't have.

We took Belinda into the house and out the front door to join her daughter.

She burst into tears, and between fits of coughs and sobs, she apologized to Molly.

FR's mother hit me with a broom as I rushed past. Unbelievable.

Fake Reyes stood livid. That's when the crazy began to shine through. Your everyday child molester-slash-abductor would have jumped in the van and run like the sissy he was. But this guy, he stood there, shaking with rage despite the sirens wailing in the distance.

"You don't even remember," he said to Reyes, his teeth clenched, his head bowed as he looked on. "You don't remember me."

Reyes glared at him, and then an instant of recognition flashed across his face. "Hale."

"I told you. I told you what I was. You wouldn't listen." The man started stabbing his own leg with a pocketknife he'd drawn. "You wouldn't listen."

"You were angry with him, not me."

Garrett placed Molly on the ground, her tiny, malnourished body convulsing from the coughing fit she was in.

I dry heaved into my sleeve, I was coughing so hard. After fending off another attack of the broom witch, I went to check on Belinda. "Reyes, what's going on?"

"So, this is him," the guy's mother said, her disgust evident.

He nodded.

"You were all he cared about," she said, accusing Reyes of some unknown crime. "It was all about you while I could hardly get the time of day from him."

After a fit of coughs, Belinda passed out.

"Reyes, we need to know what was in the fire. What chemicals he used."

People were pulling over to help, the smoke thick and acrid. Amber and Quentin ran over to warn them away.

"Stay out of the smoke!" I yelled to them. "It's toxic!"

"Even if she makes it," Hale said, a grin of pure evil transforming his features, "she'll die of cancer within a year. They both will."

"That's where you're wrong," I said, kneeling beside her. I placed a hand on her chest and let my energy flow into her. Her lids fluttered open as I hurried to Molly and did the same. They both stopped coughing instantly.

His expression morphed to one of surprise. "You're like him."

The old lady came at me again, her broom handle at the ready. "Witch! You stay away from my son!"

"Oh, that's original." I sidestepped her first swing, then turned back to my husband. "Reyes, this is getting silly. Who is he, and why is this crazy woman trying to hit me?"

Reyes bit down, disgust evident in every hard line of his face. Then, almost reluctantly, he said, "This is Earl Walker's only biological son."

19

Some people are like Polaroids.
You have to shake them violently before they make any sense.
—TRUE FACT

Earl Walker's only biological son? He could have said the man was Satan's uncle and I would've been less surprised. "I didn't realize he had another biological child besides Kim."

"None that he claimed." He said it with a smirk that drove the guy over the edge.

The woman finally hit her target, bashing me on the shin with the broom handle. Pain like I hadn't known since, well, that morning shot through me. Before I could do anything about it, Reyes had swiped the broom from her, moving so fast she didn't see him.

But Hale seemed to know a little something about my husband, probably from the monster he called Dad. He held up his hands as though to surrender, but he nodded toward his mother. She grabbed Reyes's arm, feigning a heart attack. In the split second Reyes glanced down at her, Hale dove at Belinda and jammed the knife into her jugular.

While we jumped to her rescue, Hale ran inside his house.

Blood gushed out of her by the bucketfuls. She held both hands to her throat, her eyes wide with terror as the life drained out of her so much faster than I ever imagined possible. With one touch, I healed her again, but my anger knew no bounds. Everything he did to this poor girl and those adorable children.

Hale was either going to kill himself or barricade himself inside, forcing a standoff and hours of tedious negotiations and attention from news crews. But the way I saw it, the man was joining his father in hell whether he died today or not. Why not move things along?

"Dutch," Reyes said, realizing my anger had gotten the better of me.

But I shifted before he could react. I found Hale inside the house and slammed into him, pulling a part of him with me as I passed through his corporeal body.

I dragged his soul out kicking and screaming. There were hundreds of people in the hospital, fighting for their souls. Why should this prick be allowed to keep his?

The moment his spirit left his body, hell came calling.

A black hole opened up beneath him, his shocked expression all the satisfaction I needed when claws from the underworld wrenched him from the earthly plane and into theirs. At least Lucifer had a use on occasion.

The house wasn't supposed to catch fire, but it did. His body burned, saving the taxpayers hundreds of thousands of dollars in trials and attorney fees.

I rematerialized beside my husband.

Reyes took hold of my arm. "You should have let me do that."

"Why?" I asked. "Because you're the dark one?" I laced my fingers into his. "Maybe I'm a little dark, too."

"I know you. You'll regret taking a human life."

"Yeah, well, not today."

He and Garrett carried Belinda and Molly to safety. They placed them on the steps to the Village Hall, and the two girls cried and held on to each other while Garrett grabbed a blanket and some water.

Belinda's sobs were cavernous, deeply agonizing. I knelt beside them, not sure I should've been the one to tell them, but they needed to know.

"Belinda, Meiko is alive."

She slowly turned toward me, and the look she gave me bordered on insulting. She thought I was as crazy as her abductor.

"He's in a coma, hon. Your abductor—who was not Reyes Alexander Farrow, by the way—placed him in a Dumpster. A janitor found him and called the police, but he wasn't gone. He's still alive."

"His name was Hale," she said, clearly going into shock. "Hale Walker."

"Yes. And now he's gone, and your son is waiting for you."

Gratitude with a healthy dose of disbelief swirled inside her. "Thank you," she said, simply not sure what to believe.

Who could blame her? She'd been through hell with no one there to save her.

"You're welcome. I'm going to see what we can do about getting you to him."

Uncle Bob pulled up with about a dozen cops and the entire fire department, followed quickly by Kit and her gang.

Garrett waved everybody back, explaining to Uncle Bob that he needed a hazmat crew, the smoke was toxic, and we didn't know what Hale had used.

His mother kicked and screamed when Reyes forced her to the other side of the road, away from the smoke.

I looked at her but spoke to Uncle Bob. "Arrest her."

"On what charges?" he asked.

"Taking the cold, heartless bitch thing to a whole new level."

"Well, I'm not sure that's an arrest-able offense."

"How about the fact that she helped her son keep three children locked in a box for years?"

He nodded. "That'll do it."

Ubie took the woman to his SUV and put her in back so they could take her in for questioning.

"He's still in there," she said, scanning the burning house for any sign of her son as firefighters hustled to get it contained. We were too close to the bosque to let it get out of control.

I took a dark pleasure in telling her, "No, he's not. He's with his father now."

Her face morphed into one of shock and indignation.

She wanted to hit me with her broom again.

I wanted her to try.

But just to make sure all my t's were dotted and i's were crossed, I raised my hand and marked her soul. She was now destined to join her son the moment her soul left her body, and I felt the better for it.

Uncle Bob locked her in the backseat of his SUV and set a uniform to guard her, then went to help where he could. I could see exhaustion on every face there. The town was being torn apart, and now this. We were definitely not helping the situation.

Amber, Quentin, and I had set up camp on the steps of the Los Ranchos Village Hall as the emergency crews worked. Garrett and Reyes helped out where they could as well. Watching them was the most fun I'd had all day. And Belinda and Molly were sitting in the back of an ambulance as an EMT checked them over.

Thankfully, there wasn't much of a breeze, so the smoke was drifting up and away from the residential area. And away from my two camp mates. Cookie would kill me if I gave her daughter cancer from whatever was burning in that fire after bringing her back to life.

Kit walked into my line of sight. I watched as she searched the area, only stopping when she spotted me. She shook her head as she walked up. "Davidson, one of these days, you're going to have to tell me how you keep doing this shit."

"One of these days," I said, coughing into a blanket an EMT gave me, making it look good. "Can we get Belinda and Molly to Meiko? I think seeing them, hearing their voices, would help him."

"Or maybe you would?" she asked, suspicion narrowing her lids.

"Does it matter if it's them or me?"

"No. I suppose not."

I rode with Molly to the hospital and called Cook on the way, telling her everything that happened as succinctly and metaphorically as I could, since I had an emergency tech sitting right beside me. But I wanted to keep her in the loop. And to warn her we were all a bit smoke damaged, but no one had cancer that I could detect.

"Oh," she said, surprised. "Well, that's always good to hear."

"Right?"

"But honestly, hon, you can't leave the house without causing an international incident."

"This one was totally domestic. And it wasn't my fault."

"Mm-hm." She only sounded skeptical. I could tell she was happy we were all okay.

Molly had never been outside, and she'd never been away from her mother. The spaciousness of planet Earth and the absence of her mother was causing her blood pressure to rise, so I held her hand and we sang songs together.

When we got to the hospital, word had spread about who was coming in. There were already reporters at the entrance. Security had to push them back to get us inside, and they escorted us directly to Meiko's room.

Belinda's hand flew over her mouth when she saw her son. After thinking he'd died last week, she could hardly believe her eyes.

I looked down at him as he stood beside his mother, trying to get her attention.

"Mommy, I'm right here." He tugged on her shirt, and while to him it felt very real, Belinda didn't feel a thing.

I whispered to him, "I'm going to play with your toes."

He giggled and waited for me to chase him. Instead, I reached over and touched his big toe.

Belinda had draped herself over him, his body tiny in the huge hospital bed. Molly stood beside her mother, not sure what to do or who all these people were, when Meiko's lids slowly opened.

"Mommy?" he asked, confused and bewildered.

"Meiko!" She hugged him to her while the hospital staff tried to shoo her away to check his vitals.

It *was* a miracle, after all.

Still, Belinda's mind had been fractured after everything she'd been through. I needed to get them out of town and fast.

"Kit, I need them released. Now."

She started to argue but stopped herself and nodded instead. We'd both seen all the infected when we arrived. This family had been through enough.

I walked over to Belinda. "Sweetheart, can I talk to you?"

"Anything," she said, speaking to me at last.

"I know you were abducted and were kept locked in a room for ten years, but we're going to have to abduct you again."

She tilted her head to the side, confused.

"I don't know if you're aware of what has been happening."

"He told me a little bit. We weren't allowed to have a radio or TV."

No outside contact. He wanted them completely isolated. Completely at his mercy. Dependent upon him for everything.

"But he would tell me things. He said there was an epidemic."

"Yes, and you've been through enough. We have to get you to safety."

"But, wait, my mother. She needs to know."

"I have my assistant on it now. One of the guys from the scene, Garrett, is picking her up as we speak. They're going to meet us at our headquarters, and we'll fly you all to safety tonight."

"I don't know how to thank you."

"Look," Meiko said. "I can spell my name." He painstakingly fingerspelled his name, struggling with the *K* but pulling it off to nigh perfection.

He remembered.

"I want to do that," Molly said, fascinated.

"All I know in your name is *M* and *O*."

"Here." I held up my hand. Even though Quentin should have been teaching her—it was his language, after all—I said, "I'll show you."

By the time we got back to HQ, Belinda's mother, Geri, was there. They hugged for twenty minutes before Belinda introduced her mother to her children. A part of her was ashamed, as though she'd done something wrong, but her mother had no such qualms.

She couldn't have been happier, the gratitude shimmering in her eyes so genuine, it warmed even the darkest, coldest corners of my heart. I'd just committed murder. I had to have at least a few dark, cold corners.

"You guys were amazing," I said to Amber and Quentin later. "If not for the work you did, we might never have found Meiko's family."

They blushed and took turns socking each other in the arm.

"You'll be getting our bill," Quentin said.

"Oh, didn't you hear?" My expression filled with sympathy. "I lost all my money at the card table last night. Sorry."

"Fifty billion dollars?" Amber asked.

"Hey, either go big or go home. That's my motto. Also, I suck at gambling."

They laughed and went in search of the kids, wanting to get to know Meiko in the flesh and his sister, Molly.

I went in search of a sister myself. One Miss Gemma Vi Davidson. I found her in the kitchen, talking to Reyes as he cooked. In an apron. With utensils.

I lost myself in the spectacular image before me for a few moments when Gem asked me, "Did you need something, or are you just going to ogle your husband all evening?"

Reyes chuckled as he stir-fried something delectable. And hopefully edible. Soon.

"I like ogling. I'm good at it. I feel like we should stick with what we're good at."

Gemma deflated. "There goes my shot at the Olympics, then."

Who knew my sister had a sense of humor?

Cookie was helping Reyes. "Oh, I have some info on your serial killer."

"Another one?" Gem asked, taking her turn at ogling.

"No," I said, swiping a carrot. "Same one, but he's not a killer, serial or otherwise."

"It's on my desk." Cookie gaped at Reyes. "Seriously? That's your secret? Sriracha?"

He shook his head and held up a jar of red chili paste. "Better than sriracha."

"There's nothing better than sriracha."

He chuckled. "Okay." Holding up a spoon, he let her taste his master-piece, literally hand-feeding her. At least that was how it looked when Uncle Bob walked into the room.

She moaned and made little whimper noises. I felt like I were watching porn. Reyes would be so great in porn.

"Hey," I said, ready to let him know of his imminent career change when Gemma pointed out the fact that I had a smidgeon of drool on the corner of my mouth. I wiped it away, then gestured for her to follow me. Now was as good a time as any.

We went to her room and sat on her cot.

"This seems serious," she said.

"It is. It's just—" I paused, cleared my throat, and began again. "I'm sorry to have to tell you this, Gem. More than anything, I'm so sorry."

Gemma went completely still, her face the picture of anxiety.

"There's a reason you haven't heard from Wyatt."

One hand rose to touch her mouth, a nervous gesture. "Is he . . . ?"

"No. He'll be fine. He needs to recover, but he'll be okay."

Her boyfriend had been injured while trying to stop a crowd of looters, but I'd been assured he'd be fine.

I reached forward and took her hand. "Gemma, first I want you to know, there's a way I can see all your memories. Even the ones from that night that I'm afraid you're still repressing."

"What does this have to do with Wyatt?"

"Nothing and everything. We have to stop the Shade from expanding any more. It's growing bigger every day. Consuming more every day. And for a reason I cannot possibly fathom, I need to know exactly what happened the night Mom died."

"But I told you what I remember."

"I think there may be more."

She rose and walked to the window. "No. If there were more, I'd know."

"Gemma, you're a psychiatrist. You of all people know how the mind works. How it plays tricks on us. How it wants us to believe one thing when the exact opposite is true."

She shrugged and sat back down. "So, what, you're going to do the Vulcan mind meld?"

I laughed. "In a way. I just want you to know that I love you and that . . . that you can be with Mom and Dad. You can cross through me."

"Cross through you?"

My chin shook as grief took hold. "I'm sorry, Gem. The female client who attacked you? She was infected. She . . ." I choked on a sob, allowing the loss of my only sister, the emotion of that loss that I'd been holding on to tooth and splintered nail, to wash over me at last. "She killed you."

"What?" She stood and backed away from me in disbelief.

"Think about it."

"No. No, you're wrong." She shook her head and thought back.

"Carolyn came in and . . . and I fell. She pushed me, and I fell. That was it. I was knocked out."

Tears were running freely down my face, the pain I felt excruciating. "I'm sorry. She . . . you died of multiple stab wounds before she took her own life. It wasn't her fault. It was—"

I couldn't even finish the sentiment. The truth. It was my fault. I'd killed my own sister in a roundabout, totally fucked-up way.

Uncle Bob had been dealing with her death, the autopsy, the police reports, and the funeral arrangements, while Reyes and I tried to figure out how to close what we'd opened. How to finish what we'd started. And I felt no closer to a solution than I had two days ago.

I didn't understand what any of it meant. Even with Pandu's help and Garrett's translations, none of it made sense. The box, the gold flakes, the heart, my mother's death. Nothing connected. Nothing fit together. I liked puzzles as much as the next girl, but this was getting ridiculous.

"Yours?" she asked, her voice full of venom.

I dropped my gaze.

She bounced back and glared at me. "Damn right it is. I am *so* telling Mom." She stood up and started to walk through me.

"Wait." I held up both hands, but it was too late. She'd crossed, and a thousand images hit me at once. A million memories.

I fought to swim through them, to get to the one I needed. But before I got far, Gemma did something no other departed had ever done to me. I didn't know a departed *could* do it to me. She backed out. She put herself in reverse and came back out of my light.

"Gemma," I said, appalled. Not sure if she was allowed to do that.

"What the hell?" she asked, her voice shrill with anger.

"What?"

"I'm supposed to be a part of Beep's army?"

"Wait, you saw my memories?"

"Yes, and I will never be the same, thank you very much."

"Oh, my God, that's disturbing."

"You were going to send me to the other side."

"Do you think everyone sees my memories when they cross?"

"I'm supposed to be the healer."

I snapped out of it. "Gem, that was before we set loose a hostile dimension on this plane. We've changed history."

"Like hell you have." She crossed her arms. "I'm staying put."

"Gemma, I'm convinced that most if not all of Beep's army has already crossed. I think that when she needs them, when she needs you, she'll be able to summon you, just like I can."

"But—"

"Gem," I said gently, "go. Be with Mom and Dad . . . and Denise. And good luck with that." I snorted so loud I scared Artemis. She rose out of the floor, believing I'd summoned her, growling and barking. I rubbed her ears to calm her down, then put her back to bed. So to speak.

Gemma glared at me. "You're sure?"

"Yes. Sadly, I am."

"Fine. I'm still telling Mom." Then she marched through me. Again.

This go-around, I got a foothold on her memories. Focused on different aspects of her life. And gasped aloud.

"You kissed Freddie James?" I yelled into the celestial realm. "On the mouth? While I was seeing him?"

I could've sworn I heard a giggle all the way from the other side of eternity.

And then, when I least expected it, it was there.

The vending machine. The waiting room. Uncle Bob sleeping on an orange sofa.

That's when she heard it. Gemma woke up to a strange sound and looked over at Ubie. He hadn't roused, so she stood and walked out into the hall, her tiny footsteps barely audible against the cold tile.

Nurses were rushing into the delivery room, but that wasn't what caught her attention. It was the huge demon with shiny black scales and razor-sharp teeth as long as her arm that glued her to the spot. And it was fighting her mother.

It threw her against the wall, only she went through it. She disappeared for a split second before the demon wrapped its claws around her ankle and pulled her back into the hall. It slashed its claws and opened her up, light spilling out of her, draining her of her life force.

But she wasn't real. It was only her spirit. She couldn't die, right?

Our mother, in a desperate act, screamed a name. Gemma couldn't make it out, but a second later, an angel appeared, massive brown wings spread, the tips touching the walls on either side of him.

He was young, around twenty, strong with light brown hair and olive skin. He was magnificent. And also too late.

With one slash of his gigantic sword, the angel killed the demon. He plunged it into the demon's heart while Mom dragged herself to Gemma. Gemma stood petrified. Unable to comprehend what she was seeing.

Mom raised onto her knees and whispered into Gemma's ear as a blinding light spilled out of the delivery room and filled the air. My light. I could see it from Gemma's point of view. At one point in her life, Gem could see it.

The light hit our mother. She placed a hand on Gemma's cheek, then stood. Walked toward it. Crossed.

And there it was. My mother's death recorded through my four-year-old sister's eyes. I concentrated harder and remembered. I remembered what she told Gemma that day over twenty-eight years ago.

She bent closer to Gemma's ear, the reality of what she'd gone through agonizing. The truth of what was to come devastating. No mother wants to leave her children.

And the words she spoke were no more help than any of the other clues, but she'd said them, and she'd said them to me.

"Tell her," she said. "Tell your sister. The heart is both the strongest part of the body and the weakest. Always go for the heart." She leaned back and looked into Gemma's eyes. "Tell Charley, sweetheart. Keep it safe, and tell your sister when the time comes."

Then she was gone.

The angel, the one that was too late, walked to the delivery room and fell to his knees. He buried his face in his hands, then looked toward the heavens and spoke in a celestial language that Gemma didn't understand. But I did.

"Let me stay," he said, tears glistening on his face. "I have failed You. I have failed Your children." His voice cracked, and he had to take a minute to gather himself before continuing. He closed his eyes and whispered again, "Please, Father, let me stay."

An instant later, his wings burst into flames. He arched his back in agony as they were burned from his body. The fire billowed along the ceiling, and ashes fill the air around Gemma, floating like glowing embers on the wind.

When his wings were gone, he fell onto all fours, his shoulders heaving, his breathing labored. He struggled to his feet, falling twice before he managed it.

Then he walked toward her. Again he spoke in the language of the angels when he put a hand over her eyes and told her to sleep.

Gemma collapsed into his arms.

20

My therapist says I have a preoccupation with vengeance.
We'll see about that.
—T-SHIRT

I walked down to the kitchen, stunned. The last couple of days had been some of the strangest in a life that defined strange, but this? This was beyond comprehension.

I strode up to my uncle Bob, curled my right hand into a fist, and slammed it against his face.

"Charley!" Cookie ran up to us and checked her husband's eye. "What has gotten into you? Are you infected?"

But Uncle Bob just lowered his head, the game up.

"Robert?" she said, her tone wary.

I eyed him in disgust. "You're one of them?"

Reyes grabbed me around the waist and lifted me off the ground when I went back for more. Ubie wouldn't have fought back. His crestfallen expression told me that much.

"My mother knew," I said, my voice cracking. "When she was being attacked, she called out to you. She called your name." I spoke every word with a vehemence I didn't know I possessed. "Not my dad or her doctor or even God Himself. She called you."

Without looking at me, he nodded. "She had the sight. It's why she was chosen. She saw what I was years before you were even born. She confronted me. I had to tell her what was coming. Who was coming."

"And what, exactly, did you say? What, exactly, was your job?"

He lifted his chin. "I was sent to make sure you made it onto this plane. That was it. My one job. I was supposed to go back afterwards. Robert Davidson would have died in some tragic accident or just disappeared, never to be seen or heard from again."

"Then you succeeded," I said between sobs. "I'm here. I made it at my mother's expense. Why did you stay?"

"I let my guard down." His voice grew hoarse. "It should never have happened that way. Your mother was not supposed to die."

"You think?" I said, disgusted.

He pressed his lips together. "When she passed, I couldn't do it. I couldn't leave. I had to stay. I chose to. To watch over you."

Reyes's hold slackened. He seemed just as stunned as I was.

"How could we not have known?" I asked. "How did we not see it?"

"Once I lost my wings, I became just as human as anyone else on the street."

"All this time. You could have told me. You could have explained so much. I was so . . . so lost. So alone."

"Charley, you had to discover it all for yourself. In your own time. If I had interfered—"

"Bullshit," I said from between clenched teeth. "All these years, pretending not to know what I was. Pretending not to see the departed."

Amber and Quentin ran in. "What's going on?" Amber asked.

"Ask your dad," I said, before turning and heading upstairs.

I sat on the cot, still stunned. Reyes joined me.

A combination of fury and embarrassment rushed through me. I ignored both and focused on the matter at hand. "I don't know what to think. I can't figure out how to close the dimension. Even knowing what I know, how my mother died, hearing her message to me, I still don't understand what any of it has to do with the Shade."

"What was the message?"

"Okay, word for word: The heart is both the strongest part of the body and the weakest. Always go for the heart."

"The heart?" he asked. "What heart?"

"That's just it."

"Well, every living thing has a heart, a core of some kind, an energy source that keeps it alive. Maybe we have to find the Shade's?"

I twisted toward him. "Of course. We have to find its center, what makes it tick, and destroy that." I almost laughed. "We have a plan. Now we just have to figure out how to implement it."

"The heart would be where we opened it, don't you think?"

"I do think. It has to be in our apartment. We just have to get there."

"What do you mean?" Reyes asked.

"I mean, those Shade demons are hanging around for a reason. Maybe that's it. Maybe their job is to make sure we don't find the nerve center for their little city."

A knock sounded on our door. It was Cookie.

"What was that?" she asked, her eyes wet with emotion. "I've never seen you like that, hon."

"Didn't he tell you?"

"No. He won't talk to me. He stalked out and went to work."

"Figures."

"Charley, please."

"Gemma crossed through me."

"Oh, hon. I'm so sorry."

"When she did, I saw what happened when my mother died."

"Oh, my God, he killed her?"

"No, Cook. He was supposed to protect her."

"That much I did understand, and you're wrong. He was supposed to protect *you*. He succeeded."

"I guess. But he was one of them."

She closed her eyes and asked, "A demon?"

"No. Why would a demon be sent to protect me?"

She lifted a pretty brow. "Reyes Alexander Farrow."

"Not exactly a demon, but point taken."

"So, what was he? Go ahead, tell me. I can take it. Whatever it was, we can get past it. Wait, will he grow scales?"

"No. He was . . . he was an angel."

She crinkled her forehead and thought. Then she pursed her lips and thought some more. Then, for a long moment, she just stared off into space. "An angel."

"Yes."

"As in—"

"Yep. Heaven. Wings. Celestial powers out the ass. Not to mention the sword. Those guys love their swords."

"And he gave all that up to be with you? To protect you?"

"When you put it that way."

She put a hand on mine. "There's no other way to put it."

"Oh, but there is. Traitor. Liar. Thief."

"Thief?"

"He stole my candy hearts when I was a kid."

She nodded. "He does have quite the sweet tooth."

"When I think of all the times he pretended not to see the departed or not to know what I was."

"But is that what really matters?"

"Right now, at this moment in time, yes. Tomorrow, if we make it to tomorrow, maybe not. It's all still up in the air."

"Oh, my goodness."

"What?"

"I wonder if that's why he's so good at . . . you know."

"Cunnilingus?"

She nodded enthusiastically. "And I'm not talking okay-good. I'm talking Olympic marathon."

"Okay."

"The things he can do with his mouth."

"Cook! That's my uncle you're talking about."

She smiled, satisfaction shining through her pretty expression. "Exactly."

My jaw dropped open. Fortunately, I caught it before it hit the floor and put it back on its hinges. "That was low, Cook, even for you."

"Keep telling yourself that." She handed me a file folder. "I know you probably don't care right now, but . . ."

"Thaniel?" I asked. "Any juicy goodness I need to know about?"

"To tell you the truth, I'm not sure. I thought I'd let you look it over. And, just my two cents, he doesn't look like a serial killer."

"Ted Bundy."

"Right."

She left as I opened the file. I really wanted to solve this mystery before all hell broke loose. Literally.

"Thaniel Just. What are you all about?"

I hadn't been able to shake the feeling that I knew him. Maybe it was one of those past life things, but unless he was a god, too, probably not.

I studied his file, promising myself not to devote too much time to it. Cookie outdid herself. She had everything on him. Work history. Schools. Parents. Or at least his mom. His father was never in the picture, so there's no way of finding out who he was without hunting his mother down.

Cookie had even tracked down his grandparents. His grandmother had been adopted, but Cookie managed to get the court files on the adoption. They'd been opened years earlier by Thaniel's mother.

I totally needed to give her a raise. And I would if she hadn't won all my money the night before. Now all I could offer her was . . .

The records on the adoption caught my eye. His grandmother had been adopted from the New Mexico Mental Asylum. I bolted upright. The mother was listed as an Ilsa Blaine and the father as a Richard Lund. They'd both been patients there in . . . in the fifties.

I tore through the pages. Richard had a little sister named Bella Lund who died when she was five years old from dust pneumonia. Blue Bell. Rocket's sister? Were they talking about Rocket?

If so, that meant he had a kid and, generations later, that kid was carrying on in his grandfather's tradition. That explained all the cutting. He had to write the names down. If he were anything like Rocket and Blue at all, he had no choice. They called to him.

But Rocket? With a kid? Impossible. The very thought boggled to the extreme. He was a large child himself. Either way, the fact remained that for Rocket to beget a kid, he would have to have had sex. With a girl.

I needed to have a one on one with Rocket, but for now, I needed to see a man about a horse.

After seeing to the horse—a euphemism I never understood—I hurried downstairs and told the gang about Rocket. "Is that even possible?" I asked Garrett for no other reason than he was nearest to me.

"Why are you asking me?" His gaze bounced from person to person. "I've never been committed."

"I just can't believe it. He's so . . . so . . . well, he doesn't think like that."

"Does he have a penis?" Osh asked.

When I only frowned, Reyes finished the sentiment for him. "Then, yes, he thinks like that."

I didn't believe it. There had to be some other explanation. "I'm going to talk to Rocket. In the meantime, what about the box? Have you deciphered anything yet?"

Garrett tilted his head in a noncommittal gesture. "Yes and no."

"Okay, what do you have so far?"

He took out the box, placed it on the table, and slid it over to Reyes. "Open it."

Reyes took it, his lids narrowing.

I pointed. "You just push that corner there."

He pushed it, but the latching mechanism didn't click.

"Put some muscle behind it," I said, teasing him.

He tried again. Still nothing.

"Let me try."

Reyes passed the box to Osh. He pushed the corner to no avail.

"Ugh, here." I took it from Osh, pushed the corner, which again drew blood, and slid open the lid.

"I couldn't open it, either," Garrett said, taking it back and looking inside. "It has mystical properties."

"How is that possible?" I asked.

"It's your world, Charles. I only live in it. When you opened it for me before, I took pictures." He passed a series of images around. "I'm still working on the outside carvings, which are a combination of text and pictographs. But the interior has text as well, different from the exterior."

"I hadn't noticed before."

"It's faint."

"You translated?"

"I did, partially, and if I'm correct, it's the same word over and over in several different languages."

Reyes took the now-open box and examined the text inside. "It is the same word."

I looked inside as well. "What does it say?"

"Val-Eeth."

I started. "That's the celestial language from my home dimension."

"It's you," Garrett said. "The god eater."

In my early years, I'd apparently taken it upon myself to police the gods. I devoured the malevolent ones and left the benevolent ones alone, thus earning the nickname *god eater*.

"This box was left there for you."

I exchanged a furtive glance with Reyes. "That's what Pandu said, but it's been there since the first century BC."

Reyes shrugged. "And you've been a god since before the birth of the stars in this dimension."

Osh scratched his jaw in thought. "So, does that make you older than Rey'azikeen?" He nodded toward me approvingly. "Robbing the cradle."

Horrified, I shook my head. "No. It just makes me older than the stars in this dimension. So that means I'm your elder and you have to listen to what I say."

"I do that, anyway."

"True." He was a fantastic listener. "Okay, now that we've cleared that up, I'm going to talk to Rocket. See if he did the deed with anyone at the asylum. I mean, seriously. What if this guy really is Rocket's grandson?"

"What if he is?" Reyes asked.

"He could be of use to us. And, really, how does this stuff keep happening?"

Cookie chimed in then. "It's like I said before. You attract the supernatural and those who are sensitive to it. Most people might meet one person in their entire lives who are sensitive to the celestial realm. But you have an entire team of them."

"Maybe."

"Think about it. How did you first meet Reyes? Rocket? Pari? Me and thus Amber? Quentin? Osh? Nicolette? And now Thaniel? Hell, even your own uncle was a celestial being in another life."

I chafed at the reminder. He'd kept so much from me. And he could've told me about how my mother died sooner instead of letting us go on a wild-goose chase. Still, only Gemma had the message from my mother. He couldn't have known. No. I mentally balked. That didn't negate anything.

Ignoring the sting in my heart, I stood and smoothed my sweater. "I'm off to see a Rocket about a girl."

Then I hurried out before anyone decided to defend my uncle to me. I knew the score and, sadly, I didn't know if I'd ever get over it.

I found Rocket curled into a corner again. The girls, Blue, Strawberry, and Livia, were gone, off playing hopefully. But Strawberry had been right. Rocket wasn't comfortable here. He was disoriented. Confused. Unsettled.

"Rocket?" I sat next to him and put my hand on one of his. He'd had it wrapped around his head.

He lowered it and smiled at me. "Miss Charlotte, what are you doing here?"

"I came to see you. To ask you about . . ." How was I going to put this without causing him distress? I needed to be delicate. Understanding. Supportive. And I needed to do it in 1950s language. "I came to ask you about . . . about the cat you were keen on."

"Cat?"

Too much. "You know, your sweetheart?" When he still looked confused, I deadpanned him and said, "Your girlfriend."

He frowned in thought. "Ilsa?"

Holy cow. "Yes."

He sank further inside himself. "They took her away from me. We broke the rules. No breaking rules or they take you away and you never come back."

A lump formed in my throat. "You loved her."

He didn't answer.

"Rocket, I'm so sorry. Did you know she had a baby?"

He pulled his hand back. "They took her away. No breaking rules, Miss Charlotte. They'll take you away. They always take them away."

My chest cracked open and sorrow spilled out. No wonder he was always so adamant about the rules. They made him believe Ilsa's leaving was his fault because he broke their fucking rules.

When I scooted closer, he tightened the ball he'd formed with his limbs and whispered, "No breaking rules."

I left him there, a shell of the Rocket I'd known before. We might all die soon, but I was going to do this one thing for Rocket. And Thaniel.

I asked Reyes to help Garrett with the translations and set out to Thaniel's house. The sun hung low on the horizon, oranges and pinks and purples like streamers streaking across the sky.

When I got to Thaniel's house, his Raptor was loaded. He was heading out of town, probably a good idea. I knocked on the door and peeked inside. He walked out of a side room, a towel around his neck, his blond hair hanging in wet curls around his head.

He walked to open the door, towel drying the mass atop his head.

"Going somewhere?" I asked him.

Because he wore a short-sleeved shirt, I could see the names he'd carved on his body. Unlike his grandfather, he only carved the first names. Since he had a very limited amount of real estate, that was probably a good idea.

His gray eyes sparkled with genuine humor, but he averted his gaze quickly. My light did that. "You told me to get out of town."

I handed him a pair of shades I'd picked up at a convenience store when I stopped for gas and a mocha latte. Even the powdered mixes were heavenly when faced with an eternity without one. As I was for the second time in two weeks.

"Right." I stepped inside when he held open the door. "And you should, but I'd like to introduce you to someone first."

"I've actually filled my quota for new acquaintances for the year, but I can pencil you in for January."

Ignoring him, I plowed forward as I was wont to do. "I didn't realize it until I had my assistant do a background check on you, but I know your grandfather."

He'd been stuffing shirts into a duffel bag. He stopped but didn't turn around.

"Would you like to meet him?"

"My mother told me her biological father died."

"I wish I could've met her."

His expression turned dubious, but that was okay. He didn't know me.

"Where's the other guy?" he asked.

"Research. We're trying to figure out how to close the dimension."

"The one you opened."

"Yes. Thank you for reminding me. But before all this goes down, I thought you might like to meet your grandfather. He's very special to me."

"I used to care about shit like that. I got over it." He pulled off his shirt to change into a warmer one. The names that covered his torso weren't as visible as I thought they would be. They were paper-thin scars, hardly marring the hard surface of a very well-maintained body.

He pulled the shirt over his head, but I'd walked up behind him before he could pull it down over his torso. He paused, turning his head just enough to watch me from his periphery when I raised a hand and placed my fingertips on his back, tracing the lines of a dark, freshly touched-up tat.

"What is this?" I asked, my voice hoarse with emotion.

He took off the shirt again to let me see all of it.

"According to my mother, it's a message."

My breath hitched in my chest as I stared. "For who?"

"No idea. She just used to say it to me over and over. Had me memorize it when I was a kid, before she got sick."

"How did she die?" I was sure Cookie would have put his mother's cause of death in the file, but I'd been too focused on Rocket's revelation to get that far.

"Pneumonia."

Just like Rocket's sister, Blue.

I put a hand over my mouth and backed away.

He turned. "Is it for you? The message?"

I pressed my hand against my mouth harder to stop my chin from quivering.

In small script across his upper back were the words, *The heart is both the strongest part of the body and the weakest.* Then a larger font underneath read, *Always go for the heart.* Right in the middle of the second line was a black heart incorporated into the word *for* with blood dripping down the letters around it.

Emotion jolted through me like lightning, overwhelming me so quickly, it left me reeling. I stood in what should have been Thaniel's living room as a quake shook through to my core. Despite my best efforts, tears slid past my lashes and down my cheeks.

Thaniel slipped on the shirt and eased closer. "Mrs. Davidson?"

I looked around and knew what I had to do. But first, I had to convince Thaniel. "Why do you keep the names of those who've passed on your body?"

"How do you know they've passed?"

"Because you inherited it from your grandfather. Why do you keep the names?"

"They're, I don't know, important."

"Why?"

"I don't know."

I stepped closer. Put my hand on his scruffy cheek. "Why?"

"Because it's her army. The girl's. I can see it."

I let my lids drift shut.

"There's fire everywhere. So much fire. It'll consume the world if she doesn't do anything. If she doesn't stop it. That's when she calls them. Hundreds of thousands stand at her back. Ready to fight. Ready to kill. For her."

I bit down, the image causing heart palpitations. "Do you know who she is?"

He grinned. "Your daughter, I'm guessing. She has to stop it. She's the only one who can."

"I need you here for her."

He went back to packing his bag. "Yeah, I'm not really a trial-by-fire kind of guy."

"If I can stop this thing from happening, if I can stop the hell dimension from taking over the world, I need to know you'll be here for Beep."

He frowned. "You named your daughter *Beep*?"

"No. Well, yes, but that's not her real name. Cookie said that everyone who comes into my orbit is here for a reason, including you."

"Cookie? Did you name her, too?"

"That one's not on me."

He filled his lungs and leaned against a workbench. "What do I need to do?"

"Leave town."

"You just said—"

"But first . . ." I looked past him at his knife collection, then took out the powder from my jacket pocket. "First I need you to do something for me."

I tossed the zip-top bag onto the bench, found a piece of paper, and drew exactly what I needed.

I handed it to him. "I need this. Tonight."

He took the paper and studied it. Then he plucked the bag off the bench. "That's not a lot to work with."

"It'll be enough."

He shrugged. "It's not going to be pretty."

"I don't need pretty. I need effective."

21

You know that little thing inside your head
that keeps you from saying things you shouldn't?
Yeah, I don't have one of those.
—MEME

When I left Thaniel's house, the demon horde was watching. I started to think they were a lot smarter than Reyes and I were giving them credit for. Maybe they were trying to discover if we had a plan to rip their asses from this realm. Or maybe they were hoping I'd lead them to someone or something. I hoped I hadn't just done that.

I got back to HQ just in time for dinner. A house specialty. Pretty much anything Reyes cooked was a house specialty.

We sat down to eat, some at the table, some on the sofa. Belinda and her mother were getting to know each other all over again, but Geri had already fallen in love with her grandchildren. And how could she not?

Somehow Meiko remembered us from the deepest depths of his mind. He took an instant liking to Quentin and Amber and rarely left their sides. Zoe, Garrett's ex and Pari's current, had joined us for dinner as well. So that wasn't awkward.

Actually, it wasn't. Garrett was one of the most well-adjusted guys I knew. Not that I would tell him that.

Donovan and the boys were making bets on tomorrow's outcome.

I sat next to the ball and chain with Cookie on my other side and Uncle Bob, not that he was ever really my uncle, next to her. He kept quiet. I didn't encourage otherwise.

"When does the plane leave?" I asked Reyes.

Commercial flights had been interrupted, but private flights were still a go. We were flying the rest of the gang out that night, including Eric's *abuela*. Getting them all as far away from Albuquerque as we could until this was all over.

"Three hours." My tummy flip-flopped. It was all getting closer and closer.

"Any progress on the box?" I asked Garrett.

"Some, but I don't know what it means."

"Try me."

"From what we can tell, the outside says something about staying true to the heart repeated in several different languages."

I looked toward heaven and graced my mother with a knowing smile. One way or another, she was going to get that message to me.

"How about 'always go for the heart'?"

He pressed his mouth in thought. "The word *true* in a couple of the languages could be interpreted as *always*."

Reyes downed half of his water, then added, "And *stay* could mean *go for,* as in *stay the course*."

"I know what I have to do," I said to our group when everyone was seated.

Cookie seemed the most shocked, but she usually did.

"We have to find the life force, the heart, and weaken it so Reyes and I can collapse it."

"And where is this heart?" Garrett asked.

"It has to be where we opened the dimension: in our apartment."

"How are you planning on weakening it?" Cookie asked.

"I have a weapon on the way."

Reyes lifted a brow. "Is it a rocket launcher?"

I grinned. "Close."

Osh shifted in his chair. "It won't be easy. They'll be expecting something like this. They aren't just going to open the doors and let us in."

"I know. They've been following Reyes and me. I think they're trying to figure out our next move."

"Unless they already have," Reyes said.

"Unless they already have."

He scrubbed his fingers over his face. "I suppose you have a plan."

"Don't I always?"

Cookie groaned. "No. Your plans—"

"—never work," I said, finishing for her. "I know, but this one is really good."

"They're all good!" she shrieked before draping her body across the table in typical drama-Cookie style.

She did have a point. I did have some killer plans. They rarely worked, but was that the most important takeaway?

"Okay, enough shoptalk." I raised my mocha latte. Everyone followed suit. "To victory."

"To victory," they said in unison, only Amber had signed victory wrong and a confused Quentin toasted to being single, but that was okay, too.

We didn't talk about the hell dimension—or any other dimension, for that matter—any longer that night. Instead, we reminisced about all that we had been through. Donovan and the boys told stories about being in a motorcycle club that I probably didn't need to hear, especially since they were destined to guard my daughter. Amber and Quentin talked about how their business venture, Q&A Investigations, was going. Pari told stories of clients who'd fainted on her in the middle of getting inked. And so on and so on.

It was around that time that I broke the news to Cookie.

"You're going," I said to her in the middle of a rip-roaring tale outlining the dangers of using a hot waxing kit.

The van had already made one trip to the airport, taking Meiko and his family to the private jet Reyes had arranged.

It was back, waiting to take the last passengers to the plane. Those included Amber and Quentin as well as Donovan, Michael, Eric the Prince and his *abuela*. Now I had to convince the other passengers we'd secretly scheduled that they needed to be on that last flight as well. It wouldn't be easy.

Cookie blinked at me. "I beg your pardon."

"You're going," I said even softer than before. I knew how she'd take this. After everything we'd been through, for me to force her to leave me in our darkest hour was, well, not very BFF of me.

"I most certainly am not."

"Cook, I love you so much, but I can't be worried about you and fight a demon army to get to the core of a hell dimension to try to weaken it so we can somehow miraculously collapse it and save the world."

"No," she said, in pure obstinate mode. "Absolutely not."

"Yes," Uncle Bob said, his voice soft but firm, "you are."

She gaped at him. "And what about you?"

"I'm staying."

Cookie and I had the same thought as we said simultaneously, "Oh, hell no."

She set her jaw and turned a glower on her husband. "I am not about to leave you here to be beaten to death by my best friend."

"You don't hear that every day," someone from the cheap seats said. I was pretty sure it was Eric.

"You're human now. What can you possibly do to help?"

Pain ripped through my chest, as he said sheepishly, "I can see them. And I don't have a mental illness that I know of, unless a disturbing fascination with Wonder Woman counts."

"So, what then?" Cookie asked, growing defensive. "Because you can see them, you have to risk your life?"

"Sweetheart, it's not like that."

"Then what is it like?" She tried to stand. To run.

He stopped her with a hand on her shoulder. "I have . . . experience with this sort of thing."

"You *had* experience. In another life."

"She's right, Uncle Bob." It would be suicide. We all knew it. "You know she's right. You'll just be—"

"In the way?" When I didn't answer, he prodded. "Am I so useless?"

I dropped my gaze.

He wasn't about to let me off that easily. "Charley, if I can do something and I don't and the hell dimension wins, what does that make me?"

"Mine," Cookie said, her voice cracking. She caressed his face with a quivering hand. "For a little while longer."

"Besides," Amber said, kneeling next to him, her voice shaky at best, "I just got you. I've never had a real dad and then you came along and made me believe I was worthy of one."

If the stunned expression on Uncle Bob's face was any indication, she struck a chord deep inside him. Several, in fact.

"Smidgeon, how could you ever believe yourself unworthy of love?"

Her lower lip trembled and my heart cracked when he pulled her into a fierce hug, drawing Cookie and Quentin into it as well.

"Your name is already on the manifest," I said before he could argue any further. "You're going."

I turned my attention to Garrett. "You're going, too."

"What?"

I'd offended his delicate sense of masculinity.

"Fuck that."

"Can you see into the supernatural realm?" Garrett could be as stubborn as Cookie and Uncle Bob combined. "Did you suddenly develop a way to fight demons that I don't know about?"

"Charles, this is my family now. I'm not leaving you to fight for them alone."

"Oh, trust me, hon, we won't be alone. But if something happens, I need you here for Beep."

His hand curled into fists. "You're pulling the Beep card?"

"I'm pulling it hard. As well as the Zaire card. You have a son, Garrett."

"You're the worst friend ever."

Relief washed over me. "I'm getting that impression."

We got everyone aboard the love train. Or the shuttle bus. Either way. The warehouse seemed so empty-without them, especially since I now had only Reyes and Osh to keep me company.

Reyes and I stood at the huge plate glass windows that constituted one wall of our bedroom. The view was extraordinary. The city lights sparkled beneath us.

"I think I have empty-nest syndrome."

He laughed softly.

"Speaking of which, how did you score a warehouse on such short notice?"

"I didn't. I bought it over a week ago for Rocket, but I don't think he's happy here."

The fact that my husband would spend God knows how much on a warehouse for a departed friend spoke volumes. Of course, it also spoke volumes that he was the one who'd demolished Rocket's former residence, but that was a darker time. Like, two weeks ago.

Still, for me, a century had passed.

My phone beeped. I dug it out of my pocket and my heart skip-roped with joy. Metaphorically. "The weapon's here."

I took Reyes's hand and led him downstairs.

"Is it a pipe bomb?"

"No."

"A tank?"

I giggled. "No."

"The nuclear launch codes?"

That time I snorted. "Nope."

I opened the door. Thaniel stood on the other side, holding a leather sheath. I beamed at him. "That was faster than I thought humanly possible."

"My last girlfriend said the same thing. Nice place."

"Thanks. It's home."

After showing him in, I took the knife from him.

He offered Reyes a nod hello. "Like I said, there wasn't much. I had to improvise."

I pulled it from the leather case. It was beautiful. "Improvise how?"

"I mixed the shavings with real gold."

He'd taken a blade he'd made earlier, one with ornate carvings in the metal, and filled the carvings in with the melted shavings and gold. He'd also dipped the tip in the gold for what would hopefully lessen any resistance we might have.

"It didn't dilute the strength." It hummed in my fingers, its power penetrating my skin and pulsing through me.

"I didn't figure it would."

Reyes studied it, but a part of him was demon. He couldn't hold it. He couldn't even touch it. "Is that what I think it is?"

"Yes. I found powder in the box with gold flakes, but I'm not sure where it came from."

"When you grind a blade on a whetstone," Thaniel explained, "some of the metal flakes off. The powder was from the grindstone, the flakes from whatever it sharpened."

I tore my gaze off the knife and looked up at my husband. "Zeus."

His expression was both wary and full of awe.

Zeus was a dagger capable of killing any supernatural being. We had no idea who made it, but it'd saved my life once before when I used it on myself and drained it of its power.

Now, however, with the shavings from the original knife, we had a new weapon, its power restored.

"What do you think? Will it work?" Before he could answer, I said, "Oh, I almost forgot." I cleared my throat. "Reyes, I'd like to formerly introduce you to Thaniel Just, Rocket's grandson."

Reyes tipped his head in greeting, still fascinated with the blade.

"So?" I asked, nudging just a little. "It can kill any supernatural being. What about a hell dimension?"

"It could work. If we can make it past the hordes of demons, get into the apartment, and find the heart, it could work."

"You're not really bursting my bubble of hope, but you are letting a little of the air out."

He lifted a shoulder. "We've worked with less."

"True. So," I said, turning to Thaniel, "would you like to meet your grandfather?"

Thaniel straightened his shoulders and nodded. "Sure."

"I'm going to take a shower," Reyes said.

"Okay. Don't do anything I wouldn't do."

"Don't worry, that's been my motto for years now. What's kept me alive for so long."

I gasped, pretending to be offended. He pulled me into his arms and dipped his head until our mouths almost touched. After pausing to regard me, his dark eyes glistening as though trying to read my mind, he kissed me quickly, lifted a hand to Thaniel, and headed off.

We took the stairs down to the basement.

"I have to warn you, he was traumatized recently."

"By whom?"

"That's a long story." I didn't want to give him a bad impression of Reyes when they'd only just met.

"So, your husband."

What the fuck? "No," I said, lying through my pearly whites.

"Mm-hm," he said, dubious.

"Well, yes, but Reyes really is a good guy."

"You are aware he's a demon."

"Only a little."

Thaniel stopped on the bottom rung and gave me a once-over.

"Are you okay?"

"It's just, that was an educated guess. I've never met an actual demon."

"Well, the full-blooded ones are a lot meaner. Except for Osh. But he was a slave demon. A Daeva. Maybe that makes him different."

"And what are you?"

"I'm a whole slew of awesome that you're going to get to know much better if I have any say in the matter. And if I don't die tomorrow. Mostly if I don't die tomorrow, but first . . ."

We found Rocket curled in the same corner I'd left him earlier. The vision of him broke my heart. "Rocket?"

He didn't look up.

We eased closer. "Rocket, someone's here to meet you."

After a moment, he barely lifted his head and looked out from underneath an arm.

I wasn't sure how much Thaniel could see, but every ounce of his attention was focused on Rocket. He must have been able to see him, not just a hazy outline of him, like Pari.

"This is Thaniel. Your grandson."

He dropped his arms and straightened.

"His mother was your daughter. You and Ilsa had a baby."

"Ilsa. Jill the Giant said we got married, but Nurse Hobbs said we didn't."

"Well, Nurse Hobbs was wrong. You and Ilsa were married, and you had a baby girl."

"And she was smart like you?"

I shook my head. "Smarter."

He beamed at me. "And then she got married and had him?"

"She did. She was very proud of him. She passed down your gifts."

As we stood talking, I saw Blue Bell emerge out of the corner of my eye, curious.

I motioned her over. She took another wary step closer.

"Blue, this is your great-nephew, Thaniel."

Thaniel's emotions spoke volumes. Despite what he'd said earlier, he'd wanted to know about his family for a long time.

He knelt down to Blue's level. She kept her distance at first, then something caught her eye. Recognition flashed across her face, just like it had when I'd first met Thaniel.

She dared another step, and then another, until she was right in front of him. She put a hand on his cheek and stared.

It was the eyes. Something about the shape. The gray. The expressive warmth.

She smiled.

"He has your gift," I told her, kneeling, too. "He sees the names and records them." I wasn't about to tell her how.

Blue took Rocket's hands and drew him closer as I stepped away to give them some privacy. I went upstairs, grabbed a coffee, and then headed back down, but I stayed in a corner, giving them plenty of space.

About twenty minutes later, Thaniel walked over to me.

"That was . . ."

"Amazing?"

He turned back to his family. "Humbling."

Damn it. I fell in love. I did that so often. "You need to leave town."

"I've been trying to all day," he said, teasing. "Are you going to tell me what you are?"

"How about I show you?"

His lids narrowed.

"Hold my latte." I handed him my coffee and walked over to Rocket and Blue, but I turned back. "Don't drink any."

"Like I want your cooties."

Oh, yeah. In love. Any time a grown man with muscles the size of his used the word *cooties,* my heart turned to melted chocolate.

"Rocket, Blue, if you'd like to cross, it's okay. You could be with Ilsa and your daughter," I told Rocket. "And you could be with your parents," I told Blue. They were still undecided, so I added, "Thaniel can take over now, so you can move on."

Blue took Rocket's hand.

His gray eyes sparkled with excitement at the prospect of the coming adventure.

As he stepped closer, he said in a soft voice, "Miss Charlotte." It was the last thing he said before he and Blue crossed.

Images rushed past me. Of his life on the farm. Of being bullied as a child. Of his sister always being there for him despite the fact that she died at the age of five. She never left him. And of Ilsa. He'd loved her from the moment he saw her. And if the expression on her face were any indication, she'd felt the same.

And then he was gone. I'd known him for years. He'd helped me through so many situations. Been there through so many low points in my life. I could always count on him for a hug. His hugs were dangerous and often caused internal damage, but they were better than chocolate-covered coffee beans.

With my heart ever-so-slightly shattered, I turned back to Thaniel, but Strawberry rushed up to me before I could say anything, her new friend Livia on her heels. She looked inside and laughed. "There he is. I told you I couldn't find him, and he's been there the whole time."

Alarm shot through me. "Who, honey?"

She waved. "David. Duh."

David? David her brother? He died? I'd seen him a couple of weeks ago.

Before I could ask anything else, she ran through me, stealing my breath and watering my eyes. I saw her playing with her dolls. Arguing with her brother. Stealing cookies off the counter. She was little hellion even before she died. Who knew?

And that left Livia. She stood gazing into my light, her dark eyes full of interest and awe.

"Would you like to cross?" I asked her, again using ancient Greek and hoping for the best.

She didn't answer.

"You're not really much of a talker, are you?"

The smile she handed me bordered on impish. "My father said that to learn a person's true nature, be quiet."

I laughed softly. "At least I got the language right."

I had so many questions for her, but she stepped forward and crossed before I got the chance to ask. And I was gifted with another life to live, this one in ancient Rome.

The images, the sights and sounds and smells, were all foreign to me. Exotic and rudimentary, but cleaner than I'd expected.

She'd gotten sick. Livia. Her days were filled with sunshine, good food, and family. She remembered her mother once commenting that her beautiful daughter had been promised to a prince who was seven years older than she was. She saw a drawing of him once and, even at five, she approved wholeheartedly.

She'd been playing with her cousins when she began to feel bad. Her family was well off, but the illness hit so hard and so fast, she was gone by sunset that day. The physicians could do nothing to save her.

She'd stayed for her mother. She was devastated, and Livia wanted her to know she was okay, but she had no way of telling her.

After they'd laid her to rest in the tomb, a man came to see her. A priest. He put a box in one of the pillars and summoned a beast to watch over it. A lion. Then he left, and Livia waited for centuries to be found.

Just as Livia was reunited with her mother, I drifted back to the present. Whoever put the box in the tomb wanted me to find it. And yet someone else out there didn't.

I'd almost forgotten about my guest.

"You're her," he said, astonished. "My mother used to talk about you."

"Really?" I asked, a little appalled. "So, like, what'd she say?"

A grin of epic mischief spread across his face. "I'll see you the day after tomorrow."

"You have a lot of faith there'll actually be a day after tomorrow."

"I have faith in you. Thanks to my mother."

He turned and ascended the stairs, leaving me alone in the massive room with my emotions. They bounced off the walls and boomeranged back to me, knocking my breath away. Shaking my core.

Rocket was gone.

I buried my face in my hands and let sorrow take its course.

22

Coffee makes everything okayer.
—MEME

The last two days had taken their toll, but to lose Rocket and Blue and Strawberry on top of Gemma and, hell, even David Taft. I'd just gotten them back after more than a hundred years. It was a lot to put on a girl. Perhaps I'd join them sooner than planned.

Either way, I'd lived a surreal life. Who was I to complain about the prospect of death? Most people would never experience the loves I'd seen. The heartbreak. The overwhelming joy.

No. If I were to die tomorrow, I'd die knowing my daughter was in the best hands possible. I'd lived the most joyous moments of thousands of lives. And I'd loved a god.

"This is a great room," Reyes said as he descended the stairs. "I'm not sure I want to stand in it for hours on end, but to each her own."

When he reached me, I commanded him to turn around, making a circle with my index finger. Despite his wary expression, he did as ordered. I put my hands on his shoulders and jumped on his back.

He sank beneath my weight, pretended to falter, then wobbled back onto his feet.

"I need help upstairs," I said, laughing out loud when we fell against a wall.

His long arms hooked around my legs, and he straightened with ease. "I think I pulled my groin."

"You'd better not have. You're going to need all the groin you can get later."

"Yeah?"

"Yeah. I was thinking we could go salsa dancing. It requires a lot of hip action."

"Tease."

When we reached the top of the stairs, I tightened my hold and said into his ear, "I want to see Beep."

"You couldn't have told me that two flights ago?"

I studied the perfection of his profile. The length of his lashes. The definition of his nose. The fullness of his mouth. He glanced back at me just as his molecules began to separate. And he smiled.

We materialized in a small château surrounded by snow-covered trees. A fire crackled from an open hearth with a fur rug in front of it. And on the rug lay a cherub about four months old. She kicked her legs, trying her darnedest to roll over and get to the paw of one of the three hellhounds guarding her.

It bent its head and nudged her back to the center of the rug. She giggled, enjoying the game of Test the Hellhound.

The other hellhounds were outside patrolling. Ever present. Ever watchful.

When we materialized, the three surrounding our daughter stood and emitted a low growl. They lowered their heads and studied us.

I hopped off Reyes's back and stepped closer. Their growls grew louder, forcing the hair on the back of my neck to stand.

I knelt. "You guys are the best watchdogs ever," I said as the one closest to me whimpered in excitement and threw a paw on my head. "Yes, you are." He buried his face against my neck and pushed, almost knocking me over as I hugged him to me.

The other two wagged their tails and licked their chops, excited to see us but refusing to leave their posts. I made the rounds, lavishing attention on the same hounds we once thought were sent to kill Beep. Unbeknownst to us, they'd been summoned to protect her with their lives.

And we couldn't have asked for a better sentry. Twelve of the deadliest beings ever created kept a constant vigil on the most precious thing in my life.

I lay down beside her, realizing then that the Loehrs had come into the room. Mr. Loehr carried a bottle for the little minx before me and Mrs. Loehr a diaper and wipes.

"I let them warm in front of the fire," she said, referring to the wipes. "How are you?"

"Never better." Her gaze strayed to Reyes. Her son. The one who'd been taken from her. The one she'd been denied the honor of raising.

I often wondered what he would've become had he been raised by these wonderful people. They were the perfect choice for our daughter.

Reyes had to feel the pull of Mrs. Loehr's adoration. Every time she looked at him, she basked in the man he'd become. Mr. Loehr as well. The pride he felt for his son, the unconditional love, made my chest swell.

Reyes walked over and wrapped them both in his embrace, as I turned back to the wiggle worm in front of me. Her bright copper eyes, a strange combination of Reyes's and mine, holding steady on my face. She reached for my hair, twisted her fingers into a lock, and pulled, shoving it straight into her mouth.

I disentangled my hair and pushed it behind me. "You do not need to eat my hair. There's no telling where it's been."

She squeaked in delight and tried to roll closer, putting all of her fifteen pounds into it. She made it as far as her side before giving up and rocking back in place.

I'd seen this, of course. The love a mother had for her child. I'd seen it over and over in those who crossed through me. But I'd never really understood it until I had my own spider monkey.

I ran my fingertips over her face. She grabbed them instantly and went for the mouth again. I let her this time. It gave me the perfect opportunity to attack her more vulnerable areas like her neck and her toes. I kissed every exposed inch of her. Marveled at her long fingers and chubby ankles. Laughed when she put her hands on my cheeks and tried to gnaw off my face with a piranha-like ferocity.

Reyes sat on the floor next to us. The hellhound closest nudged him, and he offered him a quick nuzzle before turning back to Beep. As tightly wound as his emotions were, as hard to read as they tended to be, there was nothing difficult in detecting the enchantment he felt every time he looked at her.

The Loehrs took the chairs beside us, more than willing to share their granddaughter.

Mr. Loehr's brows slid together. "How's the situation in Albuquerque?"

Reyes didn't say anything at first, then he answered as honestly as he could. "We'll know more tomorrow."

"What's tomorrow?" Mrs. Loehr asked.

I glanced up at her and said honestly, "The battle."

The Loehrs had gone for decades not knowing what happened to their son. I was not going to keep them in the dark about anything concerning Beep.

I picked Beep up and handed her to Reyes. He raised her high. She giggled with excitement, then did the piranha thing with him, too, trying with all her might to devour his face. And what a face it was.

Sitting up, I looked over at Mr. Wong. He stood in a corner, a place he clearly liked to be if his three-year stint in my apartment was any indication. He bowed his head in greeting.

He'd been the one to summon the hellhounds, to beckon them to our side. They obeyed his every command, but they'd been marked with

Beep's blood. They would never allow anything to happen to her, even if Mr. Wong ordered them to. They were truly the perfect guardians.

"If this thing goes south," I said to him, "you know what to do."

He bowed his head again as Mrs. Loehr covered her mouth with a hand. Her anxiety quaked inside my body, splintering my cells.

"And just what is that?" Osh asked.

I started and looked over at him. He sat on a window seat, an arm braced on one knee as the other leg dangled over the side.

"If we don't succeed, if the Shade continues to expand, Mr. Wong is to take her to our home dimension."

Having not been told that part of the plan, Osh stiffened. But he could hardly argue. If the Shade won, Earth wouldn't be safe.

He cast an irate glare at Reyes. I could still feel a part of him that fumed, his animosity directed solely at my husband no matter how hard I tried to tell him the whole thing was my fault.

"Of course," he said to me, acquiescing. "She's all that matters."

The more I saw how Osh felt about Beep, the more I thought about the prophecy about the warrior, the one who might or might not be standing by her side during the battle with Satan. His fierce need to protect her gave me a modicum of peace when contemplating all the ways this could go terribly, terribly wrong. I couldn't help but believe that, short of death, anything would keep him from her side.

Then again, a lot could happen between now and then.

We said our good-byes, drinking in our daughter's image until we'd memorized every aspect of her being, then slowly, oh so slowly, we dematerialized out of our daughter's life.

Unable to sleep, I went downstairs to make a pot of coffee. The caffeine would help me chase down a few z's. Those suckers were slippery. I'd need all the energy I could get. My stomach housed butterflies the size of Los Angeles. Only these had claws. And pincers with a stinging bite.

Still, the smell of coffee did help.

I turned on the news for the latest. Dozens more admitted. The National Guard patrolled the streets. And two more deaths.

I took my coffee to the roof of the warehouse. The cool breeze helped soothe my nerves. Walking to the edge, I held out my hand and ran it over the surface of the Shade. It rippled like water, the darkness blurring for a moment before settling.

Its radius was barely two miles when I'd arrived. Now, it was closer to twenty and growing with every second that passed.

With one thought, I summoned Osh. He appeared beside me.

"Have you been able to dematerialize the whole time you've been on Earth?"

"You haven't?" he asked, an impish sparkle in his eyes.

"I need you to sit this one out."

"I hope you're joking."

"Not even a little, but I do have some jokes if you'd like to hear a few. I have this one about a black lion that chases a girl through a series of burial chambers and ends up mauling her nigh to death. Oh, wait, that wasn't a joke."

"I'm fighting," he said, his voice so soft I barely heard it.

"Osh, I need you to watch over Beep. If something should happen to us, you're the only one who can . . . who can do what's necessary to protect her."

I didn't want to tell him that part of my decision was based on my one and only vision into the future. Of him being the warrior during the battle with Satan. Of the fact that the outcome of said battle could hinge on his participation or lack thereof.

"So, I'm your backup plan."

"Yes."

"I thought Mr. Wong was your backup plan."

"He's my backup plan if we fail to collapse the Shade."

"And I'm your backup plan if . . . ?"

"If we succeed but don't make it out before it collapses in on itself."

He put his hands in his pockets and scanned the landscape. "You have a lot of backup plans."

"I'm big on planning. My plans almost never fail completely."

He looked into the Shade, mere inches away from us now. "I'd really like to be there."

I decided to hit him with part two of backup plan B. "And I'd really like to make out with you right now."

He didn't flinch. Didn't gasp. Didn't run away in horror. He simply asked, "And why's that?"

"I told you. You're my backup plan. I need you tip-top."

He stepped behind me and grabbed the rail, bracing a hand on either side of me. "You realize even a small dose of you would last me millennia."

"Yes."

He lowered his head until his mouth was at my ear. "Turn around."

I wondered if it was bad that I was about to make out with my daughter's future main squeeze. If it made me a bad mother. It was most likely frowned upon in most circles.

I turned in his arms and put my hand on his jaw.

He watched me through hooded lids, the incredible bronze of his irises shimmering in the low light. A microsecond before he pressed his mouth to mine, he said, "Don't kill me."

"No promises."

His mouth covered mine as he closed the distance between us and siphoned out a small sliver of my soul. A cupful of my energy. His muscles stiffened, and he entered the equivalent of a feeding frenzy. He was unable to stop, my life force like a drug and he the addict.

He grabbed my throat and tilted his head to deepen the kiss, swallowing me in huge, erotic gulps. He was strong. A Daeva. A demon. But even he could only take so much before it killed him. We'd been here before, and I did not want a repeat of that night. We'd almost lost him.

I pushed gently to dislodge him, but he fought me. Twisted his fingers into my hair. Pressed harder. Drank deeper. It tugged at my very core, the exquisite sensation curling and writhing, wanting to be set free.

With a strength born of desperation, I shoved as hard as I could, dislodging him and pushing him off me. My knees gave and I sank to the floor, gasping for air.

He did the same. He fell to his knees and doubled over, his muscles straining to harness the power they'd consumed. To tame it. To control it. After struggling a solid ten minutes, doing his best to conquer the beast inside him, a calmness settled over him. He sat back on his heels, his chest rising and falling as he drew in deep rations of air.

I crawled to him. Put a hand on his shoulder. Coaxed his attention my way. "Now, you're ready to take this on."

When he looked at me, his face shimmering with sweat, he let loose a charming, confident grin. "Sugar, I'm ready to take on the world."

Despite the fact that he wasn't wearing his signature top hat, he tipped his head, then vanished, leaving me alone with my thoughts once again. It was a dangerous place for me to be.

I drew in another deep breath of air and summoned backup plan number three.

As color splashed across the horizon, I lay curled against my husband. He pretended to be sleeping, but I doubted, like me, he caught even a single one of the elusive creatures called Z.

I let my lids drift shut and shifted onto the celestial plane. Once there, I reached out until I could feel all of them, all of Beep's army, some in standby, others ready for a fight. I could feel Beep sleeping and the Loehrs watching over her. I could feel Cookie wringing her hands, metaphorically because, as always, she had a coffee cup in one of them, and Amber and Quentin praying. I could feel Donovan and Michael and Eric and Pari toasting the good times they'd had. Their families and their friends.

I could feel Osh pacing, the energy I'd injected into him pumping adrenaline into him by the bucketsful. If he survived it, he'd be even more powerful than before. If he didn't, I could add his death to the long list of my perpetual fuckups.

And I could feel Angel, my darling Angel, waiting in the wings. Waiting to be summoned. He'd be waiting a long time. This was not his fight.

Artemis jumped on the bed and struggled to get in between Reyes and me. She liked to be the middle spoon. I turned over, and Reyes let her in. We rubbed her ears and her neck and her belly. She rolled over to give us more access. She was super accommodating that way.

"We need curtains," I said, the sun slipping into the room at an astronomical rate. "Or a nice set of plantation blinds."

"Once we're in there," Reyes started, but I held up a hand.

"Not yet. I just want to pretend this isn't happening for a few minutes more."

He reached over and lifted my chin. There was no hiding the wetness in my eyes now. My only consolation was that his were just as wet. "Once we're in there, I'll keep them off you."

"Reyes," I said, choking on a sob.

"You just get to the center. Find the heart."

I nodded and fought the quivering of my chin. We both knew what was at stake. Even if we managed to weaken the dimension and cause its collapse, we could very well be trapped inside. Then again, at least we'd be together.

Reyes and I prepared for the coming battle with huevos rancheros and coffee. Lots of coffee. I sat at the table while Reyes made me a plate.

While waiting, I pulled out my phone and called Uncle Bob, hoping I'd caught him before the plane took off.

"Is everything okay?" he asked in lieu of a greeting.

"Did David Taft die?" I asked, following suit. He didn't say anything, so I prodded with an, "Uncle Bob?"

"Yes," he said at last.

Every muscle in my body weakened, and I dropped my head into my hand. "What happened?"

"He was gunned down in a parking lot in Cruces."

I could hear the engines on the plane rev, so I spoke louder. "He'd been working undercover. Did they find out?"

"We don't think so. We think he was just at the wrong place at the wrong time. He tried to stop a bar fight."

"Of course he did." My free hand curled into a fist. "You knew we were friends. You didn't think to tell me?"

"You've had a lot on your mind, pumpkin."

"Like your sudden yet inevitable betrayal?"

He didn't answer for a long moment, then said, "Among other things. Charley, let me come back. Let me help you with this."

"No."

"After everything we've been through."

"You could be killed. I can't do that to Cookie and Amber."

"You could be killed, too. I'll have your back. I've always had your back."

A pang of regret washed over me. I ignored it. "And what are you going to do? How are you going to fight them? Trust me when I say your six-shooter isn't going to do you much good."

Another moment of silence dragged between us. "Good luck to you, then," he said at last before hanging up.

23

So, when is "old enough to know better" supposed to kick in?
—MEME

"I'm pretty sure they know what we're doing," I said to Reyes a little while later.

We sat in Misery, the Jeep, not the emotion, and studied the Shade, which had invaded our humble HQ right in the middle of breakfast.

Reyes sported classic black apparel, making all the other gods jealous. He wore a black tee, black jeans, and black work boots. I, on the other hand, went for more of a dark charcoal gray.

Okay, I was wearing black, too. It just seemed appropriate.

I'd pulled back my hair and braided it to keep it out of my face. I'd considered braiding Reyes's.

"How far do you think we'll get in Misery?"

"I don't know. They're expecting us, so . . ."

"So, let's not keep them waiting."

The clawed butterflies attacked again as Reyes pulled forward. Once inside the Shade, we'd have no way to dematerialize, no way to escape, but I didn't know if we'd have access to any of our other abilities. Like spiffy comebacks or walking and chewing gum at the same time.

I took Reyes's hand, lowered my head, and summoned Beep's army. They rose before us. An assemblage of departed as far as the eye could see.

As we drove forward, the border between the two worlds crossing through us, I had only one regret: I wished I'd hugged Uncle Bob.

We got about three miles in before they came after us. One tried to rip me out of Misery, which hurt in the corporeal state. Artemis attacked at once, diving through the door and tackling the demon to the ground. They landed hard and rolled into the dirt before I lost sight of them.

The trick, we soon learned, was to pay attention to oncoming traffic while watching out for demons. Traversing two dimensions at once was not as effortless as one might think.

The demons, not anchored to the earthly plane, could take us out if we struck one, gliding through Misery and slamming into one, or both, of us. We had to keep a constant vigil, but we were getting closer.

At one point, an asshat in a Bentley cut us off.

I yelled to him. "Are you crazy? Do you know what that car cost?"

Reyes had to swerve to avoid it and instead sped through a demon. It hit him on the left shoulder, causing him to veer into oncoming traffic. I grabbed the wheel as he fought it. But a female sentry latched on to it, wrapped an arm around its neck, and wrenched it free.

We made it to within two blocks of the apartment building, at which point we had to go on foot. We scrambled out of Misery and ran for it. The sentry cleared the way, fighting the demons.

I didn't know if a Shade demon could hurt a sentry. Or worse, kill one. I quickly found out. Their claws slashed through the sentries one by one. Their teeth tearing into them, ripping them apart until all that was left were tattered pieces that disintegrated and sank into the earth.

I screeched to a halt and looked on as our army—no, Beep's army—was being killed by the dozens.

Reyes grabbed my arm and pulled me behind him. I regained my footing and followed him, my heart breaking.

As we got closer to the apartment building, they attacked in hordes, but the sentry kept them off us. Off me, anyway. They didn't seem as concerned about Reyes.

One jumped on his back. I sent Artemis. She dislodged it, but another soon took its place. He twisted around, grabbed its head, and snapped its neck. He did that again and again, as the sentry seemed to only be concerned with keeping them off me.

I cried out when one slashed Reyes's back. Blood gushed out so fast it made me dizzy. I ran forward to help, but he stopped me with a murderous glare. Then, as if it were the easiest thing in the world, he drew a blade out of thin air and slashed the demon in half.

We didn't know if we would have other powers in this realm. Now we knew.

Hope surged within me. We were almost to the front door when another wave of Shade demons descended from the roof, dropping onto us like an avalanche of boulders. One landed on top of me, knocking me to the ground. Artemis tried to drag it off, but its claws had found the tender flesh of my stomach and dug in.

Reyes tried to get to me, but he was fighting them three deep.

Then he did something ingenious. He brought forth his robe. Black and undulating, it disoriented the demons around him, blinded them, and allowed him to sever their spines one by one.

I lay on the ground at a stalemate with the Shade demon atop me. Its claws were ready and waiting to rip out my entrails, while Artemis was ready and waiting to rip out its throat, her massive jaws clamped down and holding.

With the battle raging around us, we were completely still. Deadlocked. Each waiting for the other to flinch when a sword cut through the demon, severing it in half, careful to miss Artemis.

The demon fell in two pieces on either side of me, and I looked up into the handsome face of . . . Uncle Bob!

My breath stilled in my chest. He was younger somehow. Stronger.

More determined. He reached down to help me up. Before I could say anything, Reyes appeared out of the blacks of his robe and joined us.

When I blinked in confusion, he said absently, "You weren't the only one with a backup plan."

He motioned Uncle Bob forward, and that was when I saw them. The wings.

"How?" I asked, but Reyes was already fighting again.

"Go!" he said, his voice sharp as steel.

I took off again, sprinting past battle after battle. The sentry held its own. Barely. Uncle Bob and Reyes cleared a path to the stairs, but they'd bottlenecked. Getting past them would take all day, and Reyes was bleeding from several deep wounds.

Uncle Bob had a few wounds as well, though not as severe as Reyes's.

Somehow we had to get past them and to our third-floor apartment.

"This might sound really stupid, but what about—"

"—the elevator," they both said at the same time.

Okay, so not that stupid.

They were still on another plane. It wasn't like they could cut the cable. I hoped.

We made it to the elevator and piled inside, along with Mrs. Barros, an elderly woman who lived on the second floor and couldn't see the demons surrounding her any more than she could see the gravity anchoring her to this world.

But she could see Reyes. She gaped at him, not sure what to say.

Reyes nodded a greeting. "Mrs. Barros."

"Reyes, sweetheart, is everything all right?"

"Right as rain. How's Daisy?"

"Oh, she's better. She has allergies, you know. I may need you to change the air filter in my apartment soon."

"I'll get right on that."

The doors opened onto the second floor, and Mrs. Barros got off. Slowly. Oh so slowly. Before the doors could close, three Shade demons dived inside.

Uncle Bob took one out instantly, but the others put up more of a fight.

Two sentries appeared, holding one each while the Highlander eviscerated them. Not an easy task in the limited space of an elevator.

The door opened on the third floor to a completely empty corridor. We stood shocked at the silence that greeted us.

"This isn't right," Reyes said, easing forward.

Uncle Bob followed behind me, keeping a wary eye on every nook and every cranny. "I agree."

We got to our apartment, and I could tell we were on the right path.

"I feel it," I said to them.

Reyes placed his hand on the door. "I do, too."

The energy source. The power center. It was close.

As Reyes opened the door, I tried to ignore the blood trickling down his body and soaking the floor around him.

An eerie silence wafted from the apartment. No sound whatsoever despite a blinding blue light flickering around us.

Reyes started inside, then stopped, his expression hard as he scanned the area. I hurried forward, then gasped and stumbled back. The room was filled wall to wall with the infected. Every face twisted into rage. But they stood motionless, waiting for orders.

How did we fight the demons inside without hurting the humans? Just dragging the one out of Eric almost killed him. There were over a hundred infected in our apartment, standing shoulder to shoulder, guarding the light.

At the center, the light burned like an acetylene torch, so bright it hurt my eyes.

But I'd been in the apartment after Reyes broke out of the Shade. "How did we not see this before?"

"It's using their life force to gain mass," Uncle Bob said. "All of the infected. It's using them. Siphoning their energy."

"Like Osh." I pointed to them. To the light slowly leaking out of their bodies and into the core. "It's feeding off their souls."

Reyes thought back. "That's why when the woman died in the hospital, we never saw her soul leave her body."

"I remember. You're saying the demon inside her had devoured it? Had stolen her energy?"

"It's the only explanation."

The longer we stood there, the more upset the infected became. Their heads were low, vicious scowls on their faces as though they were all being controlled by one powerful force.

Reyes swung his sword, flexing his wrist.

"We can't hurt them," I said, putting a hand on his arm to stop him. "They're still human."

"Not for long."

"Reyes, there has to be another way."

"We have to get you to that core, Dutch."

"We don't even know if it'll work. We'd be risking more lives on something that might or might not succeed, and if you haven't noticed, my plans don't always pan out."

Uncle Bob pushed me aside. "Okay, plan B, then."

I looked up at him, hardly recognizing the handsome man beside me, his massive wings foreign and surreal. "Yeah?"

"We keep them very, very busy."

"How do we do that?" I asked.

"We give them something to play with." And with that, he jumped into the crowd like a kid at a concert crowd-surfing, only he fought. He pushed and punched, trying not to do permanent damage.

They scratched and bit and snarled, drawing blood, while Reyes and I fought to get to the core. We'd made it as far as three rows deep when more Shade demons joined the fight.

Artemis jumped in, dragging one demon out after another. But Reyes and I couldn't shift. We couldn't help her.

They took Uncle Bob down, and I screamed his name. Like a horde of super zombies, they jerked unnaturally and moved incredibly fast. If we feigned left, they were already going right to head us off, as though they knew what we were thinking before we did.

All we could do was push and punch and try to knock them unconscious. But they were strong.

Sentries started arriving. They managed to get the infected off Uncle Bob, but he'd been injured. We were fighting a losing battle. I'd never make it to the core. Time for backup plan number three.

I closed my eyes and summoned the one person who could help me.

As a hundred battles were being waged around us, a soft, feminine voice wafted to us. A voice Reyes would know better than my own.

"Reyes?" she said, her lyrical voice stunning him.

He turned just in time to see his sister, Kim, appear before him. As she lovingly pressed a palm to his face, I whispered his name.

"Reyes."

Confused, he turned just as I plunged the knife Thaniel made into his heart.

He sucked in a sharp breath, looking down at the blade protruding from his chest, the metal flakes already causing damage.

Then he looked up at me with a knowing smile as his body began to crack. "I was worried you wouldn't do it."

Tears blurred my vision. "You knew?"

The horde began to grow weaker, their resistance waning. Some of them started to lose their balance. A few doubled over. Others crumpled, losing consciousness altogether. Even the individual Shade demons were losing strength.

I looked back at him. "I'm so sorry."

"Hurry," he said, his voice strained. His eyes rolled back, and he fell to his knees. He ripped at his shirt, tearing it in half as his tattoos split open and an orange light leaked out of him like molten lava. His back arched, and he threw back his head, groaning in agony. He spoke again from between clenched teeth. "Dutch."

I jolted to awareness, fighting the horror of what I'd just done.

Scrambling over writhing bodies, I hurried to the hell dimension's life force. Praying for my mother's strength, I plucked it out of the air and held it in my palm.

A fire began to leech out of Reyes, the heat blistering, and the Shade demons screeched, the sound high-pitched as though they were being burned as well.

Uncle Bob climbed to his feet, panting and covered in blood.

I concentrated on every molecule in a ten-mile radius. Separated those of the hell dimension from those of the earthly plane. Then I gathered them.

The air swirled around me as I pulled the atoms together.

A lightning storm, very much like the one from the night Reyes escaped the hell dimension, crackled and arced as a dark cloud churned above us.

I kept the core in my hand. A heat like that of the sun radiated out and fought my control. I fought harder, collecting each and every molecule for miles. I dragged them out of the infected in hospitals. I drew them out of the cracks in which they hid. I lured them out of the shadows.

Searching every inch of Albuquerque, no atom too small to escape my attention, I collected them in the palm of my hand.

Once we stood outside the hell dimension, I shifted and straddled both the earthly and the celestial planes where I could lift sand from the ground beneath our feet. Then I slowly collapsed the dimension, folding it in upon itself, crumpling it like a piece of paper. The pressure from the force heated the dimension and the sand, fusing them together, forcing the molecules to bind until it formed a ball of glass in my hand. A perfect sphere the size of a baseball.

It glistened, and though it was crystal clear, if I squinted I could still see the dimension Reyes created inside.

"Charley!" Kim called out, her voice urgent.

Reyes was kneeling on the floor, his torso arched, his head thrown back, his arms spread wide in agony. Only he was solid stone, a marble sculpture of spectacular beauty. A seasoned art critic would swear one of the masters had sculpted him.

Kim knelt beside him, frantic. "Charley, please."

I knelt on the other side, begged for this to work, then pulled the knife out of his chest. And we waited. Uncle Bob took a knee beside me, but nothing was happening.

Always go for the heart. The words repeated over and over in my mind.

I bent over him, placed my hand where the knife had been, pressed my mouth to his, and gave him a part of my soul.

A warmth spread beneath my lips. I lunged back and watched as life reflowed into my husband. As color returned.

I took Uncle Bob's hand into mine and held it to my chest for strength. He let me. He even wrapped his other arm around me. Then a wing, and I sagged against him.

We waited as color made its way across Reyes's chest, closing the fissures there. Then, in a burst of energy, he broke free of the stone and doubled over, gasping for air on all fours. He turned his head and spit blood, then looked over at me. His hand rose to block the light from his eyes, and what eyes they were.

We'd been here before. In this very situation the first time I saw him as Reyes when we were in high school. Him on all fours next to a Dumpster in an alley, reeling from a vicious attack by Earl Walker. Me, ever the doer-of-good, trying to save him.

He'd had to lift a hand to shield his eyes from the light on Gemma's camera, but now I realized he was probably shielding them from my light as well.

I eased closer and whispered his name.

He frowned in thought. "Did you stab me in the chest with a knife?"

"I did. I'm sorry."

He looked around. "Did it work?"

"Yes. How did you know what I was going to do?"

He sat back on his heels and gave me a seductive once-over. "Because you're you. What else would you do?"

Not entirely happy with that explanation, I straddled him and offered him a brilliant scowl. One that would have mortal men quivering in their boots, I was certain of it. But not Reyes Alexander Farrow.

He let his gaze drop to my mouth and held it there a long moment.

The formerly infected, a.k.a. possessed by a demon from a hell dimension that should never have been allowed on this plane, slowly awakened. One at a time, they rose and looked around, wondering where they were, if their expressions were any indication.

Taking in all the people who were now demon-free, I told Uncle Bob, "We may need an ambulance. Or two."

Reyes took Kim's hand. She brought his to her lips, tears running amok down her pretty face. We helped him stand just as another entity materialized.

I whirled around, my hands in karate chop mode. No idea why.

Michael, the archangel, decided to honor us with his presence. He stood a foot above me, his massive wings tucked behind him, the arches rising far above his head.

He looked at Reyes as though they had business. Why would they?

Then he turned his attention to Uncle Bob. "Raphael."

"Michael," Uncle Bob said in return, but he pronounced Michael's name as *Mik-ay-elle*. Like they knew each other from another time. Then the whole angel thing kicked in, the realization that Uncle Bob, *my* uncle Bob, was a celestial being hadn't quite sunk in yet. But it was getting closer. The wings helped.

Michael refocused on Reyes. "It is time."

Reyes nodded and disentangled himself from Kim and me.

"Time?" I asked, suddenly very wary. I clutched his arm. "Time for what?"

Michael spared me a glance. "The agreement was for three days."

"What agreement? Reyes?"

"Rey'azikeen agreed to sit by his Brother's side if He would lift your exile and allow him three days with you." He placed a razor-sharp stare on my husband. "It's time to go."

"That's how I got out of Marmalade?"

Michael tilted his head to the side, curious.

I stood, appalled. "Wait a minute, you sold your soul for three days?"

Reyes lifted my chin, tilting my face to his. "I would have sold it for three hours."

"Rey'azikeen," Michael said, urging him to follow.

Reyes obeyed, but I stepped in front of Michael. "Now, you listen here, buddy. We're talking days, right?"

He didn't respond. He just kept that curious gaze on me as though trying to figure me out.

"Because if we're talking days, let me tell you, where I've been for the last ten days was over a hundred years in Marmalade time." I stepped closer and poked Mik-ay-elle in the chest. "So, one day equals about ten years, according to your Boss, right?"

Nothing.

"That means I get to keep my husband for at least another thirty years on this plane. Give or take. Because it's not an exact science."

Michael scanned me from head to toe as though I were beneath him, then he did something I'd never seen him do. He almost grinned. Almost. One corner of his mouth tipped up the slightest bit, and he said, "Or, we could follow time as it is in my Father's realm."

I pointed an accusing finger at him. "Don't even try to trick me."

"I wouldn't dare," he said, unmoved.

Satisfied, I squared my shoulders and asked, "Then what time would that be?"

"It is said that in my realm, a day is as a thousand years."

I thought about that. I was so bad with the whole math thing. As I contemplated what he said, hope made a hesitant appearance. "So . . . ?"

"So," he said, "I will return in three thousand years. Be prepared."

Reyes's jaw fell open. Kim's did, too. I only realized then that mine was hanging off its hinges as well.

He turned to Uncle Bob and said expectantly, "Raphael."

Uncle Bob gave a curt nod, but I lunged forward and grabbed his wrist. "What? Are you going with him, too?"

He smiled down at me. "We made a deal."

"What is it with this guy and deals?"

"I had to help, Charley. This was the only way."

"But you can't go. What about Cookie and Amber?"

"They'll survive."

A sob wrenched from my chest before I even realized I was upset. "Uncle Bob, please." I threw my arms around him to anchor him to Earth.

He wrapped me in his embrace, his love so incredibly unconditional.

"You gave up everything to do this. To fight with us. Just like you gave up everything to stay on Earth when I was born. To stay with me. I'm so sorry, Uncle Bob. Please stay."

"I'm the one who's sorry, pumpkin. I wanted you to find your own way. I worried that if I influenced you at all, even the smallest amount, it would change the course of history. It would change your destiny."

"Raphael," Michael said, growing impatient.

"No." I turned on him with a vengeance I scarcely knew I had. "No."

"It is not up to me. It was Raphael's decision."

"Okay, your Dad likes to deal, let's deal." I lifted the globe that held the Shade and said, "I'll trade you a hell dimension for my uncle."

"Done." Michael took it out of my hands and vanished.

"Oh, holy shit, that was easy. He's probably scared to death we'll release it onto his Father's plane again." I snorted. Silly archangel.

"How did you do that?" Uncle Bob asked.

"Snort?"

"Negotiate with Michael. Nobody negotiates with Michael. Ever. You're . . . you're amazing."

"Apparently. So, when he says *Raphael*, you're not *the* Raphael, right?"

He offered me a look of pure smugness. "I didn't realize I was famous."

I clasped onto him again. He let me. He even brushed a feather over my cheek. My life was so strange.

I refocused on the ball and chain. "Okay, we have three thousand years to find another loophole. Speaking of which . . ." I punched him as hard as I could on his shoulder. He simply slid a brow up in question. "I can't believe you did that."

"What? Bargained for my wife's life back?"

"For three days?"

He pulled me into his arms. "I had to. Any longer than that and you'd start to get on my nerves."

"Ah, but the real question is, what the hell are you going to do with me for the next three thousand years?"

"I have a few ideas."

24

Charley Davidson and Reyes Farrow:
That thing that happens when an irresistible force meets
an immovable object.
—TRUE FACT

We could've stayed at the apartment, but there were still a dozen formerly possessed people getting medical attention, so we decided to stay at HQ one more night. The fun part of our evening was calling everyone and telling them the good news. Mainly that we'd stopped the hell dimension and traded it to Michael for Ubie.

Good times.

I had to threaten my uncle, however. He wanted to call Cookie, but she was my BFF. I wanted to call her. He acted like he had some kind of spousal rights to break the news, but I threatened to tell her about his wings, which were gone again, but I had a feeling he could bring them back whenever he needed to.

She was so going to love that.

Once that was out of the way, and I could hear again after Cookie's high-pitched shrieks of joy, Reyes made dinner. Yes, the man had been shredded, stabbed in the heart by his wife, died, turned to stone, and brought back to life and still managed to whip up a batch of green chile burritos. He was a keeper.

While he was cooking, I ran to the roof to see the lights of Albuquerque without the haze of the Shade obstructing my view. The quarantine would be lifted soon and martial law rescinded. But the total loss, besides the sanity of many an individual, was thirteen. Thirteen had died as a direct result of something I'd done.

The thought was unbearable. All thirteen had severe mental illness. This could not have helped their situation.

As I contemplated how I could get away with healing them all, a feminine voice wafted toward me. "I think you're being too hard on yourself."

I turned to see a departed woman standing in the dark, her monochrome features coming through in Technicolor. Except she was monochrome.

But she was pretty and . . .

I paused and took another look, blinking in disbelief. It would be several minutes before I could speak, and when I did, I could only manage one word.

"Mom?" I asked, almost afraid to say it out loud. Afraid she'd disappear if I broke the spell of her existence.

But a smile widened across her face. "I'm surprised you remember me since we only met the one time. And you were covered in afterbirth."

At long last, I knew where I got my sense of humor from.

I rushed forward and threw my arms around her. "Mom, how are you here?"

"You summoned me."

"What?" I leaned back to take her in. She was so beautiful. "I summoned you? How? I didn't even know I could."

"You summoned my strength in the battle and thereby me. I'm glad you followed the clues."

"Mom, how did you know I would need them?"

"I was a seer. When I was alive."

"A seer? You mean a prophet?"

"Yes. When that demon killed me, I was bombarded with vision after vision. That's why I gave the message to your sister."

"How is she, by the way?"

She laughed softly. "She's beautiful. Just like you."

I covered my mouth with one hand, but kept a firm grip on her with the other, afraid to let her go. "Can you stay?"

"No. I've crossed over, so even if you summon me, I can only stay a little while. But I wanted to talk to you. Something has been bothering you, and I wanted you to know that anytime anything bothers you, anything niggles at the back of your neck, it's usually important. You need to take heed."

"How did you—? Never mind. Take heed. Gotcha."

She began to fade. "Wait," I said, trying to grab her, but she'd gone too far. My hands slipped through her.

"I'll be back," she said, her voice fading as fast as she was. "When she's older."

"She?" But my mother, the woman I only had a vague recollection of, was gone. "Wait! I have to know! What was with the lion?"

Receiving no answer, I turned back to the grid of city lights. I loved this place so much. I was glad I got to stay a little longer, though I wasn't sure three thousand years would be long enough.

So, what was bothering me? Besides . . . well, besides the obvious.

And I had my answer. It had been staring me in the face.

I ran downstairs. Uncle Bob was there, hovering in the kitchen, asking Reyes how much longer. He was like a kid, but I could hardly blame him. Reyes's burritos, like everything else Reyes, were delicious and addictive.

"I have a solution."

"Good," Reyes said, folding a tortilla around the burrito innards and handing it to the renegade angel. "I was worried."

"I know how we can keep Beep safe and watch her grow up. Also, I met my mother."

That got his attention. "How?"

"I accidently summoned her."

"No, how can we keep Beep safe?"

"A haven, like the one around the Vatican keeping you out."

"You can't go to the Vatican?" Ubie asked, surprised.

"And the Shade. It was a type of haven. We couldn't dematerialize inside it."

"Okay," Reyes said, still not catching on.

"So, we create a haven around Beep. Around a city. Any city in which the Loehrs want to live, and we get to see her every day. We get to watch her grow up without the fear that a demon, or any other supernatural being, can get to her."

"And how do we get to see her every day?"

"Our energy will be the source of the haven. It will be us, guarding her and protecting her, just in a very different way." I stepped closer to him. "Remember what Pandu said? Your darkness is a void. It simply needs to be filled with my light. I think that's how we do it. We'll be together. And one day when she needs us most, we'll be there."

Reyes gave me a look of bewilderment. "It's brilliant."

I nodded, just as bewildered. "I know, right?"

It was like once the solution took hold, we could think of nothing else.

As we ate and planned and talked to the Loehrs about where they'd most like to live, a news story was playing on the TV, proclaiming the area allegedly infection-free.

"It stopped as suddenly as it started," a male news anchor reported. "Remarkably, only thirteen people died in an epidemic the CDC feared could kill tens of thousands."

Then a female reporter came on and said, "In other news, scientists are scratching their heads over a large pool of glass that showed up in the Sahara Desert over the weekend. They're baffled as to what caused it. So far, there is only speculation about what could have heated such a large area of sand so much, it created this spectacular sea of shimmering blue, but people from all over the world are already flocking to see it. Some are even calling it a miracle."

I caught Reyes staring at me, his expression warm and curious at the same time.

"What?" I asked, suddenly self-conscious.

"You know, if we do this, we can't question the Loehrs' parenting style."

I had the presence of mind to look offended. "I would never."

A grin so sensual it should have been outlawed slid across his face. "So, if they force her to eat spinach, you won't interfere?"

"First of all, forcing a child to eat spinach is cruel and unusual and should carry a prison sentence. Second, I trust them implicitly."

The decision made, we asked Uncle Bob to give everyone our good-byes. He agreed, understanding. I worried how Cookie would take it, but she had Ubie. What more could a girl ask for?

Still, I sat there astonished that this man, my very own uncle, was an angel. A supreme being. A celestial warrior. I couldn't fathom what prompted him to stay on Earth. To take a thankless job, one full of death and deceit and disillusion. To be surrounded by humans he couldn't possibly see as his equal.

And yet, he'd stayed.

Wingless once again, he pulled me into a long hug. He smelled like lightning and rain and cinnamon.

I breathed deep and whispered, "I'm sorry, Uncle Bob."

"Don't you dare."

I hugged him harder, memorizing the feel of him against me before stepping away.

Without another word, Reyes and I dematerialized and rematerialized in the town the Loehrs had chosen, a.k.a. Mrs. Loehr's favorite place on Earth: Santa Fe, New Mexico.

Once the decision had been made, we couldn't stop what we had to do even if we wanted to. The gravity of it, the force, drew us together like two planets on a collision course.

Standing on a deserted street with stars sparkling overhead and a warm breeze on my face, I stepped into Reyes.

My light spilled into his darkness, filling the void that was Rey'azikeen. Our molecules fused, becoming one. And then, in an instant, they separated. Expanded. Surged in all directions until we had created a haven over the city for our daughter to grow up in. Where we could watch her from the heavens. Where she'd be completely safe. Where nothing could touch her until the time came for her to make her mark on history.

After we ascended, I looked on as Mrs. Loehr sang softly to Beep, rocking her until the chubby darling drifted to sleep. It was then that a thought struck me. I scanned the area we watched over. Then I scanned all of New Mexico. From there, I branched out and scanned the entire planet and then the entire universe.

"Reyes?" I said as he nibbled on my ear. Metaphorically, as we were this huge incorporeal mass now.

"Yes?" he said back, his voice still deep and still smooth and still able to weaken my nonexistent knees.

Not wanting to cause a commotion unnecessarily, I looked again just to be sure.

Then I nudged the god next to me and asked, "Where's Osh?"